EDUCATING

Cattleman's Club 5

Jenny Penn

MENAGE EVERLASTING

Siren Publishing, Inc.
www.SirenPublishing.com

A SIREN PUBLISHING BOOK
IMPRINT: Ménage Everlasting

EDUCATING CASEY
Copyright © 2015 by Jenny Penn

ISBN: 978-1-63259-187-6

First Printing: April 2015

Cover design by Les Byerley
All art and logo copyright © 2015 by Siren Publishing, Inc.

Printed in the U.S.A.

PUBLISHER
Siren Publishing, Inc.
www.SirenPublishing.com

EDUCATING CASEY

Cattleman's Club 5

JENNY PENN
Copyright © 2015

Chapter 1

Saturday, May 24th

The music was pumping. The margaritas were flowing. Patton was buried in Casey's closet, and Casey's nose was buried in Patton's sketchbook. It was just like old times.

Casey smiled at that thought, recognizing the ridiculousness of it. Patton had been gone only a few months, and she kept coming back. So it wasn't as if Casey really had a chance to miss her, but she did.

As best friends, business partners, and former roommates, they'd been inseparable for the past several years. That had all changed, though, when Patton had gone home a few months back and ended up deciding to stay there.

Not that she could abandon Casey entirely. After all, they still owned a store together. Their small lingerie boutique catered to upper-end clientele with certain adventurous, adult-minded interests.

"This!" Patton spun around holding up a nude bandage dress Casey hadn't worn in years. "You *have* to take this."

"Why?" Casey asked with a scowl. "I'm going to a sex club. I'm hoping that I'm not going to be wearing any clothes...and if I am, I am going to be very disappointed."

That was the honest truth.

Casey was headed off toward the Cattleman's Club first thing in the morning, and they had a reputation for liking to keep their women naked and stuffed full of cock. The rumor was the club was populated by an incredibly talented and insatiable group of hot men who enjoyed a woman in every dirty, orgasmic way possible.

That was according to Felicity Foster.

She was a regular at the club, which said something about the place because Felicity was one hard bitch to impress. Everything had to be custom. The woman drove Casey and Patton nuts because she couldn't order anything out of the catalog but always demanded specific creations made only for her. At the prices she was willing to pay, though, they were more than willing to indulge her whims.

Of course, Felicity had to have something to do with all her custom-fitted negligees and teddies or, more appropriately, some*body* to do. As she always said, she certainly didn't spend that kind of money on her outfits for any low-rent ride. Instead, she reserved her skilled favors for her stable full of stallions—that's how she'd described the Cattlemen when she'd offered to get Casey into the club.

She'd made that offer more than once over the past years, but Casey had always turned her down. That is she had until Patton realized that her three fiancées, the Davis brothers, were the founders and owners of the club. The brothers wouldn't allow Patton through the front doors, so Casey was going undercover to infiltrate the club and report back all the dirty secrets Patton's men were trying to keep from her.

Not that Casey expected there to be any great secret to discover, but Patton was insistent that there had to be a reason for them refusing to let her into the club. She wanted to know what it was, and Casey just wanted to get laid. So, she'd agreed and finally taken Felicity up on her invitation.

"If you're not planning on taking clothes, what's with the bag?" Patton nodded to the open suitcase sitting at the foot of Casey's bed as she returned the dress back into the closet.

"Take a look for yourself," Casey told her, her concentration caught by the drawing before her.

"Oh, *nice!*" Patton nodded her approval as she picked up a tiny pink lacy set of crotchless panties. "You've been raiding the store."

"Yes, well, being a partner in a lingerie shop, I figured I might as well do a little advertising. Hell, I could write this trip off as a business deduction," Casey shot back as she turned the sketchbook around. "If there had been time, I would have asked you to make one of these because this is *nice!*"

Casey mimicked Patton's earlier exaggeration, drawing a laugh from Patton as she dropped the panties back into the suitcase and stepped up to admire her own drawing.

"That it is."

"But not in yellow." Casey was too pale to look good in yellow. "At least not for me, but this would look amazing against a darker skin tone."

"That's what I was thinking," Patton agreed with a quick grin. "Actually, I was thinking of—"

"—Aysia!"

They spoke in unison in a habit they'd had almost since they'd first met, but it was Casey who continued on. "She'll love it. Get me a finished piece in her size, and I'll give her a call."

"I can have it done in a week," Patton assured her, dropping the sketchbook back down onto the bed. "You can pick it up before you head home when you come by to give me your report."

"Works for me." Casey rolled off the bed, snatching up her empty glass in one smooth move. She cast a pointed look at Patton's nearly finished drink. "Refill?"

Patton drained the last bit from her glass before handing it over to Casey with a smirk. "Thanks."

Wandering down the hall and through the open living and dining area into the small kitchen that served her purposes well enough, Casey squinted against the bright flash of headlights that cut through the window over the sink. She peeked out, half expecting to see one of Patton's men arriving to collect her, but instead of an oversized pickup, she caught sight of an all-too-familiar black sports car pulling into the parking spot next to her own two-door compact.

Josh was home.

Home and looking good as ever.

Casey couldn't help but admire the graceful flex of the thick muscles highlighted by his custom-tailored suit as he stepped out of his car. The high-performance vehicle was a perfect match for the cool, urban sophistication that Josh went out of his way to project. In some ways, it was an accurate reflection. He was smart and successful, driven by a relentless ambition that was sexy unto itself.

At the same time, the image was a lie. He might look smooth and polished in that attractive preppy, slightly jaded sort of way, but Casey knew the truth. Beneath the cold glitter of his calculating gaze lay the heart of a sweet geek, who preferred playing video games to going to art galleries and could skin a fish or tack a deer better than he could pick out a decent glass of wine off of any list.

Josh might be highly educated and given toward using big words, but he'd grown up in a pair of well-worn jeans and a stained T-shirt, hanging out at honky-tonks just like Casey had back when she'd teased her hair and worn her jeans too tight and too high. They came from the same place—Nowhere, Georgia. Both had shed that life to build a better one in the big city, which was the basis of their friendship.

"Oh, is that Joshy?"

Patton's overly excited question cut through Casey's idle thoughts, making her realize that she'd been standing there for longer than she should have. Now she'd drawn Patton's attention, and Josh wouldn't be thanking her for that.

"Don't start," Casey warned Patton, knowing the effort was futile.

Casey had lived next door to Josh going on four years now, which meant that Patton had too. Not surprisingly, the two of them hadn't gotten along. Instead, Patton had bonded with Dylan, Josh's non-identical twin brother. That made sense. Dylan was loud, rude, and wild. So was Patton…in a less annoying kind of way, or maybe not.

"Oh come on," Patton sang out as she danced out of the kitchen. "I have to go say hello to Joshy!"

Casey groaned, already knowing how this conversation was going to turn out. Like a gawker at the scene of an accident, though, she couldn't resist the urge to watch the disaster about to unfold. Following after Patton, Casey reached the front door in time to almost get hit by it as Patton threw it opened and ambushed Josh.

"*Joshy!*"

Patton launched herself at him, engulfing Josh in a bear hug from behind as he fumbled with his keys in front of his door. She plowed hard enough into him to make him drop the keys with a curse, not that Patton paid his clearly foul mood any mind.

"Miss me?"

In answer, Josh groaned and pounded his head against the door before turning around to offer Patton a politely fake smile. "Peyton, it's been…too long."

Josh paused just enough to assure that it was clear that he was lying, which only egged Patton on.

"That it has! So long in fact that it almost requires us to share a drink to toast this momentous occasion," Patton declared with a dramatic flair as she looped her arm through his and all but dragged him into Casey's apartment, forcing Casey to step back to let them pass.

She caught Josh's eyes for a second, but his gaze cut quickly away. He wasn't fast enough, though, to disguise the gloom darkening his normally brilliant gaze. Casey could only assume he'd had a rough day, and Patton wasn't making it any easier either.

"Hey, Josh." Casey offered him a quick, apologetic smile, but he didn't return the gesture. Instead, he responded with a curt tone that was cut with enough of a sharp edge to make Casey cringe.

"Casey."

He didn't elaborate on that greeting but remained tight-lipped and tense looking, leaving her to wonder just what was wrong. For the first time that day, Casey silently cursed Patton's presence as she wished she could have a moment alone with Josh because it was clear that he needed a friend tonight.

"Have a seat and I'll get those drinks ready," Patton informed Josh as she all but shoved him down onto the couch.

Patton tossed her a wink before rushing off toward the kitchen, and Casey could all but read her friend's mind. Not that it was hard to figure out what Patton was up to. Hell, she'd spent the last four years trying to convince Casey to go after Josh, but he had a girl, and that just wasn't her style.

Even if it had been, she wouldn't have stood a chance. After all, Josh was engaged to a Brazilian swimsuit model who was a perfect match for the suit and the car, even if Casey didn't think Maria matched Josh all that well. The woman was kind of a bitch and tended to make Josh's life more difficult than easy.

"Sorry about"—Casey hesitated, having to remember that Patton preferred to go by Peyton in Atlanta—"Peyton."

She claimed it was part of her urban persona, but Casey knew the truth. Patton had worried her name came off as too hick for the big city. Casey had worried over the same thing about her accent. They'd bonded over the insecurities, whereas, with Josh, she'd bonded over their shared love of toffee, dogs, and video games.

That was, apparently, all that was needed for love to grow. Those three things and years' worth of routines that had bonded them like family. That's what Josh was to her—family. That bond felt distant, though, that night as Josh sat there bent forward with his elbows resting on his knees and his gaze locked on his hands.

"Don't sweat it," he muttered, not bothering to elaborate with any of his usual rejoinders.

Instead, an awkward silence enveloped them that was broken only by the distant rumble of an all-too-familiar engine. Dylan and his obnoxiously loud motorcycle were home. Casey swore the bastard had bought that damn machine just to drive her insane by revving the engine every time he returned home at three in the morning after hitting the sheets with yet another nameless, big-titted conquest.

"Dylan!"

Patton shrieked, running right out of the kitchen, clearly having completely forgotten about Josh's drink. She flew past both Casey and him and out of the front door. Screaming her way down the walkway, she acted as if she were greeting some long-lost lover she hadn't seen in years instead of simply a pal who she had lived next door to and hadn't seen in weeks.

"Well." Josh roused from his brooding silence as he slapped his knees and shoved off the couch. "This has been fun, but—"

"Wait!" Casey leapt to her feet as she quickly reached a hand out to stop him. "Is everything...I mean, are you all right?"

"Sure," he said, all too quickly, refusing to meet Casey's eyes, even as he shot a tight smile in her general direction. "It's just been a long day. Lots of meetings and stuff, so I'm just going to—"

"Go to bed at nine o'clock tonight?" Casey lifted a brow, not buying that for a moment, but that was the lie Josh was sticking to.

"I guess I'm getting old." Josh offered that tired joke as he shrugged. "I'll see you later."

"Josh?"

Casey didn't know if it was the concern or the hurt in her voice that brought him to a stop, but he hesitated for a second, long enough to give her an answer to the question buried in her tone.

"Maria left me."

With that, he trudged out the door, leaving Casey too shocked to do much more than watch him go. As much as she disliked Maria, her heart ached for Josh. He'd looked more defeated than tired, except that Josh was never defeated. Not even when Maria went completely nuclear could she turn him into the shuffling zombie he appeared to be right then.

Maria hadn't just dumped him. She'd hurt him, but Casey didn't have a chance to chase after him. Instead, she had a different problem to deal with, and it came barging right into her living room with an arm looped around Patton's shoulders and a bottle of Jack clutched in his other hand.

"It's a party at the pixie's house," Dylan declared, as if he wasn't completely aware of how much she hated him calling her that. "How is it going way down there, my itty, bitty pixie pal?"

"I'm not your pal," Casey snapped back, wishing she could come up with a better comeback, but Dylan always managed to fluster her enough that she couldn't seem to think straight. Tonight was no different.

"Whatever you say, squirt."

"I say you're an ass," Casey shot back, meaning every word.

Brothers and roommates, it amazed her that Josh and Dylan had ever once shared a womb, much less that they managed to continue to live together. They were as opposite as brothers could be. Where Josh had been a math prodigy by the age of eight, Dylan had been winning spitting contests and breaking his bones in rodeos. Now Dylan was a detective in the narcotics division, and Josh ran his own highly secretive computer security company.

Whatever the hell that meant. Casey didn't know, and Josh wouldn't say. The only assurance he offered her was that if she ever needed his services then she'd know what they were. If only Dylan would be that cryptic, but subtle was not in his nature. Instead, he loved to regale everybody with gross and lewd stories from his undercover work.

He had tales about prostitutes, pimps, dealers, and perverts of every variety. Patton ate them up, and so, secretly, did Casey. She didn't mind lewdness. She minded Dylan.

He was loud, rude, and macho enough that she kept waiting for the day, when in the middle of one of their infamous arguments, he finally tried to win by ripping off his shirt and pounding his overly developed chest with his fists in an attempt to intimidate her into conceding defeat.

That was never going to happen.

The man might be hotter than the sun and tall enough to reach it, but Casey didn't even notice. Even if she did, she'd never have admitted it. After all, Dylan had enough bimbos hanging off him. Besides, looks didn't matter. Talent did. A man had to be good at something more than bragging, and it had been her experience the more a man bragged, the less likely he was to actually be good.

That thought brought a smile to her face, and she was just about ready to share it with him when the sudden prickle of claws pierced through her jeans and had her glancing down into the sweet, innocent face of Dylan's newest groupie.

"Ah, there is my little Kacey Pussy." Dylan smirked as he pulled free of Patton to reach down and scoop up the small, black cat that had wandered into their lives not but three months ago. "Come here, Kacey Pussy. I don't think you've met Peyton yet."

"Oh, he's sooooo cute," Patton cooed, shooting Casey a smirk that assured her she got the joke. Not that she could miss it. The damn man had named the cat after her for God's sakes, and it was a male...well, not anymore.

"Where did you get him?" Patton asked, glancing up at Dylan.

"I didn't. He kind of just wandered in one day and refused to leave." Dylan shrugged as if that was all there was to it, but Casey knew the truth.

He'd lured the cat in and given it every reason to stay, including more than just food and a bed. Casey had caught the big, tough man baby-talking to the rat-catcher more than once, which would actually be kind of sweet if he hadn't insisted on giving the damn thing her name.

"I'm surprised Josh let you keep him," Patton murmured as the cat mewed so pathetically and reached for her, melting yet another heart in its endless attempt to conquer the entire world. "Oh, what a sweetie."

Patton folded just like that, even though Casey knew she didn't care for cats, but Kacey was different. Everybody loved Kacey...everybody but maybe Josh. He had his reasons, though, for disliking the most likable cat ever.

"Yeah." Dylan let her take the cat and watched as she cuddled it close. "He wasn't too thrilled, especially when Kacey decided to pee in his laptop."

That got a laugh out of Patton, who lifted to cat up to look him right in the eye and give him a stern talking to in a voice better reserved for small children.

"Did you do that? Did you? Were you a naughty kitty?"

"He's a pussy," Dylan corrected her before nodding toward Casey. "Thanks to her. She took his balls."

"And Maria took Josh's," Casey shot back, knowing just how to get rid of Dylan and his pussy. "She dumped him."

"What?" Just as Casey expected, that caught Dylan's full attention because there was at least one thing they both agreed on. "That bitch. I'm so sick of her shit."

Turning to head for the door, he was about ready to storm out, and Casey was more than glad to let it hit him on the ass as he went. Him and his cat.

"Hey!" Casey called out as she stepped up to retrieve the cat Patton was loving all over. "Don't forget your pussy!"

That drew Dylan to a stop and had him whipping a wicked grin over his shoulder. "And which one would *that* be? You or the cat?

Because I got an idea on how we can cheer Josh up and make him forget all about his problems."

There was no disguising the blunt suggestion in his tone or the wicked curl of his grin, but the rapid pound of her heart and the heated rush that shot through her were easily masked by Casey's scowl as she thrust the little rat-catcher back at Dylan.

"Take this one. It *doesn't* have standards, just like the rest of your girlfriends." With that, Casey slammed the door on Dylan's smirk, only to turn around and be confronted by Patton's.

"I still can't figure it out. Is it Josh or Dylan? Which one are you really getting wet for…or is it *both*?"

Chapter 2

Dylan slammed into the apartment he shared with his brother, intent on finding out just what had gone wrong between Josh and Maria so he could get back to harassing Casey as soon as possible. God, but she was fun to pick on. The way her delicate little pixie features scrunched all up and flushed red, she was so damn cute he found himself laughing.

The beauty of that was Dylan knew his amusement drove her nuts. Driving Casey nuts was sort of Dylan's secret hobby. Truth was, he couldn't get enough of her and plotted almost every damn day about how to irritate her anew. Hell, he made up half the shit that came out of his mouth just to piss her off.

One day he was going to give her the education of a lifetime, but not tonight. Tonight, Josh needed him. His twin took precedence over everyone else, even Casey. As much fun as she was, and as grim as Josh looked, Dylan wished he wasn't half as loyal as he was because part of him just wanted to turn around and flee as he entered the apartment he shared with his brother.

He found Josh sitting on the couch, staring blindly down at the floor with his shoulders slumped in defeat. Only Maria could make him look that depressed, which was one of the many reasons why Dylan hated the woman. She might have been hot, but she was also a drama queen.

If Dylan had to listen to another chapter in the endless saga that was Josh and Maria's relationship, he was going to need a beer. Josh looked as though he could use one too. Actually, he looked as though he could use something stronger, but beer was all they had.

Without a word of greeting, Dylan dropped Kacey on the floor and strutted straight through the living room that was nearly identical to Casey's and into the kitchen, leaving Josh brooding on the couch as he silently, pointedly, refused to look in Dylan's direction. That was his way of saying he didn't want to talk about the matter, even though they both knew that he really did.

That's why he needed the beer. It would help him let go of the attitude. Carting two cold ones back to the living room, Dylan set one on the coffee table's glass top before settling into one of the two oversized recliners that swiveled to face either the couch or the oversized TV hanging on the opposite wall.

His ass had no sooner hit the leather than Kacey jumped up onto the chair's arm to demand the affection he'd grown accustomed to. The cat crept into his lap as Dylan took a swig from his own bottle, allowing the silence to thicken. Truthfully, he kind of liked the quiet and really wasn't in the mood to hear whatever woeful tale Josh had to tell.

It hadn't been like this in the beginning of their relationship. It seemed hard to remember right then, but there had been a time when they'd been happy, when Josh had been happy. Dylan knew that his brother had his whole life mapped out, and Maria had fit perfectly into those plans.

She still did. The problem was that the plans no longer fit Josh, and he was just too stubborn to admit it. Try as hard as he might have, Josh still couldn't escape who he really was, and it wasn't no sophisticated, urban yuppie. He was just a country boy in a really well-tailored suit.

"So?" Dylan finally broke the silence as that thought cut through him. Josh needed him because he was the only one who understood his brother. "Casey says you and Maria had a falling out."

Josh didn't answer but dug into his pocket and pulled out the ring he'd wasted way too much money on as far as Dylan was concerned.

On the other hand, Maria wouldn't have said yes if the ring had been anything other than what it was—a big, gawdy statement of wealth.

"Ah," Dylan sighed, unconcerned by Maria's overly dramatic gesture. She was known for them. "Don't worry, dude. She'll be calling you first thing in the morning demanding that stupid thing back."

"I don't think so." Josh closed his fingers around the ring, curling it into his fist. "She's found somebody else."

"What?" That caught Dylan off guard, not that he was shocked. Maria was a smart woman with an agenda. She knew to keep a bird in hand while hunting for a better pet. Apparently she'd found one.

"An investment banker," Josh stated with a complete lack of emotion as he dropped the ring onto the coffee table and snatched his beer up. "They've been going at it for a while now."

"That bitch."

"She said I had it coming. That it was my just desserts."

"That's because she's a psycho." Dylan knew his brother better than anybody else and knew there was no way Josh would have done anything to hurt anybody.

"I thought you liked Maria." Josh finally looked up to meet Dylan's gaze, and what Dylan saw there about broke his heart.

"I did," Dylan lied. "Until just now and don't give me that look and don't *even* try to defend her."

Because Dylan could see that Josh wanted to. More than that, he could see the guilt glinting in his brother's eyes and knew he was blaming himself, though there was nothing that Josh could say that would justify what Maria had done.

"She thought Casey and I were having an affair."

Dylan about choked on the chug of beer he'd just taken when Josh dropped that bombshell. At first he didn't know what to say, but there really was only one thing to ask.

"Did you?" Because if anybody could make Josh defy everything he stood for, it probably was the little pixie…or not.

"*No!*" Josh spat in disgust. "God! Why does everybody keep asking me that?"

"Who the hell else asked you that?" Dylan shot back, caught off guard by that revelation.

"Who hasn't?" Josh's shot back before snapping out a long list of names that did not leave Dylan feeling comforted. Especially not the last one.

"Anna?" Dylan leaned forward as his stomach twisted into a tense knot. "When did you see her?"

Anna was Maria's best friend and accomplice. She also happened to be a real estate agent, who, along with Maria, had been pressuring Josh into buying a house. Dylan knew the women thought if they got Josh to spend a million or two on a house then he'd be more likely to follow Maria's engagement ring up with a wedding band. Hell, he couldn't even blame the women for trying to pressure his brother.

It had been four years.

Four years of more excuses than Dylan could remember. Even he had begun to wonder if Josh really wanted to get married. Of course, he'd assumed if the answer was no, it was because he had enough sense to recognize that life with Maria would be miserable. Then again, his brother tended to cave where she was concerned.

"You bought the house."

Not just any house. *The* house.

It had a pool and sauna, along with ten thousand square feet that Josh didn't really need. Maria had shown Dylan the pictures, and it had been clear that she was in love with the place, but what wasn't to love? It had cold marble floors and statues of little kids peeing into fountains, not to mention enough rooms to need a map to navigate the damn place. It was definitely not Dylan's style, or Josh's either for that matter.

"I thought it would make things better." Josh seemed to understand how bad that sounded and almost immediately corrected himself. "I mean, I thought it would show her that all this time I've been spending on the new project was worth it."

"You got the bonus?" Dylan asked, his attention perking up finally.

Josh couldn't talk about the specifics of his work, but that didn't mean he hadn't let a few details slip, like that the contract he had been currently working on came with a bonus if completed in time. It wasn't some dinky bonus either, apparently.

"Five million."

"Woo–hoo, man," Dylan hooted, momentarily forgetting all about the Maria situation. "Can I marry you?"

That earned him a dour look. "You joke, but I got a house that I don't want, a ring that I don't need, and I am supposed to be leaving tomorrow on a two-week romantic tour of Paris and have nobody to go with!"

"Then come with me," Dylan suggested, the idea springing into his head as he perked up.

"*You* want to go to Paris?" Josh asked, clearly appalled by the very idea.

"Oh, good God, no." Dylan wrinkled his nose at the very thought, shaking his head as if he'd just smelled something unpleasant. "I'm talking about *you* coming with *me*."

"And where the hell are you going?"

"Alabama." Dylan savored the word and the thrill it sent through him before sucking in a sobering breath and focusing in on the moment. "You remember Chase Davis?"

"How could I forget?" Josh snorted. "You two went head-to-head at more rodeos than I care to remember."

Growing up in South Georgia, Josh had only ever dreamed of getting the hell out of it. Dylan, on the other hand, had reveled in the open plains and hard work. Hell, if Josh hadn't come to Atlanta to go to college, Dylan would have never done the same.

Not that he minded the city. It had its benefits, namely women. He'd had to travel with the rodeo to find as many available and good-looking women as he did within a block of their apartment. Of course, most of them weren't half as wild as the rodeo girls had been, and even they hadn't been half as kinky as Trina.

She'd been enough of a pervert for Dylan to think he'd found love. He hadn't realized he had just been another conquest to her. That is, until he found her in bed with his good friend. He could have gotten mad about that, but instead, Dylan had just decided to join them and use Trina like she wanted to be used.

That was about the time he'd decided he was done with relationships. There was no point in committing to one flavor when the whole world was full of all sorts of women to dine on, and Sunday he was going to a banquet that promised to be a bounty of many flavors. A bounty Chase was no longer indulging in.

"Yeah, well, Chase has finally decided to settle down with that little girl who used to come around with him and his brothers."

"I remember her." Josh nodded. "She was a tiny little thing, cute as the button…didn't she have a man's name?"

"Patton." Dylan filled in, remembering it only because Chase had mentioned it when they talked last night.

The girl, on the other hand, he couldn't recall other than a faint memory that all the Davis brothers had been very protective of her. Apparently that hadn't changed.

"So you headed out for a wedding?" Josh asked with a heavy hint of disgust coloring his tone. "Because I'm really not in the mood to watch and see if you can fuck your way through another bridesmaid chain."

"All in one day," Dylan boasted, savoring that memory for just a second before focusing on the real point. "But no, the church bells aren't set to ring yet. I'm talking about a job and getting paid with all the pussy you can fuck in one week."

Despite his grin, Dylan could tell his enthusiasm was not catching, as Josh continued to glare at him with a look Dylan knew all too well. Josh was thinking he was a dick. Maybe he was being a little insensitive, but Dylan had to do something.

If he didn't and left Josh there all alone, he knew he'd return to find his brother had hooked up with Casey. It was all but a sure thing. After all, the two of them were perfect together, which probably explained why everybody thought Josh was cheating on Maria.

He should have been, but Josh wasn't that kind of guy. Neither was Casey that kind of girl, but now that neither of them had to worry about their consciences, it was almost guaranteed that they'd be hitting the sheets in the near future. For some reason, that thought really bugged the crap out of Dylan.

"Come on, man, don't give me that look," he begged Josh. "It'll be fun."

Even as the words came out of his mouth, Dylan knew they were the wrong ones. Josh knew it too. His brows lifted, his lips parted, but before he could speak, Dylan beat him to the punch.

"I know. I know." Dylan held his hands up in surrender. "I have a history of promising and not delivering…at least not by your standards." Which were far afield from Dylan's. "But, this time, I swear it will be your kind of fun."

"Really?" Josh sounded far from convinced, and Dylan could sense he was losing the battle.

"Look, Chase called because he needs some help," Dylan rushed out, desperate to pique Josh's interest. "His barn burned down."

"I'm not a fireman or an architect," Josh reminded Dylan, as if that were necessary, especially since they both knew Dylan wasn't done explaining.

"With his girl in it," Dylan snapped.

"Oh." Josh appeared to consider that for all of a second. "Bad news for the girl. I assume she survived?"

"Yep." She hadn't been hurt thankfully, not that that made much of a difference to Chase or his brothers. "And now it's time to find the arsonist."

"Are they sure it's arson?"

"Yep."

"And don't they have local authorities to handle the matter?"

"Apparently the local sheriff is preoccupied."

Actually according to Chase, the sheriff was "balls over heels" for a chick who was doing a good job of making a fool out of him, but that problem wasn't worth mentioning. Especially since Josh appeared to be caving.

"I can't imagine it'd be that hard to find one arsonist, especially in a small town," he mused, sounding intrigued despite himself.

"Arsonists are a bitch to find," Dylan corrected him, knowing he had Josh hooked. "And Pittsview might be small, but thanks to the Cattleman's Club, it has a hell of a lot of tourism."

"The Cattleman's Club?" Josh scowled in confusion before asking the question Dylan had been waiting all night for. "What the hell is that?"

* * * *

Later that night, Josh lay in his bed, staring at the ring Maria had given back to him and wondering what the hell he was going to do now. That was the big question. One he didn't have an answer to. All he knew was what he wasn't going to do—a bunch of strange women at some kind of sex club.

That really wasn't his thing.

Looking for an arsonist, that held more appeal. Enough that he'd agreed to go. If nothing else, the distance and time would give Josh a chance to figure out what he was going to do next.

He really had no clue, and that was very unsettling to him. Josh always had a plan. His plans were always successful, or they had been. Then Maria had happened.

She was exactly what he'd been looking for, fitting into the role of girlfriend so perfectly it was as if she'd been made for his plan. The only problem was she hadn't been perfectly made for him. That meant his plan was askew, that it didn't fit him.

That was the revelation that had him floored and shocked and, in a very real way, panicked. He didn't know what he was supposed to do now. That didn't mean he didn't know what he wanted to do. Technically it was a who—Casey, to be specific.

Heaving a deep sigh, Josh dropped the ring back onto the nightstand and stacked his hands behind his head as he stared up at the ceiling and considered how right Maria had been about his wandering eye. What did it matter that his hands had never followed? His heart had.

He was in love with Casey, and he was so screwed because Josh knew Dylan was too. Not that his brother would admit it, but Josh suspected that was part of what had driven his desperation to get Josh to the club. Dylan didn't want to leave Josh alone with Casey.

He wanted Casey for himself.

He could have had her too, but Trina had really screwed him up. She'd helped twist Dylan into such a pervert that Josh didn't know if any one woman would ever be able to satisfy him. What he did know was that he was screwed no matter what because Josh was pretty sure Casey had it bad for his brother, too.

As for him, Josh was the best friend, the good guy, the one who was too straight-laced and boring to ever keep up with a woman like Casey. Or, at least, that's what she thought. Maybe it was time to change her mind and prove to her that he could keep her just as satisfied as his brother.

After all, Josh had always wanted to try a few things.

Chapter 3

Sunday, May 25ᵗʰ

Dylan woke up the next morning, as he usually did, before the sun. He didn't need the light to see as he pulled on a pair of baggy shorts and stepped into his well-worn sneakers. It took only seconds to lace them up, and he was waiting by door when Casey finally appeared wearing a very similar outfit. Unfortunately, she'd also put on a shirt.

He'd left his off, knowing that, despite her best efforts not to, Casey couldn't help but take sly glances at his body. She liked what she saw. Dylan knew it. He liked what he saw, too, as he fell in step behind her. Casey had a great ass, and he loved to watch it bounce. It was so round and plush. His hands fairly burned with the itch to reach out and touch.

Casey would probably bite his hand off, though. He knew she thought he followed her just to be obnoxious, just as he knew it irritated the crap out of her. That was just too damn bad. She was too cute, and as a cop, he knew how dangerous jogging alone could actually be for a woman, especially women who had ritualized habits and routes, which Casey did.

Every morning, exactly at six, she ran a five-mile loop before showering, dressing, and joining Josh for breakfast. So, every morning Dylan was home, he got up at five minutes to six and joined her. He'd have liked to have joined her for the shower afterward, too, but, in four years, Casey had never once extended that invitation.

Not once…

That depressing thought echoed through his head as it dawned on Dylan he wouldn't have a chance to make a move after Josh made his. He and his brother had competed over a lot of things, but never a woman. That wasn't going to change, but his running in her shadow was.

Picking up speed until he was running beside her, Dylan made a silent point to Casey that she responded to in kind. Without a word or even a glance in his direction, she picked up speed in a blatant attempt to outrun him. Dylan couldn't let her get away with that.

He matched her step for step until finally Casey was running flat-out, and he was still jogging. It wasn't fair. It wasn't right, but Dylan still couldn't help but smile. His grin didn't last long, though. It ended abruptly as Casey tripped over her own feet and plowed into his side, sending both crashing to the ground in a tangle of limbs.

Thankfully, they landed on mostly grass. It was softer than the pavement but not nearly as soft as the breast his hand ended up covering. Actually, she was kind of firm. Instinct had his fingers curling around the generous curve of her soft mound just as it had her nipple hardening against his palm. That didn't stop Casey from snapping at him as she all but threw his hand back in his face.

"What the hell do you think you're doing?" Casey demanded to know as she scrambled back to her feet.

"Well, I was trying to get in a morning jog." Dylan began his explanation as he stared at the puckered tips of her breasts pressing out against the worn cotton of her shirt.

Casey had a nice rack, but that's not why he stared. He stared because he knew it would irritate the crap out of her. Sure enough, she flushed and crossed her arms over her chest as her tone sharpened with her impatience.

"You were racing me," Casey accused him, as if it were the worst of all sins.

"Nope." Dylan shook his head, unfazed by her attitude as he leapt back up to his feet. "*You* were racing me."

"I was not!"

"Then why are you the one sweating?" Dylan retorted with a smile. "Or are you panting because you're excited to see me?"

"*If* I were racing you, you wouldn't stand a chance."

"Okay, now we're on." Dylan didn't ever back down from a challenge, especially not one Casey issued.

She knew it. She knew exactly what she was getting herself into and didn't hesitate for a moment to line up beside him along the path and nod her agreement as he began to count down. Casey took off the second he said go, but Dylan hesitated.

He allowed her to run ahead for most of the way back, not bothering to put much effort into chasing her until they turned back into their apartment complex. Only then did he pick up speed, sailing right past her and up the steps to land in front of his door before she made it to hers.

Of course, he couldn't just smile and be contented with the knowledge that he'd bested her. Oh, no. Dylan had a victory dance, one that came with ever-changing lines but always ended with Casey storming away. She was a sore loser, which just made it all the more fun to beat her.

Dylan chuckled to himself as he headed in to take a quick shower. By the time he was clean, shaved, and dressed, Josh already had the coffee going and breakfast cooking. It was eggs that morning with a hash that had Dylan's mouthwatering, but he knew to stay on his side of the counter. Josh didn't like people getting in his way.

No sooner had Dylan settled down into his normal seat than Kacey appeared, jumping onto the stool beside him and using it to climb up onto the counter. The cat joined Dylan in watching Josh as he finished prepping the plates.

"You cook those potatoes in the bacon grease?" Dylan eyed the hash and all but licked his chops. He was hungry.

"Huh? Oh, yeah." Josh nodded as he glanced over at Dylan, his gaze darkening into a scowl as his eyes narrowed in on Kacey. "Would you get that thing off the counter?"

"Kacey is not a thing,"

"Off the counter."

"You heard the grouch." Dylan picked up the cat and gave him a quick hug as he murmured in a baby voice he'd have never used in front of anybody other than Josh…and Casey. "He's just a mean, old, grumpy bastard, isn't he? Yes, he is. Yes, he is. Yes, he is."

Whether he agreed or not, Kacey wanted to be freed. He squirmed, making his want known. Dylan dropped him onto the floor as the door cracked open and Casey stuck her head inside without bothering to knock.

"Hello?"

"In the kitchen," Josh hollered back, drawing Casey through the living room toward the island bar that separated the kitchen from the dining room. Dylan kicked the stool beside him out in a silent greeting that she didn't bother to thank him for, though she did take a seat.

"Breakfast is ready," he informed her as he considered that Maria had a right to be jealous of Casey. After all, Maria might be gorgeous, but she wasn't perfect. Casey was, with that smile and those eyes and those firm, large—

"Do you mind not staring at my breasts?" Casey snapped as she crossed her arms over her chest. "You're acting like you haven't gotten laid in—"

"Weeks," he finished for her. That was just the pain of having to live life undercover. No sex. No fun. No Casey.

"Yeah, right." Casey snorted in obvious disbelief. "What happened? You have to wait for the medicine to clear up something down *there*."

Casey stressed that last word as her eyes dipped down to Dylan's crotch in a pointed look that had him flipping her off. She was forever insinuating that he had some kind of sexually transmitted disease, but he wasn't dumb. He wore a condom every time, with every woman, and always turned down pussy that either looked weird or had a funny smell. He did have some standards.

Unlike some people.

"Oh, that's right. I ran into Jeb down at the prison and he said not to worry. The itching will go away," Dylan shot back, lying as he referenced one of the many bozos Casey had dated, thankfully, briefly.

"Really? Because I ran into Janet shopping for strollers. She said the baby's due in a few weeks and here I forgot to get you a card," Casey retorted, matching Dylan's dirty look as they shared a moment before she dismissed him and turned her attention to Josh, who was sliding a plate of smiley-faced eggs with bacon eyebrows and hash-brown hair.

"Here, I made this for you." Josh offered Casey a bashful smile that had Dylan rolling his eyes.

He knew what was coming. Josh always got weird around women he liked. Weird, awkward, even gawky, it was so embarrassing. Embarrassing but effective.

"Feeling creative this morning?" Casey's tone and manner softened, no doubt in response to Josh's sudden onset of shyness. She was folding.

Just like every woman before her, Casey was falling for Josh's big doe-eyed look. It wouldn't be long before her clothes were littering the floor and Josh had her screaming down the rafters. Dylan wasn't sure what Josh did to a woman, but he made most of them thank God loud enough for every saint in heaven to hear, not to mention the sinners down in hell. That's where Dylan felt as though he was being sentenced, too, as Josh gazed longingly down at Casey.

"I find myself feeling strangely...."

"Optimistic?" Casey offered, earning her another smile from Josh.

"Yeah." He nodded. "Optimistic, that's how I feel."

"That's because you are bitch-less." Dylan lifted up his glass and lifted it into the air. "And I say we celebrate your new single-man status."

"Here, here." Casey could agree with him on that much at least. She lifted her glass, clinking it against his as Josh gave them both a sour look.

"Maria wasn't that bad."

Dylan snorted right along with Casey as they shared a glance and shook their heads.

"He's hopeless." Casey sighed.

"Well, he's had sex with her," Dylan quickly reminded Casey. "Sex, especially *good* sex, can make up for a lot of flaws."

"And you would know," Josh muttered as he handed a plate over to Dylan.

Casey snickered as she picked up her fork, but before she could take a bite, a set of claws sank into her jeans, and a second later, Kacey was hoisting himself up onto her lap as she sat there clearly simmering or, at least, pretending to simmer. Dylan could see through Casey's act.

She liked his cat.

* * * *

Josh watched Casey's brow wrinkle into a scowl as she glared down at Dylan's cat and had to admit that he was amazed Kacey hadn't disappeared one night. He wouldn't put it past her to relocate the cat to a good home somewhere. Of course that would crush Dylan, and Josh was pretty sure Casey would never hurt his brother. It didn't matter if she did hate his cat because Casey liked Dylan.

She would just never admit to it.

As far as the cat went, Kacey didn't help matters when he shoved his face into her eggs and began eating without any concern of retribution. He didn't have to worry. Dylan was there to keep him safe. Plucking the cat off Casey's lap with one hand, Dylan swapped plates with her using the other. In less than five seconds, Kacey was settled back down on his brother's thighs and shoving his face deeper into the eggs as Dylan leaned forward to eat around the cat.

"That is so gross." Casey stared at Josh's brother with a look of disgust.

"What?" He glanced up as if checking to see if she were really talking to him. When he realized she was, Dylan's indignation couldn't be masked. "Why? It's not like I'm eating where Kacey is. There is a little buffer."

"Whatever." Casey waved away his explanation. "I'm not kissing you, so it's really none of my business where you stick your tongue."

In response to that, Dylan stuck his tongue out and wiggled it at her, but he quickly retracted it when she lifted her fork higher and eyed him with malicious intent. Josh bit back a laugh as he watched the two of them. They really were a matched set, and he loved them both.

That truth hit him then and there as he gazed over at Casey, amazed at how beautiful one woman could actually be. The sunlight streaming through the kitchen window made her skin glow until she nearly glimmered like an angel. Of course, the devilish twinkle shimmering in her eyes assured a man that Casey was no saint. Far from it. She was a flesh-and-blood goddess who was meant to be worshipped both in bed and out of it, like maybe on the kitchen table…or bent over the couch, or even—

"So, how you holding up?"

Josh blinked as Casey's question cut through his wayward thoughts. It took him a moment to remember Maria and their breakup. He was supposed to be emotionally torn up, but he was more nervous about what came next than worrying about what he'd lost.

"I'm fine." Josh finally offered her that answer, knowing it had taken too long. She wasn't going to believe him.

"Shit, you're better than fine. You're free," Dylan proclaimed with a grandeur that Casey quickly seconded.

"To freedom." Casey lifted her glass in a salute. "May we all use it wisely and never waste it."

"I'll drink to that." Josh lifted his coffee cup and clinked it against her tea, but whereas Casey took a big gulp, Josh simply sipped. "So, what about you? You excited about your trip?"

"Oh, yeah." Casey broke out into a big grin. A grin that kind of unnerved Josh.

"I take it you got big plans, huh?"

"The biggest."

"Really?" Dylan perked up at that brag. "And what are they?"

"To spend as much time naked as possible," Casey shot back obnoxiously, making Dylan snort and roll his eyes as Josh swallowed and tried not to picture her without clothes. It was pointless.

"I assume you have similar plans?" Casey lifted a brow in Dylan's direction. "I mean, given your weeks-long fast and all, you must be kind of...desperate by now."

"Honey, I am *never* desperate." Dylan tossed her a wink before throwing Josh under the bus. "But I do have big plans, and this time, I'm taking baby brother with me."

Josh felt the ground shift beneath him as he silently started praying that Dylan would leave it at that. He didn't want Casey to know about the sex club. It was embarrassing. It wasn't as though he was going for the sex.

"Is that right?" Casey glanced over at Josh for confirmation and he quickly tried to change the direction of the conversation.

"More like I'm going along to bail him out just in case he gets into that much trouble," Josh assured her, earning him a laugh from her and a dirty look from Dylan.

"I'll have you know I have *never* been arrested," Dylan said, defending himself.

"That doesn't mean you shouldn't have been," Josh muttered. He could think of a few times when they'd been teenagers and Dylan hadn't been such an upstanding citizen.

"You know you two argue like an old married couple," Casey commented as she lifted up a piece of bacon and dangled it over her mouth.

Josh watched as she lowered it all the way down and felt his breath catch as she ate the whole piece in one bite. He was hard and hurting in an instant. Thankfully, the counter hid his body's reaction to Casey's innocent provocation, but he couldn't hide the truth from himself. How sad was he? He was getting turned on by watching the damn woman eat bacon. Maybe Dylan was right. Maybe he needed to get laid. What he really needed was Casey.

"You know, I was going to say the same about you and me," Dylan cut in, drawing Casey's attention back to him and reminding Josh that he wasn't the only one who needed her.

"Please, like I'd marry you." Casey laughed. "I don't even think that is legal."

"What do you mean?" Dylan puffed up indignantly.

"I think there are laws against marrying dogs."

"Ha. Ha. Ha," Dylan shot back. "You're so funny I forgot to laugh."

"And that's just like the *lamest* comeback ever!"

"Enough, children," Josh intervened before their argument could really get started. "If you can't be creative and clever with your insults, then keep them to yourselves."

"Yes, dad," Casey and Dylan echoed together in a harmonized routine that almost made Josh smile. His grin didn't last long as Casey returned to the very topic he didn't want discussed.

"So? Are you guys really headed out somewhere, or are you just going to beat around the bars in town?" Casey looked from Josh to Dylan, who snickered.

"Why are you so curious?"

"I was just asking."

"Oh, really? So, where you going?"

"It's where *are* you going," Casey corrected Dylan as she stuck her nose up in the air at him. "And that's none of your business."

"That sounds like a singles cruise to me," Dylan declared as he drew Josh into the middle of their argument. "What do you say, baby brother?"

Josh blinked, his mind going blank as his gaze caught Casey's. He found himself instantly captivated and suddenly uncertain. "Uh…"

"You should come with us." Dylan moved on quickly as he shot Josh a disgusted look before turning a lecherous look back on Casey. "You can lay around naked all damn day where we're going, and we'd *love* to have you…join us. Wouldn't we, Josh?"

"Uh…" Yes. Yes. A million times, *yes*! But that wasn't going to happen. What was going to happen was Dylan making a complete ass out of not only himself this time, but Josh as well.

"Let me interpret for you." Once again Dylan filled in for Josh. "That's a yes."

"It didn't sound like one," Casey disagreed as she studied Josh. "And why is he blushing?"

"Because he's afraid," Dylan admitted, crushing all of Josh's hopes with his next revelation. "He doesn't want you to find out I'm taking him to a sex club."

Chapter 4

A sex club. Dylan was actually going to do it, too. He hadn't been kidding. Why she should care? Casey didn't know, but that didn't mean she didn't. Three hours later as she found herself hesitating at the turn-off to the highway that led up beneath the ornate arches that welcomed guest and members to the Cattleman's Club, she still couldn't escape her thoughts of Josh and Dylan.

She was torn between disgust, jealousy, and the strange fantasy of running into them at the Cattleman's Club. That would never happen. The entrance conveyed a sense of wealth and privilege that Dylan couldn't afford and Josh wouldn't waste his money on.

That meant she was on her own.

Forcing herself to put aside her thoughts of Dylan and Josh, Casey turned her attention to the reality of what awaited her at the end of the drive. An education in ecstasy—that was what Felicity had called it, which was saying something because Felicity knew Casey wasn't exactly inexperienced, far from it.

Her carnal curiosity had led Casey to try just about every kink that wasn't too gross or out there. Every kink, that was, but the one that unnerved her the most—domination. When it came to sex, Casey was always in charge. The idea of not being in control, though, sent a tingle of anticipation racing down her spine and had her turning off the highway and easing her compact down the long drive.

It curled around one grassy knoll after another, which added to that sense of prestige garnered by vast feel of the club's estate. She couldn't even make out the hint of a building in the distance when she finally came to a fork in the road. A beautifully carved wooden sign directed staff to the right. Members went straight and female guests to the left.

The butterflies that had been gathering in her stomach for the past several hours began to synchronize their fluttering as she turned the wheel toward the left. Casey wanted this. She needed it.

That didn't change the fact that the fear gripping her muscles grew only stronger as she neared the small guard shack blocking the road. The adorable little building looked quaint and cute compared to the very large man who stepped out of it. He rippled with muscles and moved with a lethal grace that had Casey's heart doing a double beat.

If the guard was any indication of just what the Cattlemen were like, then she'd hit the jackpot. That is if she didn't end up arrested. A whole new worry blossomed in her as the guard asked to see her identification.

Along with the fake name Casey had used to get into the club came a fake driver's license that she could only pray was good enough to get her past the guard. It was.

Breathing a sigh of relief, she took the fake license back, along with her visitor pass while he gave her directions to what he referred to as the harem. Those two words alone evoked an image that had the butterflies fluttering again.

Casey was shaking by the time the guard stepped back to press a button that had the wooden arm blocking the road lifting upward. She eased her car forward, feeling a sense of finality as the gate closed behind her. There was no turning back now, not that she wanted to.

It had been months since she last hooked up, and that guard was delicious looking. He was a hell of a lot better than the pickings she'd been wading through, but that was life in Atlanta. The competition was fierce thanks to the fact that the women outnumbered the men.

It didn't help either that half of the men preferred other men and a half of what was left were already married. It also didn't help that a lot of the women were affluent enough to afford better than good.

Not Casey. Patton's and her boutique might be doing well, but they'd invested most of their money back into the business. That meant Casey's white teeth came from drugstore strips, along with the rest of her beauty supplies. At least, her clothes were custom made thanks to Patton.

Patton.

Casey sighed as her thoughts strayed toward her friend and her comments from the previous evening. Patton was too insightful by half, but that didn't change anything. Whether Casey wanted Dylan or Josh didn't matter because she'd never be able to have either one, but she could make one of her fantasies come true.

What better place to make a fantasy come true than a perfectly groomed garden paradise where amazingly hot and talented men roamed free?

Apparently that wasn't all that was roaming free. Casey's attention caught on the sight of the woman clearly waiting for her as she turned into the parking lot the guard had directed her to. It was large, but the wide stretch of asphalt was broken up by large islands filled with lush, decadent landscaping. Not that Casey really noticed the shrubs.

Her gaze remained fixed on the raven-haired beauty standing there wearing a smile and not much else. Pulling her car into the numbered slot she'd been assigned, Casey tried not to ogle the woman as she stepped out of the compact, but it was impossible. The woman was gorgeous and perfectly formed from the top of her head all the way down to her elegant little feet.

Suddenly Casey found herself feeling very outclassed.

"Morning." The woman stepped forward wearing nothing but a smile and a pair of heels. "I'm Lana, director of female services."

"Casey." She shook the woman's hand and tried not feel like a complete oaf as she did.

"It's nice to meet you, Casey, but we don't use real names around here," Lana assured her with a smile warm enough to make the sun jealous. "So for now, you're The Cherry."

"The Cherry?" Casey repeated, thinking that was a little on the nose.

"It's the one given to all new girls." Lana offered her an apologetic smile. "Don't worry. The guys will come up with a more specific one once they've gotten to know you."

She meant once they'd fucked her. That thought sent a thrill racing down Casey's spine that was equal parts apprehension and anticipation.

"Come on in to the admissions office, and I'll explain how things are run around here." Lana nodded toward the small wooden alcove that protruded out from the stone wall that rose high above.

It loomed over them like an old guard, its sense of strength not weakened by the vines running up its rugged length. Instead, the colorful flowers blooming across its surface only served to heighten the illusion that the wall protected something great and glorious, and Casey already knew what. The harem.

If she was about to join such a forbidden group of women, Casey wanted to be dressed for the occasion.

"Just let me get my bag," she called out as she circled around toward the trunk.

Lana watched her with an amused expression. "You did note on the invitation that it said no clothing was necessary?"

"This isn't clothing," Casey assured her as she pulled out the small sack and slammed down the trunk. "I have a friend back in Atlanta who owns a lingerie boutique. You share some…clients."

So she thought she'd bring some samples, but Casey knew better than to be so bold as to finish that thought aloud. Instead, she simply returned Lana's smile as the other woman's gaze shifted to the bag Casey had slung over her shoulder.

"I take it that's how you learned about our club then?" Lana asked politely as she led Casey toward the admission office. "I believe you were nominated by Felicity, right?"

"That's right." Casey nodded, distracted by the room Lana escorted her into.

Admission office sounded more professional and sophisticated than this small, wood-paneled room. Hell, a bus depot had more class, Casey thought, considering that the ambience was more psycho-killer, horror movie-ish than resort sex-club-ish. She had a feeling it was intentional.

It was too pointedly stark, too opposite of the image presented outside. There were no windows, no paintings, no anything but the outdated fixture overhead and a metal table that would have looked right in any prison in the country. That observation led Casey to the only obvious conclusion.

The room was designed to unnerve and scare…but why?

"You'll have to forgive the way the office looks," Lana spoke up, drawing Casey's attention toward her as she recited what felt like a well-rehearsed line. "I assure you the rest of the grounds are better kept. Please, have a seat."

She gestured toward the nearest chair before circling the small, metal desk that took up most of the room. Other than the table and the two folding chairs flanking it, there wasn't much left in the room except a folder with Casey's fake name on it and a pen resting beside it.

"Is this just a temporary space?" Casey asked as she settled down into her own seat. Perhaps there were renovations going on that had forced them into using this small space.

"No." Lana shook her head. "I know this room doesn't look like much, but it serves its purpose well."

"And what purpose is that?" Casey asked. "Scaring the hell out of the newbies? Is this some kind of initiation?"

Those two blunt questions had Lana's gaze narrowing on Casey before her eyes began to twinkle with an honest sense of amusement. "Something like that."

"Job well done," Casey assured her before giving into her curiosity. "So I have to ask, why?"

"For the obvious reason," Lana answered with a shrug. "This club is about pushing boundaries and exploring new levels of delight. While most women arrive eager to participate, not all of them are actually willing to pay the price for such divine ecstasy."

Casey got that. Giving one's will completely over to another person was frightening enough, but giving it over to strangers—even she wasn't certain she was ready for that.

"Obviously, it sort of dampens the mood if ladies get in who really can't participate. So, it's part of my job to weed out the panickers and make sure that the women who make it through are actually willing to play."

Those words awakened the new fear in Casey. To be intimidated was one thing. To flee was another. But to be rejected? That would be the worst.

"The Cattlemen's Club is about enjoying the experience," Lana explained. "Trust me, nerves can make all sorts of things feel so much more intense."

"I get that." And Casey did.

The light, excited feeling that had filled her with giddy bubbles on the short drive from Atlanta had been strong enough to leave her feeling drunk for most of the way. That sensation had given way to an apprehension that was no less potent and even more thrilling.

"And you will be getting a lot more of it," Lana informed her. "I'm not going to lie. The men here will strive to make you nervous, but rest assured that none of them will actually hurt you or do anything you don't want them to. This isn't about force, but submission, and any time you want to stop, all you have to say is 'pygmy.'"

"Pygmy?" Casey repeated, unable not to smirk at the very word. It was just so weird.

"Yes, pygmy," Lana repeated with a nod, quite serious. "That is the club's universal safe word."

"Safe word. Got it."

"You say pygmy and the men stop, and you *leave*," Lana stressed. "Men engage with women at their discretion. The choice of partners is not yours."

"You mean I'll be having sex with complete strangers, and I don't get to choose who," Casey stated evenly, managing to control the shiver that thought gave her. The butterflies in her stomach were in full flurry now, and Lana's assurance didn't calm them a bit.

"The likelihood is you won't even get to see them," Lana explained before qualifying that strange comment. "At least, not at first, but before we get into that, we must go over the rules."

Flipping open the folder in front of her, Lana pulled out a sheet full of bulleted points and passed it over to Casey, who began to read through the list.

"All females are to remain naked at all times unless dressed by their masters in appropriate club costumes."

Casey smirked at that one, unable but to wonder what appropriate meant. The next one, though, left no doubt of its intention.

"All females are to be collared. Any female who removes her collar opens herself up to claiming, and yes, that means exactly what it sounds like. They hold a public competition where the men fuck you one right after another and the audience judges who you responded best to."

"Wow." Casey blinked as Lana's words painted an image that both tempted and terrified her. "That's…"

"Been done more times than you would think," Lana assured her. "But normally by more experienced female members. My suggestion is you leave this generic collar on until a master claims you."

Lana leaned back to fish a small strip of black lace out of one of the desk's drawers and slid it across to Casey as she continued her explanation. "Tomorrow there will be a festival followed by an auction where you'll be sold to your master and he or they will provide you with a collar that allows all other members to know who you belong to."

Casey looked down at the piece of black lace that had the word Cherry embroidered on it in pink thread before glancing back up at Lana's bare neck.

"No. I'm not wearing a collar," Lana answered before Casey could ask the obvious question. "I'm not a servant to these men, but to the women. I'm in charge of all female services. So if you have any questions, any problems, I'm the one you should speak to."

"Is that after I say pygmy?"

"Just say my name and somebody will come and get me."

Casey nodded, accepting that Lana was just the type of person she'd want on her side if she needed a voice to speak for her beside her own. The woman just had that kind of commanding authority, one that left Casey wondering if Lana didn't have a man collared somewhere.

"Of course, I won't be of any assistance to you tonight," Lana stated bluntly. "You have to survive your initiation on your own. If you can't, then, frankly, you don't belong here."

Casey wanted to belong there, but the word "initiation" had the knots tightening again in her stomach. "Initiation?"

"It is a rite of passage for all new females, and it can be very intimidating." Lana paused, her smile dimming for the first time as her full lips tightened into a serious expression. "Honestly, a good quarter of the women don't make it past the first night, and I'll give you the same advice I give every woman who passes through this office.

"Surrender. Don't fight how good things feel. Don't try to think of how right or wrong something is. Just breathe, relax, and enjoy. If you can do those three things then—"

"—I'll be treated to an education in ecstasy?"

"Yes." Lana's grin reappeared, along with the twinkle in her eyes. "I don't think I could have said it better myself."

"I didn't come up with the line," Casey confided in her. "But I am curious to find out what it means."

"Well, I can appease a little of that curiosity and, at least, tell you what to expect," Lana offered.

"I'm dying to know." Actually, Casey was creaming, but she kept that information to herself.

"Very well." Lana nodded before clasping her hands and meeting Casey's gaze with her own direct one. "You will be spending the night strapped and blindfolded. You will be put on display in the main room where all members will be allowed to play with you as they please."

That sounded naughty, dirty, and like the kind of fun Casey had never dared to dream of. It was then that she began to realize that this wasn't the place where her dreams would be fulfilled. This was a place where her fantasies would be redefined.

"I assure you there will be no vaginal or anal intercourse."

That dampened the lust boiling through her veins, but it flared back hotter as Lana continued.

"Though there might be penetration with any sorts of toys, and you will undoubtedly be demanded to suck more than one cock...you do like to suck cock, right?"

"I've been assured that I'm pretty good at it," Casey answered, avoiding explaining that blowjobs weren't her favorite pastime. She was willing to go there, though, as long as a man was willing to return the favor.

"If that's true, then you will probably fetch a very high price at the auction tomorrow. Speaking of tomorrow, I mentioned there will be a festival in celebration of the holiday. There will be all sorts of competitions where you will be offered either as part of the challenge or as a prize if you make it through the night."

"I'll make it," Casey assured her.

Whatever it took, however many deep breaths she had to suck down, she wasn't going to punk out before she got to the festival because the very notion of being considered a prize had her wetting her panties enough to leave her feeling a little uncomfortable.

"Something tells me you will," Lana agreed with her, though Casey suspected she gave all the women she met the same kind of encouraging support. "The fair will close with an auction where the men will be bidding on—"

"—me."

"You." Lana nodded. "As I explained before, whoever buys you will be your master for the rest of your stay. Now keep in mind, masters share, lend, and trade women constantly. You can't take it personally or get jealous. This is not about fidelity. It's about gluttony. Now, I need to know if you can accept these terms."

Have sex with untold number of strangers? Be put on display? Used? Traded? Sold? Casey's heart was pounding, her palms sweating, and her panties dripping. There was really only one answer.

"Yes."

Chapter 5

Monday, May 26th

Josh stared up the steps of the ornate entrance to the Cattlemen's Club. The place looked like an upscale resort with its lush landscaping and beautifully designed Spanish-style buildings. It reeked of wealth and privilege but not the kind of elite sophistication of some intellectual society.

Despite the large cobblestone carport that was well-manned by valets, who were both quick and respectful, and the butlers who stood at attendance, dressed in full uniform with long coattails, there was still a sense of forbidden perversion that lingered over the club's entrance. It might have had something to do with the gilded, wrought-iron gates that were custom fitted into the entry arches that led up into the club's main lodge.

Eat. Drink. Be Merry.

Each arch bore its own welcoming message, and while Josh was all for the eating and drinking, his mood was far from merry. A whole bunch of easy pussy wasn't going to change that because sex was not his problem. Neither was it the solution to his problem.

What Josh needed was a plan, a new plan because his old one was all blown to hell, which was just a shame. It had been such a good plan. It had gotten him this far, after all, and he'd racked up quite a number of accomplishments.

He'd been valedictorian, gotten into his first-choice college on a full scholarship, worked the right internships, maintained straight A's, gotten the right job, and made all the right contacts. He'd started his business, met the perfect girl, gotten engaged, and bought the house.

Everything had gone just as planned. Now he was supposed to get married, have children, travel the world, and retire to a tropical location. Along the way, there would have been grandchildren and lots of happy memories. That was the perfect life spent, but now he was off script, swimming in unchartered waters, and it was all Casey's fault.

She'd come along and ruined everything...or saved him. Josh honestly didn't know whether to blame her or thank her right then. All he knew was that he was twisted up into knots and had enough lady problems to not be eager to complicate the matter with even more women.

A good puzzle, though, was just the kind of distraction Josh needed.

"I guess ranching has gotten more profitable since we left the country, huh?" Josh commented as he cast an eye around the entrance. "It certainly pays better than security."

"Please," Dylan snorted. "I'm betting this place pays for itself. I mean, seriously, how much would you pay to enjoy what is on the other side of those gates?"

"Trust me, you can't afford it," Chase answered for him, appearing on the other side of the *Merry* gate with a grin that Josh remembered all too well.

Back in the day when Chase had competed in the same rodeos as Dylan, he'd been known for two things—winning and grinning. It looked as though he was still at it.

"Chase," Dylan broke out enthusiastically, stepping up to greet the other man as the butler opened the gate for him. "It's been a while."

"Too long," Chase agreed, taking Dylan's hand and stepping up to engulf him in a quick, one-armed hug as he pounded him on the back with his other hand. Dylan returned the affectionately macho gesture that Josh was thankfully spared when all he got from Chase was a quick nod.

"Josh, been a while."

"Time that seems to have served you well." Pointedly glancing around, Josh shook his head. "These are some fancy digs."

"And that's got to mean the women are..." Dylan didn't fill out that hopeful conclusion but instead wagged his brows, eliciting a laugh from Chase, who stepped back and gestured for Dylan to step through the gate.

"Why don't we take a tour, and you can decide just how the women are."

"That is an offer I cannot resist."

Dylan didn't have to be invited twice. With the eagerness of a child rushing toward a Christmas tree, he stepped through the gates and entered paradise. Josh followed with the tolerant acceptance of a parent but soon found himself caught up in the moment as they wound through the massive club.

After seven years of sex with a woman who expected a man to do all the work and didn't reward him with much more than the right to ride her from behind, Josh found himself captivated as they entered the main hall. Everywhere he looked, women not only allowed a man to ride them from behind but also in it.

How many times had he dreamed of indulging in that pleasure? Enough that he couldn't help but stare, stare and hunger as he glanced about at the forbidden fantasies being played out all around him. There were threesomes, foursomes, and even fivesomes. Women were bent in every position imaginable, taking the men in every physical way possible and making Josh realize just how much he'd been missing out on.

He'd suppressed his redneck genes for far too long. They'd withered beneath the constraints of domestication that was necessary in the modern world of political correctness. Here those restraints were ripped away. Here women were adored and worshiped for the sexual goddesses they were while the men proved just who commanded those passions.

Deep within Josh stirred that primitive male, awakening to the challenge of being strong enough to claim a woman for his own. There was only one woman he wanted with that kind of feral lust, only one woman he ached to see glancing up at him from her knees with her big eyes hungry and pleading, his cum dripping from her lips.

Casey.

God help him, it was her face he saw as they wove through the main hall to check out the dining room and the men's den. Everywhere he looked, he saw her. Even when they paused by the punishment pen, where masters left their naughty slaves for any and all to discipline as they so desired, Josh saw Casey's face staring up at him from the woman stretched out over a table.

Tied down like an offering, she was being punished, and Josh couldn't deny that his palms itched to feel the leather-strapped handle of a flogger in his fist. He watched with fascinated hunger as the tassels rained down over her tits, turning her large breasts a beautiful blush color before they danced down to lick over her pussy.

Spread wide and completely bared for all to see every inch of her intimate flesh, her cunt creamed as the woman cried out, but instead of begging for mercy, she demanded to be fucked. It was that insolence that had landed her in trouble, Chase explained.

Women didn't demand, but Josh kind of liked hearing the filth coming out of the woman's mouth and couldn't help but wonder what it would take to make Casey beg like that. Probably not much, actually. Casey wasn't exactly a prude, not with her body or her language.

"Normally things are a little more busy," Chase assured them as he led Dylan and Josh outside into a garden that swept back farther than the eye could see. "Most of the ladies are in the harem, getting ready for the festival this afternoon."

"A *harem*?" Dylan gaped at Chase in wide-eyed wonder. "Are you kidding me?"

"Nope." Chase paused to cast Dylan and Josh a wicked grin and quick wink. "Most of the men are resting up."

"Gonna be that kind of party, hu—*oh*!" Dylan nearly tripped over his own feet as his grin fell open into a look of shock.

Josh shared the moment with him, his eyes rounding at the sight of two women tag teaming a third while a man relaxed in a recliner watching the show as a fourth woman knelt between his legs, sucking on his cock like a lollipop she couldn't get enough of.

"That's what we call a cube." Chase gestured to the glass hut tucked into a small curve in the garden's wall. "There are a couple of dozen of them built into the maze's main paths. I've reserved one for the two of you while you stay here. They all have a bedroom and a bathroom in back, and you can order up room service whenever you want."

"Forget room service," Dylan shot back. "I want to know how many ladies come with the place."

"What do you think I meant by room service?" Chase smirked before nodding down the path. "We got more to see."

Josh didn't need to see more. He was seeing just what he wanted—one woman eating out another while a third fucked a double-sided dildo into her own cunt and the other woman's ass. Girl-on-girl action…Casey had been with a woman before, at least in his dreams. Of course, in Josh's dreams, Casey had done a whole lot more than that.

"Come on, man." Dylan smacked him on his chest, breaking the trance Josh had gotten caught in with that last thought. "We better move before you bust that zipper."

Moving didn't actually help his condition. It made it only more painful because there was nowhere to look, nowhere to turn where they weren't confronted by one wicked fantasy or another being played. As they wove their way through the carnal delights hidden within the garden's maze, Josh started taking mental notes of things he'd like to try.

"As I mentioned, we'll be having a party later," Chase repeated as they came to the end of an intricately designed garden. The opening in the tall fence of pine trees gave way to a massive field that was busy with activity.

Tents were being erected in a large circle around a bonfire with what appeared to be a catwalk encircling it. Josh could easily figure out that they planned on parading naked women around a roaring fire in some sort of rite that would probably tempt him into doing something stupid.

Or somebody.

As hot as the women were and as hard as they made him, Josh knew that if he gave into that temptation he'd probably lose any chance he had with Casey. Of course, if he kept playing it like a good boy, he wasn't going to stand a chance anyway. He was done being the nice guy, but that didn't mean he was going to play the stupid one either.

"There'll be competitions throughout the day and an auction in the evening."

"Competitions?" That sparked Dylan's interest more than the naked women frolicking in the field down below. "What competitions?"

"All sorts."

"Like?" Dylan prodded.

"Like the pussy-eating competition. Whoever makes their woman come first wins ten buckles. That one runs every half hour. So does the dick-bobbing competition, which is the same idea in reverse—the woman goes down and the winner is whoever last the longest."

"Oh, man, I am so there," Dylan swore, wearing a grin and a boner that said it all.

Josh would have been too, except for that nagging bit of conscience that kept making his thoughts stray to Casey. It just wouldn't be the same without her. It just wouldn't be worthwhile.

"Later, man," Chase assured him. "The fair is not starting for another hour, so why don't you come on up to my office and we can go over the details of the fire that brought you here."

"Sure thing, boss." Dylan nodded as he threw an arm around Josh. "Josh and I are here to help."

If they could, but Josh kept that pessimistic rejoinder to himself as Chase led the way back through the maze and past the main lodge to a smaller but no less elegant hut surrounded almost entirely by a private lagoon that was clearly also a swimming pool.

"This is nice." Dylan turned in a circle, admiring the full view. "All you need is a couple of naked mermaids and it'd be perfect."

"We used to have them, but then Patton came along, and…" Chase shrugged.

"You sent them all over to the main pool," Dylan filled in for him with a lecherous grin. "Naked women swimming…that was my kind of pool, man."

"Yeah? Well, just remember *you'll* need a pair of trunks," Chase shot back before shoving open the door and nodding for Josh and Dylan to precede him. "Come on in and have a seat. We have a lot to talk about."

That they did, and Josh tried to focus. He really did, but it was hard. Despite his best efforts, Josh felt his mind slipping back toward everything he'd seen and wondering how much Casey would let him get away with.

* * * *

"How did you enjoy last night?" Lana asked that question of Casey, making the other woman blush and glance quickly away.

That could only mean she'd enjoyed her initiation. Most women did—that is, if they didn't panic. Lana remembered hers. Of course back then there hadn't been a club, just three horny brothers with way too many ideas and a barn that had since burned to the ground.

Those times had come and gone, along with Lana's ability to blush.

"Are you interested in enjoying more?"

A smile grew across Casey's face that curled with a satisfaction that left no doubt of her answer.

Yes.

Lana wondered if Casey realized that first *yes* was only just the beginning. By the time she left the club, the other woman would be permanently changed. Everything would be different for her. All of her expectations would be altered, and the hunger for more wouldn't leave her.

Just the opposite, it would grow into a craving that would have to be filled. Lana knew what Casey would soon learn. Sex was the greatest addiction of all.

"Last night was…entertaining," Casey finally answered. A husky note that hadn't been there yesterday infused her tone as her smile crept ever wider. "An education in ecstasy that I think I'd like to continue."

"Well, then," Lana sighed, recognizing the gleam in Casey's eyes and knowing the other woman was as doomed as her. There was nothing left to do but enjoy. "I guess we should get you signed up for the fair this afternoon."

That didn't take long, given Casey had been tanned and waxed the day before in preparation for initiation. Lana left her with the rest of the women lounging around the harem's pool waiting for the fair to begin. She wouldn't be participating this year, but that didn't mean Lana wasn't responsible for assuring that the women were ready and the staff organized.

Normally she had more help, like the Davis brothers, who had joined in the celebration in the past. They were no longer circulating, though, and had appointed GD to manage their old tasks. Unfortunately GD was off at some church fair of all things. That left Lana alone to assure everything went smoothly.

As if she didn't have enough to see to, Chase sent a butler out to inform her he wished to see her in his office. For a moment, Lana considered ignoring his call, tired of the ache that always pained her when she saw him. He was supposed to be hers, but he belonged to somebody else now.

She had to live with it, or she could just run away. That was just what part of her wanted to do, but Lana couldn't leave. She'd been with Chase since she was sixteen. She'd been a friend, a lover, and a business partner. She didn't know anything else of the world other than that she'd never find the satisfaction in it that she did at the club.

That thought used to fortify her, but now it saddened her. Her nest had become a cage, one that she held the key to but was too afraid to use. So with slow, heavy steps, she made her way to the private hut that served as the Davis brothers' lair and knocked on the thick wooden door.

"Enter!" Chase hollered from inside, even as Lana was already turning the brass knob.

"You wanted—Dylan?" Lana stumbled to a stop, her mind going blank as she took in an all-too-familiar face. It was him. He was just older now…and more filled out. "*Dylan!*"

"Well, holy shit!"

Dylan broke into a wide grin, jumping out of his seat to catch Lana just as she launched herself into his arms. They closed around her, tightening with a strength had had only grown over the years, sort of like the rest of his muscles. Of course, she hadn't seen him since she'd been nineteen.

Back then all three of them had traveled the rodeo circuit, competing and partying hard. In fact, Dylan and Chase had been her first ménage, and it had gotten only wilder from there. Dylan was probably the only man that had ever been able to keep up with the Davis brothers when it came to an inexhaustible carnal curiosity.

"Chase said there was a familiar face I'd enjoy seeing, but I never thought it'd be you." Dylan's grin took on a lecherous curve as he finally released her to step back and give Lana a once-over. "And might I say I am *definitely* enjoying seeing you."

"Perv," Lana shot back with a laugh as she slapped him on the shoulder. "I'd say the same about you but…"

Lana gave him the same once-over he'd given her. Though she liked what she saw, she still shrugged and wrinkled her nose, earning her own laugh as he grabbed his chest and stumbled backward.

"Oh, you *wound* me."

"I somehow doubt it," Lana stated dryly, not believing him for a minute. "Even if I did, I'm sure you got all sorts of honeys to make you feel better. After all, you were always rolling in them."

"Like a pig in mud," Chase muttered, but there was no disguising the twinkle in his eyes as he gazed over at the two of them.

That's when it hit her—what Dylan was really doing there. He was her consolation prize. Chase was clearly hoping they'd hit it off, and rekindle their old romance, appeasing his guilt for breaking her heart.

Suddenly, her joy in the moment dimmed, but Lana held on to her smile as her gaze shifted to the man seated behind Chase's desk. He was hunched over, working on the computer and trying to avoid looking at her. There was no disguising how uncomfortable he was or that he looked faintly familiar.

"You remember my brother, Josh." Dylan followed her gaze, nodding toward the other man who bore a very striking resemblance to him.

"Oh, yeah, the shy one."

That was putting it politely. From what she recalled, he'd blushed and begun stuttering whenever a good-looking woman came around.

Apparently he'd gotten over the speech impediment, but his cheeks still flamed bright red as he glanced quickly up at her and away.

"Actually, he was engaged to a Brazilian swimsuit model until recently," Dylan informed with a hint of pride in his tone that couldn't mask the undercurrent of disdain lingering as well.

Clearly the "recently" hadn't ended well, and that was something Lana knew all about. Realizing they shared that bond made her feel a sense of compassion for the strangely hot geek, and he was hot. Hot enough to make Lana notice. Good-looking genes clearly ran in his family.

"I'm sure you are better off without her," Lana assured him with a tender smile. "After all, if you were with her, then you couldn't be here."

She didn't add on the "with me," though Lana knew Chase was hoping that it was implied. That much was clear by his smile and the suggestiveness in his tone as he offered up her services for the rest of the day.

"I was just telling the boys all about our annual festival, and I thought you might be interested in showing them around."

Chapter 6

Dylan couldn't take his eyes off of Lana. She was still gorgeous. All tanned, toned, curvy, and naked except for the high heels she managed to wade gracefully across the grass in, she was just like he remembered. She'd filled out a little, grown a little extra muscle, but then so had he.

Of course, his breasts didn't look half as good as hers. Then again Lana had always had a nice set of tits and never been shy about showing them off, or anything else for that matter. Unable to help himself, Dylan allowed his gaze to skip down past her gorgeous tits to her soft, bared mound.

Lana's slit glistened with just a hint of arousal, assuring him he'd find her wet if he reached out and tested those folds. He remembered her cunt well. She'd been all tight and slick, an absolutely excellent fuck.

Just the memory had him getting hard, and he barely heard a word she said as she rambled on about her job until she started talking about the harem. Then he was all ears.

"It's a female-only area where the ladies can relax and be prepped for whatever the men call on them to do." Lana came to a stop at the crest of a hill to gesture down to the crowds beginning to swell in the fairgrounds below. "As you can see, we have a lot of ladies."

Dylan barely spared a glance toward the long line of naked women filing into a small, closed tent. He really had eyes for only one woman. Besides, he could get to the rest later. That thought brought a smile to Dylan's face as his gaze shifted back over Lana's generous assets, assets that were puckering and straining toward him in obvious delight at being ogled.

He could have bent her over right then and there and taken her without any hesitation, but still Dylan hesitated. Lana was hot and lots of fun, but when would he ever have another chance to engage in a pussy-eating contest?

He wasn't missing out on that experience, so he better be both quick and good if he wanted to have his appetizer with Lana before the fair started. With that in mind, he moved in close and dropped his voice to a husky purr that left no doubt of the move he was making.

"Lots of ladies," Dylan agreed, casting a pointed glance back down at the long line of lovelies below. "But none as beautiful as— *ohmyGod!*"

Dylan forgot everything he was about to say as his gaze locked on the sight of the red-headed, naked pixie chatting with the other women as they all shuffled steadily forward into the tent below.

It couldn't be…

She wouldn't dare…

But it was…it was Casey. *Casey!*

And she was naked. She hadn't been kidding when she'd said she was going somewhere to be naked most of the time. She'd just forgotten to add, "and stuffed full of cock," because that's exactly what she would be once he got his hands on her.

God, was she better formed than he'd ever imagined.

Casey might have been tiny, but her curves were anything but. They were lush and full, and Dylan was going to devour them. Devour her. He was going to fuck her. Fuck her in every single position he'd ever imagined while she'd been smarting off. Even better, he was going to make her beg for it. Beg and plead and call his name, and then he was going to cram every single inch of his aching erection up that tight ass and take her for a ride.

That was just the beginning.

"Dylan?" Lana's concerned voice broke into his rampaging thoughts and brought him back to the reality of the moment as she stepped intentionally into his line of view. "Are you all right?"

No. Far from it.

"Dylan?"

"Where is the redhead going?" He paused, scowling as he heard the echoes of the crowd. "And why are all those guys calling her firecracker?"

* * * *

Casey couldn't help but laugh as the men shouted outrageous comments at her. It was a rush not only to be naked and put on display but also to be praised for her abilities. It only added to the liberating sense of freedom she had discovered last night. Being singled out, though, *that* was the best feeling.

Thankfully her popularity with the men didn't erode her popularity with the women. Lana hadn't been lying when she'd said the club was no place for jealousy. At least not about the men—the samples Casey had brought with her were a totally different matter.

By the time the other women were done raiding her luggage, Casey had given out every single business card she'd brought with her, making it a *very* good day indeed, and it looked as though it was going to get only better. Maybe, possibly even better than last night, which would be a hell of a feat.

Casey still blushed as she felt her blood heating over just the memories of what all those horny, talented men had done to her. She'd let go of her fear and anxiety and just enjoyed the feel of being touched and touching complete strangers with such great intimacy. Besides, in her mind, they hadn't been strangers.

Instead, they'd all been Dylan...or Josh, depending on the roughness of their demands. That was the real secret to how hard she'd come. Not that the Cattlemen weren't very talented, but the pleasure was more intense whenever she let her mind go and allowed the fantasies to run free.

That's what this place was all about after all—living a fantasy.

That fantasy was getting a whole lot kinkier, and Casey couldn't wait. The fair was set, the booth ready, and carnal excesses were beginning, and she couldn't wait to join in. Hell, she was wet for it.

Finally the moment came, and the attendants called her name—Firecracker. Casey felt a burst of anticipation flood through her as she stepped into line to have her collar leashed to the woman in front of her. A second later the world went dark as the attendant wrapped a blindfold around her head, leaving Casey to rely on her other senses as the leash tugged forward and she was led out into the heat of the day's sun.

The soft breeze teasing her naked flesh felt like an intimate caress that fueled the sense of exhilaration, making her heart pound and her palms sweat. This was just how it had been the night before. She'd felt as though she was flying so high that she was completely free of all restraints, despite the fact that she was actually bound in a line full of naked women being offered up as some kind of prize to the men hooting and hollering all around.

There was nothing like being appreciated, or desired. Casey felt her cunt swell and thicken with the proof of her excitement. The thick cream scented the air around her as she felt her nipples pucker beneath the lewd and dirty comments being hollered at her. She couldn't deny that she reveled in the attention, not feeling the slightest bit threatened.

Though she was a tad anxious, uncertain about what came next, but just as Lana had promised, that little tinge of unease only heightened the experience as she was instructed to sit down on a stool. Mindful of the rules she'd learned the previous evening, Casey didn't hesitate to obey. She even spread her legs wide so her pussy was open for all to see without having to be reminded.

Almost instantly her cunt went soft, swelling with joy as she felt the gazes of dozens of men rake over her intimate flesh. It was a heady rush to know that each one wanted a chance to lick, suck, and fuck her creamy folds. One lucky man was going to get a chance to…eventually.

That thought had her blushing in all sorts of inappropriate places. Casey could feel the heat spreading out from her cunt as the crowd began to chant "Firecracker," roaring with approval as the warm tide rushed upward to consume her breasts. They swelled, growing heavy with a need that almost distracted her from the attendant's orders as he commanded her to lift her breasts up and together.

He had to prod her, making Casey rush to obey before she got expelled. The disembodied voice explained that they were participating in the Hit the Tits competition as he tucked a small funnel into her cleavage. Apparently the men all had water guns and would be aiming for the funnel, which would allow the water to run down and fill up the small cup hanging from the chain attached to the clamps.

It was the word "clamp" and the sound of the woman next to her gasping that caught Casey's attention, but she didn't have time to put the two together before a set of cold metal teeth bit down over her nipple. Her breath caught as a sudden bloom of pain mushroomed out of her chest, growing in intensity as a second clamp closed over her other tender tit.

Casey was barely aware of the attendant adjusting the little cup that hung down against her stomach, but she felt every motion of the chain. Every tug and shift unleashed a new wave of agonized delight that crashed through her with the force of a tornado and left Casey panting for breath as she fought the sudden urge to reach down and stroke her clit.

The pounding beat of her pulse condensed in the tight bundle of nerves, making her clit swell and throb with a demand that was only fueled by her motions as she squirmed on the seat, wanting to do so much more but not daring to. Besides, the waiting made the release only that much more intense.

She'd learned that last night.

"You okay, Firecracker?" The concerned voice of the attendant helped Casey fortify her control, allowing her to enjoy the deep, delicious ache pulsating out of her clamped tits.

"Oh yeah," Casey breathed out with a smile that left no doubt of just how she was feeling. "Everything is just perfect."

* * * *

Dylan's heart seized as he watched the grin spread across Casey's face when she spread her legs wide, opening up that pretty, pink pussy for his gaze to devour. She was flushed, swollen, and wet. More importantly, she was smiling with the welcome he'd always dreamed of.

Actually she was more than he dreamed of because it was clear now that his little pixie was actually a red-hot firecracker. Sitting there with her nipples clamped and her big breasts heaving as she flushed with her excitement, there was no masking the truth behind her new nickname.

Casey was dangerous to touch and ready explode.

Really, he should have known. Whether she was smarting off to him, playing a video game with Josh, or yelling at whatever movie had her all hopped up, Casey was full of passion and carnal appetites, which she'd clearly been hiding from him.

Well, not anymore.

Now she was fair game.

With every intention of winning her favors, Dylan joined the crowd as the attendant opened up the booth, hollering out a greeting that welcomed one and all to the Hit the Tits competition. The men surged forward, forcing Dylan to move quickly, but he still wasn't fast enough and ended up second in the long line that formed before his firecracker.

It was torture standing there waiting to see if the idiot before him actually managed to win and claim the "breast job" that belonged to Dylan. All he knew was that he wouldn't be responsible for his reaction if that happened. He also knew the other man would end up bloody and Casey would end up being carted out of here over his shoulder.

That thought brought back his smile as a surge of barbarism had his muscles tensing in anticipation. He tried to squelch those urges with the reminder that Chase would be pissed, not to mention Casey, but in the end, his fingers still curled into fists, readying themselves to do what was necessary.

Thankfully it didn't come to that.

The idiot ahead of him was more frat boy than a true competitor. He let out a hoot as he doused Casey's breasts in the milk streaming out of his water gun. The moron didn't even try to hit the funnel. Instead, he aimed for Casey's lips, which parted to allow her tongue to lick out and catch the creamy drops.

Dylan cheered her on along with everybody else, enjoying the show. After all, Casey did look good in white. She looked even better in the henna tattoos that curled around her body, highlighting her curves and making them appear lush and full.

Those lines were so damn sexy. They made Dylan ache to trace them. He'd start with the tip of his finger and find out just how ticklish she was before he followed with his tongue, tasting every last inch of her. His fists tightened at that thought as the drool puddled in his mouth.

The crowd broke into a roar as a winner was declared down at the other end of the line. It took a few minutes for the attendant to escort the winner and his prize over to the winner's circle, but then finally it was Dylan's turn. He didn't waste time playing around like the fool before him had.

Dylan aimed straight for the funnel, which turned out to be harder than he imagined, given he had to hold the water gun down by his crotch. He still managed to claim a victory, though.

"Congratulations, sir." The attendant nodded toward him as he came down the line to unhook Casey's leash from the chair she was perched on. "If you'll follow me, sir."

He didn't ask Casey to do the same but led her over to where comfortable, oversized chairs waited in the winner's circle. In plain view of everybody, Dylan settled down into his seat while Casey followed the attendant's commands and knelt down between his legs.

Dylan ignored the lookie-loos, having eyes only for his firecracker. A part of him ached to rip off her blindfold and watch her pert, pixie features go wide with shock when she realized who had won her favors, but that moment would be better savored when he had her pinned and penetrated beneath him.

Then he'd reveal his identity and explain how he'd been the one to win all her favors in every competition because that is just what he planned on doing. Nobody, absolutely nobody, was going to touch Casey but him.

That possessive thought hammered through Dylan as the attendant began to run through the rules. He didn't fight it, simply accepting that he was too jealous to withstand the sight of her with another man. Another woman—that was different matter altogether.

"You're allowed to touch, stroke, and pet any part of your prize. You are not allowed to kiss, lick, suck, or penetrate any part of her body. You have five minutes. Enjoy."

With that, the man left Casey completely at Dylan's mercy, not that he planned on showing her any. Of course, he didn't have any plan at all, just a bunch of ideas and no sense of where to start. Part of him was just content to sit there and stare down at Casey.

She made a lovely sight wearing nothing but a set of clamps and a smile that made his balls sweat. With her legs spread and the scent of her own hunger perfuming the air, Casey had his cock swelling painfully large. In fact, he didn't even think he'd ever been this hard before.

An erection that size should be put to good use. It should be put some place hot, wet, and tight...or someplace soft and velvety. Eyeing Casey's plump tits, all flushed and swollen and swinging softly with her every breath, Dylan found the perfect place to start with.

"Come closer."

Growling over his words, he tried to mask the familiarity of his voice beneath a harsh tone. That was easily done thanks to the savage satisfaction that cut through him as Casey obeyed his command. That was sexy, almost as hot as the husky tenor in her soft murmur.

"Is that better, sir?"

Even thick with lust, there was still no disguising the hint of laughter lurking in Casey's question. She was trying hard to act submissive, but Dylan knew her well enough to see the truth. Casey was amused, amused and plotting, which meant she was up to no good. Given the circumstances, Dylan figured he had a right to start sweating, especially when she shifted, allowing her breasts to brush up against the inside of his thighs as she bent forward over the thick bulge tenting his jeans.

With a smile that assured him that she was having fun, Casey nuzzled her face into his crotch, making Dylan squirm as she nibbled her way up his length to capture the small, metal tab of his zipper in her teeth. She pulled it down with a slow, teasing motion that had the crowd around them going wild.

They cheered for her to take him down and teach him not to mess with the Firecracker. That demand drew Casey's attention as she cast a quick smile over her shoulder at the other men and wiggled her ass in a move that had them going wild and Dylan about ready to kill.

He would have, too, if any of those idiots had dared to step up and take advantage of that invitation. None did, though, and Casey's attention quickly returned to where it belonged, to him. She wasn't done yet with him yet.

Leaning down, she recaptured his zipper's tab and finished tugging the rest of the way down. Dylan's dick sprang free the moment the pressure eased, and Casey was there to greet him with a kiss that had her tongue swirling down his naked length as her lips sucked him into the warm, moist heaven of her mouth.

She milked him with three quick pulses of her cheeks before releasing his enflamed length into the cold air and bringing a complaint instantly to Dylan's lips. He grumbled over his own incoherent demands, forgetting his complaint as Casey pressed her breasts forward, blindly capturing his cock between the heavy mounds.

The flushed, sticky head of his dick peeked out at him as she dipped her chin to lick him clean. His cock wept in a blatant attempt to gain more of her mischievous tasting, but Casey denied him, daring to make him growl once again.

That feral sound turned to one of tortured delight as her hands lifted to cup her breasts and fold them around his enflamed flesh as she began a slow massage that had one plump mound pulling his taut, sensitive flesh down while the other one pushed the other side up. The pleasure was exquisite and quickly became an agony that had him fighting the urge to cover her hands with his and force her into a harder, faster pace.

He didn't give in to that urge. The seed boiling in Dylan's balls threatened to explode, but still he held back, savoring the moment as the firecracker lapped at the angry, swollen head of his cock as it wept for mercy.

She had none.

"Mmmm," she murmured as she began to pump her breasts in rhythm together. "So thick and long, you're very meaty, sir. It makes a girl kind of ache...for a taste."

With that, she caught his dick in her lips and began sucking him in earnest, clearly relishing her role as the tease and living up to his dirtiest of dreams as she reached down to fondle the tight sac of his balls. It was too much, and he couldn't take anymore.

Allowing his eyes to drift close, Dylan let the rapture rip through him as the seed shot straight down his cock and into the hungry mouth greedily nursing his length. Casey swallowed the first load before pulling back and using her hands to milk the rest out over her breasts.

"That's it...you're so hard, so hot..." Casey moaned, encouraging him with her words as well as her touch. "I wish I could feel your dick buried deep inside me, riding me hard and fast, because that's how I like it. I like it rough. I like it wild, and I like to go all the way down."

"Shit!"

Dylan gasped, his eyes flying open as Casey matched that naughty declaration with a whip of her tongue. It led the parade that had his cock being swallowed whole, taken into the moist suckling depths of her mouth and straight down the back of her throat. Then with a whoosh of those puckered lips, she squeezed the strength right out of his cock, leaving him soft and limp as the crowd broke into applause.

Rearing back on her knees, she smiled up at him, not done making him sweat. With slow, deliberate movements, she rubbed the milky liquid covering her breasts into her silken flesh, marking herself as his even as she marked him as hers. He felt branded, claimed, nothing more than a puppet on her strings, and she knew how to pull them.

Rising up to her feet with a slow, sensual motion that had every one of her naked curves sliding over him, Casey hesitated to press inward, allowing the hot wash of her breath to warm his ear.

"We weren't supposed to take a taste, but I just couldn't resist. You..." Casey paused to pull back far enough for Dylan to watch her drag a finger across the pearly white globes of her breasts.

They still dripped with his seed, and Dylan expected her to take that finger and lick the seed from it as she told him once again how good he tasted. What he hadn't expected was that then she'd gather up both breasts in her hands and lift them up so that she could dip her chin and lick them clean, sucking the droplets hanging off her puckered tits with a moan of such delight Dylan thought he might come again right then and there.

God, but she was hot. With the dark lines of the henna tattoos leading a happy-trail around her curves, she was hotter than any dream he'd ever dared to entertain. Definitely hotter than any reality he'd ever touched. As if she could read the compliments running through his mind, Casey released her breasts to smile down at him.

"I could dine on you all night long and still wake up hungry for more."

For a moment, Dylan got lost in the fantasy her words painted, but it was wrecked by the arrival of the attendant. Courteous as he was, the man still rounded Casey up and led her away, but Dylan wasn't going to let her escape that easily.

Chapter 7

Josh stared at the monitor and scowled. It had taken him way too long to hack into the local police department's files, especially given they weren't exactly secure. It should have taken him a half hour at most to access their system, but he kept getting lost in his thoughts and his memories of what waited on the other side of the office's walls.

It was a paradise, and he was too afraid to indulge.

"You don't look happy. Is something wrong?"

That question broke through the still air, startling Josh. He jerked back in his seat, his gaze cutting toward the man now smirking at him from across the room.

"Sorry, man. Did you forget I was here?"

He had, but in Josh's defense, it was easy to forget that Slade, the middle Davis brother, was working on the books in the other corner of the room. The man was quiet and thoughtful in a way that Josh hadn't suspected any Davis of being.

"I don't know." Josh sighed as he relaxed back into his seat, his attention shifting once again to the monitor in front of him. "I've made it into the police department's system, but...other than the original complaint, there is not much in the electronic file."

"Complaint?" That caused one of Slade's dark brows to rise. "We're not exactly complaining. We're pissed."

"Yeah."

Josh could get that. If Casey had gotten caught in a fire, he'd do whatever it took to find the asshole who'd started it. Hell, she was the reason he was the one denying himself…at least for now, though he didn't expect that he'd be able to hold back forever.

"Well," Josh sighed, forcing himself to focus on the moment, "maybe that's why there isn't anything in here because all the other files are pretty well filled out. Maybe the sheriff figured you were going to hire help and wanted to make sure we didn't find anything. That possible?"

"Anything's possible with Alex." Slade scowled, not appearing to care too much for the sheriff. "But if you are thinking of breaking into his office to try and find any physical files, I'll save you the effort and let you in on a little secret—the only thing in the paper file is an incident report."

That didn't sound right, and neither did the implication that somebody had already broken into the sheriff's office. It did, however, explain why the Davis brothers had called in Dylan. They were running out of options…and so was he.

Josh had a decision to make, whether to take a risk and make a move on Casey or not. If he did make one, what kind of move should it be? He normally went for romantic and sweet gestures. It wasn't so much that he didn't think Casey deserved to be showered in rose petals and dressed in diamonds, but a part of him burned to give in to the more rustic and rough style that Dylan normally used to lure women in. It certainly appeared to work on Casey.

Why not steal a few moves from his brother? After all, Josh would already be betraying Dylan no matter what move he made. That didn't sit well with him at all. Neither did the idea of what Dylan was, no doubt, up to right then.

His brother clearly wasn't abstaining, so why should he? Besides, if Casey ever found out about this trip, Dylan's chances with her would be nil. Casey might like to run a little wild, but even she had standards.

* * * *

Casey hoped she hadn't just made a complete fool of herself. She'd gotten caught up in the moment, in her fantasy, because that was what it had been. Just as she had the previous evening, Casey couldn't help but pretend that the man she'd just gone down on was Dylan.

Not that the man had been any good at the role. Hell, if it had been Dylan, he'd have curled his fingers into her hair and forced her to take him hard and deep. Really, his tentative touch and gentle caresses had been more in line with Josh's more subdued personality, but the idea of Josh at a sex club was outrageous enough. Casey certainly couldn't imagine him participating in any competition known as Hit the Tits.

Josh had too much dignity for that, which was just a shame. With the intent focus he normally applied to things, she was betting he'd make a real good master.

Dylan, on the other hand, fit the role of king better. That was just the way she imagined him, lazing back in his chair like some noble lord. That made her the good little servant, catering to his every need. That thought got her hot, and she was all too eager to hear her name called again.

Soon enough, it was, and Casey was lining back up, blindfolded again before being led back out of the waiting tent where all the ladies were kept between challenges.

This time she was taken to the Cock Bobbing tent that was just as the name suggested, a dick-sucking competition. According to the attendant escorting her into position, the rules were simple. The women gave head. The men took it. Whoever lasted the longest won.

That didn't sound hard to her.

What really piqued Casey's interest was the strange sense that she knew the man she was ordered to kneel before. She couldn't see him thanks to the blindfold but still recognized the musky scent of arousal thickening in the air around her.

Her fantasy Dylan had returned.

He smelled divine and tasted even better, like wild, raw passion. It was an addictive combination, one she savored as she took him deep and slow, thrilling at the way he grunted out a gasp. Whoever her mystery admirer was she could feel the thickness of his thigh muscles and knew well the meatiness of his cock. He wasn't a small man, but he was under her control.

She relished that knowledge as her mind once again painted an image of Dylan at her mercy. Perhaps, maybe, once she returned home, she would find the courage to dare and offer him the option of her riding him all night as long as he let her tie him to the bed and do as she pleased.

Casey didn't know what Dylan would say to that, but she didn't allow that to spoil the moment. It was too good to ruin. He was intoxicating, and she was obsessed with getting more. Forgetting all about the competition or the fact that she was supposed to be making this last and really challenging her admirer, Casey lost herself in the moment.

She enjoyed it for all it was worth, and it was worth remembering for a long, long time. He was so hard, so hot, and tasted so good. She couldn't get enough. Quickly losing control of her desires, Casey devoured the erection trapped between her lips with an enthusiasm that had the man above her cursing.

He tensed, fighting to hold back, but she wouldn't let him. Intent on driving him past his control and claiming her own victory, Casey was barely aware of the attendant ringing the bell as he declared a winner. Given her mystery lover hadn't come yet, she knew just who had won.

He didn't wait to celebrate his victory but gave over the battle, coming in a hard, thick blast that challenged her to swallow every drop. She managed, taking pride in the words of praise that came huffing out of her fantasy Dylan. The words, the sound of his voice—it was as if Dylan himself had spoken.

While Casey was certain it was only her imagination, it still felt real enough to have her preening beneath his lewd compliments. He vowed all sorts of retaliations that probably should have concerned her, but they didn't. Just the opposite. They sent a thrill of anticipation through her that left her wet and quivering.

She was almost too excited to stand but was left with no choice as the attendant came down the line to take command of her leash. He led her over to some kind of strange seat. Casey couldn't see it, but it had vinyl cushions that stuck to her ass as she slid onto it and made an embarrassing fart-like sound as her ankles were grasped in strong hands and pulled forward.

Positioned so that her ass hung off the edge of the seat and her feet were nestled into a set of stirrups, Casey didn't need her eyes to figure out that she was being strapped into some kind of exam chair, only she didn't suspect she was about to get a physical.

It was more like she was being put on display, as the stirrups were spread wide apart just like her legs. The position left her pussy open and exposed to the world. As if that weren't intimidating enough, her wrists were stretched over her head and bound, forcing her back to arch and her tits to thrust up into the air.

She probably should have been alarmed about her current position but couldn't work up the fear. The club was a magical place. Since the moment she'd been led out into the main hall the other night, Casey felt nothing but sexy and confident…and, perhaps, a little unnerved as she heard her mystery lover speak once again in a voice that was achingly familiar.

"You wouldn't happen to have a clit clamp to go with these nipple ones, would you?"

That question about stole her breath. It caught in the back of her throat, afraid to pass through her lips in an audible gasp and draw any more attention in her direction. Casey knew, though, that she couldn't escape her fate, especially when the attendant quickly assured her mystery lover they did, which meant she was in a lot of trouble.

It was in that second that, for the first time, Casey was thankful that her soon-to-be mystery tormenter was not the real Dylan. God only knew what the real Dylan would do, probably just what the fake one did. Whatever sweetness had softened his approach in the last competition, it was lost now that he had her bound and at his mercy.

"Well now, Firecracker, you ready for an education?"

That smug greeting assured her she was right. She had a secret admirer, though there was no doubt about what he admired about her. With a quick flick of her clit that had Casey squirming in her seat as a shiver of delight shot straight up her cunt, he laughed, clearly enjoying teasing her.

"Again," Casey moaned, arching her hips up in hungry demand. "Please."

"That's nice," the man drawled out. "Begging is a very nice touch, but you know the rules, Firecracker. You don't ask. You don't demand. You do, and you get punished."

That word sent a fierce fizzle of sensation racing up her spine and unleashed the gasp of air she'd been holding on to as her entire world flashed red before her blinded eyes. Every single nerve in her body ignited with a sensation so sharp it bordered on painful as her clit was suddenly caught in the tight grip of a clamp.

Quickly the sensation dulled into a throbbing ache that pulsed in beat with her trapped bud in a rhythm that was soul-deep and pounding. It was too much and yet only the beginning. Before Casey could manage to get her rioting body back under control, her breath was stolen again by another bright flash of molten rapture.

The beautiful bloom of pleasure blossomed out of her breast as the hard bite of another clamp bit down over her nipple. Casey had barely even managed to suck in a hard breath before a second detonation had whole body arching upward with the searing rush of delight when her second tender tit was caught in its own clamp.

For a moment, Casey thought she might come right then and there. That's how exquisite the ecstasy flooding through her veins was, but it wasn't rushing fast enough to hurtle her over the edge of a release. Instead, she drowned in the sensation, writhing in the searing tide of delight that all but consumed her.

The bliss rippled and popped with small fissures of piercing ecstasy as deft, callused hands leashed each clamp to the other with a chain that was pulled taut enough to make every breath a torturous experiment that she relished. Casey shivered, not bothering to even try to stay still but wiggling within her binds as she chased after the gluttonous pleasure building inside of her.

She was being naughty, knew that she would get punished. That's just what Casey wanted, and that's just why she welcomed the velvety tassels that cracked over her cunt. Each one licked across her molten flesh and over her throbbing clit, setting her entire world on fire. The flames seared upward as he whipped her with relentless strokes that had her crying out when her world exploded into one endless climax.

The pleasure was so intense, and it didn't stop, soon becoming an ache that cut deep and left her weeping with a need for more. A need to be fucked, which was just what Casey begged for.

* * * *

Chase stood at the top of the hill, surveying the fair in full swing below him while Lana stood back in his shadow, watching him. It wasn't fair that a man should be so good-looking, so strong and capable, and yet so dense to think that she could be so easily pawned off onto another man. She wasn't some stray puppy, looking for a new home. It was just as obvious that Dylan wasn't looking to adopt.

At least, not her.

Lana's gaze dipped to where Dylan had Casey strapped into a sex seat that had been set up in the middle of the festival's main walkway. There were several of them staged around the fairgrounds, but none with the size of crowd the Firecracker had drawn.

"They are drawing a lot of attention." Chase finally spoke, proving that he was not only aware of Lana's presence but also the direction of her thoughts.

It was an unnerving talent of his, and one that had once proved to her that they were meant to be. After all, Chase was not considered by most people to be insightful. He wasn't even known for being sensitive, but Lana had seen the heart he kept hidden beneath his rough exterior.

She knew the truth.

He'd had to grow up too young, thanks to his daddy being sent to jail and his mom passing on. Chase had assumed the responsibility of providing not just for his brothers but for Patton too. Back then, of course, Patton had only been his obnoxious little sister. She wasn't related by blood, though, and she hadn't stayed little.

"Things didn't work out the way you thought they would, huh?" They certainly hadn't worked out the way she'd hoped they would.

"I didn't have any thoughts about the matter at all," Chase denied, cutting her a look out of the sides of his eyes as she stepped up. He didn't look directly at her very much anymore. When he did, his gaze stayed locked on her face.

"Yeah, right," Lana muttered, finding her soured mood lighten as she stared down at Dylan and Casey.

They really did look like a perfect match, and they were putting on quite a show. For his part, Dylan was acting like a man possessed, absolutely intent on driving the woman bound before him past all her boundaries, but that seemed like an impossible feat. The harder he tried, the more Casey begged.

Lana could see why the men had crowned her the Firecracker. Between her flushed coloring and her outrageous responses to everything Dylan did, Casey really was like a living inferno that just seemed to grow hotter, louder, and wilder by the second.

She demanded more when he whipped her cunt, moaned for it deeper when he fucked her with the handle of the flogger and screamed for it harder when he pulled it free and shoved it up her ass instead. Then Dylan was going to his knees and burying his face between her legs, causing Chase to heave a heavy sigh.

"I just didn't want him to become distracted."

"You invited the horniest man we both know to a sex club full of naked women and *hoped* he wouldn't become distracted?" Lana had a hell of a time keeping a straight face as she asked that absurd question.

Chase didn't have an answer. He didn't even bother with trying to come up with one. They both knew the truth about why Chase had really called Dylan.

"Well, I didn't expect him to turn you down." Chase sighed as he gave up denying the obvious and turned to face her. "I mean, really, who would turn you down?"

Lana snorted, amazed that he had the audacity to even ask her that question. "I can name at least one man."

"Lana—"

"Forget it." She cut him off, not interested in hearing any more excuses. "It doesn't matter anyway. Some things are just meant to be."

And some weren't.

"Oh, God," Chase groaned and rolled his eyes. "Don't start with that romantic bullshit."

"Who knows, it could have been love at first sight."

It had been, both for her and Dylan. They just hadn't fallen in love with each other. That was a shame. It really would have been easier if they had, at least for her.

"What a bunch of crap."

"You don't—"

"You should know better than to finish that question." Chase never had come close to being a romantic. That didn't mean he hadn't fallen in love.

"What about Patton?"

"I don't think you can use her to prove your point because, unless you've forgotten, she was a baby when I first laid eyes on her," Chase pointed out. "And, besides, Dylan isn't the kind of man to fall in love that easily."

"Okay then." Lana conceded the point but didn't give up the argument. "What about attraction at first sight? You believe in that, don't you?"

"Fine. You win." Chase held up his hands. "They're a perfect couple. If that's true, you better make sure nobody else gets a taste of the girl or Dylan might be likely to rip the guy's tongue out."

He had her with that one, and Chase knew it. He also knew how to make an exit. Pausing only long enough to shoot her a dirty look, he turned to saunter off, giving her a nice view of his tight ass. Damn the man, he looked good going.

It was just a shame that he was dense as shit.

The good-looking ones always were. Lana heaved her own heavy sigh at that thought and turned her attention back to the show Dylan was making of Casey. The two of them really did look good together. There was just something there.

It had been awakened the very second Dylan had laid eyes on the little redhead. Chase might not want to believe it, but it had been love. Instant love. Lana knew that look, knew that feeling, and knew Chase was right. She better make damn sure that nobody else got a chance to touch Casey, or Dylan really might get violent.

Chapter 8

Dylan didn't know what lucky star was shining down on him behind the cloak of the day's bright sunlight, but somewhere up there. somebody was watching over him. What else but fate could explain how Casey had ended up here with him? Who else could be thanked other than God when he managed to win her favors in every competition he entered?

Never one given much to prayer, Dylan offered up one of heartfelt gratitude that day. God, fate, or just luck—whatever it was, he was grateful to be so blessed as to get a taste of almost every delicious delight Casey's body had to offer. That didn't mean there wasn't so much left he wanted to try.

Try, and savor.

Savor, that's just what he planned to do, as he trailed Casey into the next booth. The attendant welcomed one and all to the best Cat Lick competition east of the Mississippi. It was a pussy-eating contest, and sure enough, as he reached the head of the line, Dylan could see Casey waiting for her turn next.

They met minutes later over yet another examination chair. Once again she was strapped down and spread eagle before him as Dylan knelt in his assigned place. The attendant quickly went through the rules, which were pretty simple.

Contestants could only use their mouths, tongue, and teeth to make their women come. First to get a taste of that sweet cream was winner. Dylan wasn't a loser, but Casey stole his concentration as she smiled down at him.

"I know it's you, my mystery lover. I'd know you anywhere. The feel of your hands, the heat of your breath, the very scent of the air around you…I'll never forget."

That soft whisper wrapped around Dylan's heart as Casey's words filled him a contentment that he'd never dared to believe existed. In that moment, he completely forgot about the contest. Dylan growled as the attendant rang the starting bell, offering up Casey one assurance before feasting on the creamy treat of her pussy.

"I'm right here, Firecracker."

With that, he dipped his head and followed the intricate, flowing lines of the henna tattoos that led down the curved mound of her cunt, and he got lost in the heady taste of her arousal. She was so sweet, so addictive, and she squirmed so delightfully, her motions driven by the rapid whirl of his tongue over her clit. He circled her sensitive bud, sucking it past the hard scrape of his teeth and making her squeal loud enough to assure that every man there knew who commanded her passion.

They were chanting her name again. Dylan couldn't help but notice that the louder their cheers grew, the hotter Casey burned. Her pussy pulsed and wept, sucking his tongue deep when he pumped it into her spasming sheath. He could feel the ripples of her release beginning to race across her velvety walls and felt his dick swell with a need to join her, to pound into her until they were both crying out—

Clang! Clang! Clang!

"We have a winner!"

And it wasn't Dylan. He'd completely forgotten about the contest. Now he'd lost.

Lost. Lost! Lost?

His mind just couldn't comprehend that thought. Instead, it got stuck on it, simply repeating that word as he obeyed the attendant's demand for all other contestants to step away from the women. In a stupor that lasted only as long as it took for him to walk away, Dylan didn't even realize what he was doing until he heard some cheeky-ass bastard say that he was finally going to get his turn with the Firecracker.

Over Dylan's dead body!

Turning back around with every intention of shoving the man's teeth down his throat, he didn't even make it a step before a hand latched onto his arm. He'd have thrown it off, but the warning that came with it had him pausing to glance over at the woman who'd materialized at his side.

"Don't," Lana ordered, pulling him back as she stepped past him. "I'll take care of it."

And she did with just a nod of her head. All it took was a look in Casey's direction, and the attendant was pulling her out of the lineup, a fact that didn't go over too well with the man kneeling in front of her. His gaze cut, quick and sharp, past Lana to pierce Dylan with a promise that he recognized well.

The other man was vowing retribution.

Dylan didn't need an interpreter, and neither did he need the stakes explained to him. The other man wanted Casey, and he wasn't going down without a fight. That was just fine with Dylan. He had no problem with putting the man down.

"Come with me."

Lana wasn't asking but took Dylan by the hand and all but dragged him away from the other man's grim look. She muttered over every step she took, complaining about Dylan causing her nothing but trouble. When she had the audacity to accuse him of wearing his heart on his sleeve, Dylan had to object.

"Excuse me?" Digging in his heels, he pulled Lana to a stop so he could pin her with a pointed look. "This doesn't have anything to do with the heart, honey, but an organ a good deal farther south than that."

Lana rolled her eyes, clearly unimpressed by his denial. "Don't start with me, Dylan. I know you better than you think."

"You haven't seen me in almost ten years, woman," Dylan reminded her, not about to give up his stance. "Whatever you think you know…it's old news."

"People don't change that much," Lana assured him before insulting Dylan in the worst kind of way. "And you were always a big-hearted fool."

"*I was not!*"

That earned him another sour look from Lana, who didn't even bother to argue the point but, instead, went for the kill. "Really? So you don't mind if I put the Firecracker back into rotation? Maybe let another man have a taste of her?"

Dylan didn't answer that. He didn't dare because he might say something he regretted, like threatening Lana, but God only knew what he'd do if Lana dared to take Casey away from him.

"Yeah, that's what I thought." Lana snorted and shook her head before narrowing her gaze back on him and asking with a deceptive-sounding curiosity, "Can I ask you a question, Dylan? Do you believe in love at first sight?"

"No." Dylan didn't even have to think about that. Love was something that built over time, kind of like an addiction.

"Then why are you so into this girl…oh," Lana breathed out, as if the answer had just dawned on her. "You know her, don't you?"

"She's my neighbor," Dylan admitted with a shrug. Casey was a hell of a lot more than that, but he didn't think Lana needed to know all those details.

"So…you two planned this?" Lana brow wrinkled into a scowl as she worked to figure it out.

"No. In fact, I got a feeling Casey's not going to be too thrilled to find out that *I'm* her mystery lover," Dylan admitted with blunt honesty. "But she'll get used to the notion."

"The notion?"

"That she's mine," Dylan stated simply.

He didn't question his own conviction but accepted the truth in his words. Casey was his. If he had to tie her to his bed and prove it to her, that's just what Dylan would do. One thing was for certain. He wasn't going to let her go. That must have been clear in either his tone or his look because Lana seemed to hear his unspoken vow.

"Well then, you might not want to piss off too many of these men," she advised him. "Because there is nothing more they like than the challenge of taking a woman away from a man who is obsessed."

"Obsessed? I thought you said I was in love."

"Is there a difference?"

Dylan didn't rightly know, didn't really care either. What did a label really matter anyway?

"There is only one truth," Dylan finally admitted. "Anybody else touches Casey and I'll kill them."

"Well," Lana breathed out, not sounding particularly shocked by that declaration, "then I guess I better make sure nobody else touches her, huh?"

"You are my guardian angel." Dylan smiled, realizing it wasn't God he should be thanking, but Lana.

"Yeah? Well, until we get your collar on her, just remember she's technically still available to any and *all* takers," Lana stressed. "So try not to aggravate the situation. 'Kay?"

"Cross my heart and hope to die," Dylan pledged.

He matched his words with actions as he made an X over his chest with his finger. Despite his solemn gesture, he couldn't keep the grin off his face as he vowed to do no harm...sort of.

"I won't bloody up any of your pretty boys as long as none of them touches what is mine. 'Kay?"

"It's amazing you ain't been killed yet," Lana shot back, her old accent thickening her words as shook her head at him.

"Trust me, honey, they've tried," Dylan assured her as he threw an arm over Lana and began leading her toward the refreshment booth.

It was time to toast their deal. While they were at it, he filled her in on the past few years and the several attempts that had been made on his life while undercover. Needless to say, they'd all been less than successful. In the end, the incidents had made for good stories.

Lana had a few of those herself. Her own life might have been a little less dangerous, but no less adventurous or exciting. While she painted a rosy picture, Dylan had been around enough blocks to figure out what she wasn't saying. She could smile and laugh all she wanted, but he could see beneath her smiles to the hurt she tried to hide.

He didn't call her on it, though. As much as Dylan might sympathize with Lana, there wasn't anything he could do for her. So he kept his opinions to himself and allowed her to spin a happy tale, knowing that's what she needed to hold on to.

He kept his smile firmly locked in place until she finally abandoned him at the Bucking Bronco booth with the promise that the Firecracker would be waiting for him at the head of the line. With that, she told him to enjoy himself and turned to walk away, taking Dylan's gaze with her.

He felt bad for Lana and worried that he might be staring into his own future. After all, just because Casey liked fucking around with him didn't mean she was going to fall in love with him. In fact, she had a history about as colorful and short-term as Dylan's. Unlike Lana, though, Dylan wasn't ready to give up the fight.

In fact, he'd only just started.

He didn't know how long he had, but Dylan knew he was good enough to make sure Casey ended up panting his name whenever she closed her eyes and started petting herself. He was going to be her dream, her fantasy, the very thing she needed to get off.

Love was fragile. Want was binding. Dylan knew which of the two he was a master at.

With that thought, he turned to try and catch a glimpse of the latest competition he'd be entering. The line was too long, the crowd too thick for him to get a good look. The whispers rustling down the long line that twisted around the booth like a snake, on the other hand, were too wild to be believed, but Dylan should have known better than to question the perverseness of the Cattlemen. They were deviants of the highest order.

The challenge was called Bucking Bronco for a reason, a very obvious one Dylan learned as he finally caught a peek of the stage through the never-ending shift of men. His breath froze in his lungs as his heart seized and his eyes widened over the sight of a woman bent over a saddle and strapped down while a man behind her rode her ass as the platform shifted and whipped the couple from side to side. It was a mechanical bull ride with the ladies as the heifers.

Dylan knew that thought would have gotten him smacked every day of the week by Casey if he'd had the balls to say it aloud. That didn't change the fact that a half-hour later she was being escorted past his nose and strapped down before him. Then the attendant was slapping a condom into Dylan's hands and assuring him that the woman had been lubed up.

He didn't want to think about how that had happened, but concentrating on what was about to happen had Dylan hands shaking too much to rip the foil open. Forcing himself to take a deep breath and steady his fingers, he concentrated real hard, finally managing to sheathe his dick in the too-tight latex.

It was a challenge, though, to roll it down his cock without making the damn thing go off. Dylan had never been this hard or in this much pain, and he could only pray that he lasted long enough to actually get inside Casey before he embarrassed himself.

The little pixie was bent over the saddle with her ass arched high into the air. Given her position and what was to come next, Dylan would have expected her to show some kind of anxiousness, but Casey was far from being intimidated. In fact, she was giggling and wiggling those sweet cheeks in a bold invitation that had the crowd going wild.

Just as he noticed before, she seemed to love the attention. It made her burn hotter and cream harder, proving that she was more than just a pervert. She was also an exhibitionist.

Dylan, on the other hand, had sweaty palms and a pounding heartbeat that left him half out of breath as he knelt down behind her. All day he'd been dreaming about fucking something other than her mouth, but now that the moment had arrived, Dylan felt nearly overwhelmed by it. He wasn't going to last. Not two minutes. Not two strokes. Not if he didn't get himself under control.

Control was something that Dylan wasn't exactly known for. He enjoyed riding the wild waves of passion. Giving in to the raw intensity had never felt half as good as it did with Casey, who responded to him in kind. She was as untamed as the wind and as savage as the sea, demanding equal measure from him.

Which was why it was clear now to Dylan that they were perfect for each other. They were like oil and fire, and both of them were addicted to the burn, only before it had scalded them as they tried to deny the truth, forcing their needs to twist into aggravated, angry arguments, but no more.

From now on, they'd have nothing but honesty and pleasure before them. Dylan swore to that as he reached out to trace the tattoos that highlighted the graceful curve of her spine and led down to the luscious globes of Casey's ass. Splitting her sweet cheeks wide, he flexed his hips forward, allowing the thick, flared head of his cock to brush up against the clenched ring of muscles guarding the shadowed entrance to her ass. He hesitated there, biting down on his lower lips as every muscle in his body tensed with the strain of holding back.

"Ride lasts five minutes. If you make it past the first two, you're a winner. You're only allowed to hold on to the woman's hips. No teasing. No petting. No pumping. You start fucking, you're disqualified. Now mount up…oh, and don't forget the hat."

With that the attendant slapped a wide-brimmed cowboy hat onto Dylan's head and retreated back to the control panel to wait for Dylan to obey the rest of his instructions. The crowd was chanting and cheering, eager for the ride to begin, but Dylan wanted to savor this moment. No matter what the future held, this day would live on as the best day of his life and this moment as the pinnacle.

"I know it's you."

Tossing a smile along with that assurance over her shoulder, Casey pressed backward and down the heated crest of his dick, allowing her tight muscles to clench around him and hold him prisoner as she shook her ass again.

"I've been waiting all day for this moment. You're not going to deny me now, are you?"

He wouldn't dream of it, but Dylan didn't assure her of that. Instead, he answered her challenge in the only way worthwhile—with action. Not even pausing to take a breath, he slammed his full length into her tight channel, forcing her muscles wide and fucking a pant right out of her.

It was like diving into a heated pool of pure, white-hot delight. The shock sent a wave of frenzied delight racing up his spine, stealing his breath. There was no time to reclaim it as the attendant flipped the switch that set the saddle Casey was draped over into motion. It began to tip and sway as the platform beneath his knees moved in opposite directions, causing his dick to bump and grind into the muscles tightening down around him like a vise.

Her grip strengthened as the ride picked up speed, making Dylan's fingers grip her all the harder until he was white-knuckling it and grunting with every second as he strained to hold back the seed boiling in his balls. God help him because he didn't think he could do it. It was all too much.

The pleasure, the speed, the very feel of Casey beneath him all sweat-slickened and mewing with pleasure, Dylan couldn't take it. He wasn't going to last. It didn't matter how many searing breaths he gulped in. Nothing could ease the inferno flaring into epic proportions.

He was hard, hot, and hurting. Casey was clinging to the saddle, panting out one giggle after another. That sweet sound enflamed Dylan's seething senses, wrapping around his heart and making it swell with the same endless need churning in his balls.

Casey was having fun, and he wouldn't dare to ruin that for her. At least, he didn't want to, but he didn't have the strength left to control his body's raging response to finally being buried balls deep in Casey's tight ass.

It rippled with a pulse he knew she commanded as she showed off her muscle control, making her ass milk the very seed from his balls as she claimed the ultimate victory. Not that Dylan felt like a loser, far from it. The only thing he felt was the glorious rush of a release so intense and powerful his whole body arched with it as his hips began moving, began pounding back and forth as he gave in to the moment and rode Casey right over the brilliant edge of a climax brighter than anything he'd dared to touch before.

It burned through him with such force that he didn't even notice as the ride came to an end and the crowd went wild, cheering him on as Casey came apart beneath him. All that Dylan knew then, all that mattered to him, was the rapture ripping through him, leaving him a broken, quivering shell with only one thought in his head.

He was *so* doing that again.

Chapter 9

If Casey lived to be a hundred, she'd still never forget this day or this moment. The excitement fueled by the crowd's chanting paled in comparison to the feel of her secret lover's thick cock pounding into her ass. The sensation was absolutely divine, making every cell in her body begin to glow with a euphoric delight that could not possibly be contained.

It seared through her, along with the sharp edges of her climax as her ass convulsed around the latex-covered dick pumping an endless load of hot seed deep into her body. Her lover's erection had thickened to the point where she could actually feel the mad pound of his pulse beating against her sensitive walls.

Casey's heart fell into rhythm with his as her ragged pants began to heave in time with the rough gasps coming hard and fast behind her. They were as one, and for a moment, she lost herself in the beauty of that truth, but all too quickly, the contentment flooding through her along with her release was doused by the cold, hard reality of the moment as the attendant appeared to pull her lover free.

"You would have won, but you broke the rules…so, sorry, dude, you're disqualified."

Those words barely registered through the fog of lust still muddying Casey's thoughts. She didn't have the strength left to care, much less listen. She could have passed out right there draped over the saddle like a used, wet rag, only she wasn't allowed to.

With quick, efficient motions, the attendant unlatched her and pulled Casey to her feet. She stumbled over them as he dragged her off the stage, assuring her that she was being sent back to the harem to get prepped for the auction coming up in a couple hours.

Casey couldn't ask help but ask if that meant she could take a nap, which earned her a chuckle and a swat on her ass for talking back before the man handed her off to another attendant who led her across the field and down the silent path back to the harem. Only then did he bother to remove her blindfold and leash, allowing her freedom to move off into the harem's gardens alone.

The gardens were magnificent and full of hidden surprises that Casey had already become addicted to, like the mud baths and the massage gazebo. She hit up both of them, allowing the female attendants to rub the aches from her muscles as she replayed the day over in her mind. It really had been one of the best, but in hindsight, Casey began to worry that she'd made a tragic mistake with her mystery lover. She'd spent all day imagining he was Dylan and could feel the effect of that shifting her heart toward thoughts that were too dangerous to entertain.

Not only were they dangerous, they weren't exactly fair. After all, her mystery lover had earned the right to be judged as his own man. He would be, too, because once she saw him the fantasy would be over. That was a sobering thought, one that brought the tension back to her muscles, which had the masseuse working even harder to get it back out. Naturally she commented on Casey's wound-up state, causing Casey to offer her up a half-hearted, lame excuse.

"I'm just a little nervous about this auction." That wasn't a lie, not exactly.

"Oh, yes." The masseuse drew out that agreement, clearly reveling in getting to gossip. "You new girls always worry, but you have nothing to fear. Your man will bid on you."

"My man?" Casey repeated, strangely thrilled at the sound of those two words. "You mean my mystery lover?"

"Whatever you wish to call him." A shrug sounded in the other woman's voice. "We've been hearing the whispers all day. The man is quite smitten."

"I guess."

Actually, Casey hoped because she was kind of smitten too, which probably wasn't a good thing. After all, she was breaking one of Lana's rules. She was starting to feel a little possessive.

"The other men are not happy that he's been hogging your time," the woman confided, clearly up to date on all the news. "Everybody is expecting you will go for the highest bid tonight."

Casey didn't believe that for a moment, but it made her feel good to hear it anyway. "Hopefully, my mystery lover can afford me then."

"I wouldn't worry about that. Rumor is he's one of the owner's good friends. How else do you think it worked out that nobody else got to play with you?"

That question brought a frown to Casey's brows. She hadn't actually considered that point before, but in hindsight, it seemed like a valid one.

"The games were rigged, and everybody is expecting that auction to be too," the woman declared. "Trust me, the men are not happy about that."

* * * *

Josh was not happy. He wasn't happy with the missing information in the police report. He wasn't happy that the background checks he was running were turning up squat. He wasn't happy that he'd been stuck in that office all day, brooding over the computer when, technically, he could have been back at home planning his move.

He'd decided to make one…he just had to figure out a way to tell Dylan.

"You know, you don't have to get everything done tonight." Slade broke the heavy silence that had, once again settled over the office.

This time it had stretched on for several hours. During that time Josh hadn't spoken a word or even taken a break. He didn't dare. Every time he paused, even for a second, his mind drifted back to Casey, back to wondering just what she was doing...if, maybe, she was doing herself. That thought always had him trying to imagine just what that would look like, what she'd look like naked, wet, purring...his name—

"You're not paying me any mind, are you?" Slade asked, drawing Josh's attention back toward him and the realization that the other man had started talking to him a few minutes ago.

"I'm sorry." Josh shook his head. "I just sometimes get lost when I'm working on a...problem."

"Yeah? And tell me something, does this problem maybe come with a few curves and smell real nice? A woman, maybe?" Slade asked as he shoved out of his seat and crossed the room to the wet bar.

"Her name is Casey," Josh admitted as he eyed Slade for a moment. "And how did you know?"

"Please." Slade snorted as he returned with a bottle and two glasses. "You're at a sex club full of naked women, and you spent all day staring at a monitor. Either you're gay or you're taken...or I guess you could be both. Not that it matters because I know the solution to your...problem."

"Whiskey?" Josh lifted a brow at that. "I'm not sure drinking is going to help me think any more clearly."

"The liquor isn't to help you think. It's to help you listen," Slade assured him as he measured out two healthy doses. Settling back into the seat across from Josh with his own drink, he nodded toward the one he'd left on the desk. "Go on. Trust me, you're going to need it."

He did need it. His mind was in a twist, his stomach knotted, and his muscles bunched tight enough to make them ache. He needed something. Josh kind of thought he might need Casey, but the whiskey would have to do.

Lifting his glass, he offered Slade a silent salute before he threw back the entire shot and slammed the glass back down. Grimacing as the heady liquid seared its way down his throat, Josh took a second to take a deep breath and throw off every bit of tension he could, which wasn't much.

"Okay." Bracing himself, Josh lifted his gaze to meet Slade's amused one. "Hit me with it."

"Fuck her."

"What?"

"Fuck her," Slade repeated as he poured another round. "Trust me, there is no problem that can't be resolved after a few hours of sweating it between the sheets...or on the floor...up against a wall...or—"

"I get that idea." Josh cut Slade off, guessing the man could go on all night listing different positions. "And, while I appreciate the advice, I think you might have been hanging out here at the club for too long."

"Oh, God." Slade sighed and banged his head against the back of his seat as he lifted his eyes toward the ceiling. "Spare me the feminist lecture and just let me ask you one thing. When you're done fucking, do you have the energy left to argue?

"No," Slade answered for him as he straightened back up to give Josh a pointed look. "When you disagree with your woman, then fuck her, and afterward, I assure you, you both will be feeling good enough to resolve your issues without everything blowing up."

"That's insane."

"Works."

A lot of things worked for Slade Davis that Josh wasn't sure he could get away with. That didn't stop him from wondering. It would assuage a lot of his guilt if the choice wasn't him *or* Dylan. Maybe it could be him *and* Dylan…fucking Casey, bending her over and shoving—

"I lost you again, didn't I?" Slade smirked as he shook his head at Josh. "Would I be wrong to assume that the fact that you're here brooding and not back at home taking my wise advice is because this is about your recently broken engagement?"

"No. This is about the reason for my broken engagement." Josh nodded when Slade lifted the whiskey bottle and gestured toward his empty glass.

"Ah." Slade measured out another healthy dose for both Josh and himself before settling back to offer Josh a sly smile. "The plot thickens. So Casey isn't your ex-fiancée."

"She's my neighbor." Josh hesitated, his tone dropping as he slowly admitted the rest. "And I think my brother has a thing for her…and she might have a thing back. I mean, you should see them together. They just pick at each other and yet seem almost magnetically attracted to each other."

"And that's a problem for you?" Slade asked, the laughter fading from his tone as he studied Josh and the blush he could feel streaking across his cheeks. "No. It's not. You actually like the idea."

Yes. He did. He liked it a lot, enough that he couldn't hold Slade's gaze as he made his confession. "I've never shared a woman like that…before. I'm not sure how it would work."

"You mean the sex or the relationship?" There wasn't a hint of hesitation in Slade's blunt question or his offer. "Because all you have to do is take a stroll and you'll figure out the positioning and, as for the relationship, fuck her."

"You know, you sound a lot like my brother." That kind of shocked Josh.

He'd thought Slade had a more even and reasoned temperament. That was far from any description anybody would have given of Dylan, who, as if on cue, exploded into the office with the frenzy of a teenage girl about to wet herself. He was shrieking just like one, too.

"Oh my God! *Oh my God! OhmyGod!*"

Dylan stumbled to a halt, suddenly appearing to realize that Slade was there, not that he had the dignity to act embarrassed. Instead, he pointed a finger at Slade and hollered out to him as if the man wasn't standing only feet away.

"This place is *awesome!*"

"We get that a lot," Slade assured him, taking the compliment in stride as he shoved out of his seat. "And clearly you've had a taste of something you liked."

"You wouldn't believe it." Dylan took a deep breath and let it out with a contented sigh that matched the smile spreading across his face. "It was the *best* day of my life."

"Well, I'm glad we could make your dreams come true," Slade snickered as he gave Dylan a quick pat on the back. "Hopefully, you can help your brother return the favor."

"Don't you worry," Dylan shot back, his voice rising as Slade moved farther away toward the door. "We'll get you your arsonist."

"Don't you want to talk to me before making that kind of promise?" Josh spoke up, unnerved by Dylan's blatant confidence.

He'd always found it best not to overpromise or sell. Dylan, on the other hand, liked to talk big and never seemed to worry about living up to expectations.

"You are just the man I want to talk to." Dylan turned his attention and his grin back on his brother as he slunk down into Slade's abandoned seat. "Because you will not believe how I spent my day."

"Actually, I can take a pretty good guess," Josh muttered before catching Slade's eye as he hesitated by the door. "You done for the day?"

"Yeah," Slade drew out the word with a yawn before offering Josh the use of the office, along with the reminder that number one on the speed dial would ring up a butler who would be happy to assist them in any and all their desires. With that, he wished them both a good night and escaped, leaving Josh to handle Dylan's grin.

He really wasn't interested in hearing how Dylan had spent his whole day whoring his way through a list of women, especially not when his own thoughts had kept him half hard all damn day. Maybe Slade was right. Josh shouldn't waste so much time on trying to figure out how to romance Casey as he should be plotting to seduce her. That sounded like more fun anyway.

"Okay, check this out," Dylan began, appearing completely oblivious to Josh's impatient attitude. "You will never believe who—"

"I don't care," Josh cut him off, coming to his decision. "We need to have a talk, Dylan."

"What? No!" Dylan shoved back in his seat with a sullen pout. "No serious conversations. I can't manage them. I just spent the entire day—"

"Fucking your way through a bunch of pretty girls," Josh finished for him. "I get it."

"You think so?"

"Yes, and I'm glad you're having fun—"

"—but?"

Josh shot Dylan a hard look for that obnoxious interruption and very pointedly continued on. "*But* I'm not interested in any of these women. I already know who I want."

"Let me take a guess." Dylan cut back in with a dramatic flair. "Casey."

Josh scowled, not caring for the laughter still coloring his brother's tone. "As matter of fact—"

"I want her," Dylan finished for him, making his own claim at the same time and giving Josh reason to both hope and dread just what his brother really meant by that.

"What about all the other women?"

"What other women?" Dylan blinked, looking honestly innocent, or at least as innocent as he could.

"What do you mean what other women? What about today?"

"Oh, now you want to talk about today?"

"No!" Josh snapped before forcing himself to take a deep breath and focus on regaining control of his emotions.

It took a lot of effort because Dylan knew just how to irritate the crap out of him. More than that, Dylan enjoyed irritating him. Josh wasn't going to let him get away with it. Not this time. He said what he had to say and could offer Dylan only one final assurance.

"If you want Casey…then that's between the two of you. That doesn't change my plans." Josh couldn't be more blunt than that. "Now if you could focus—"

"Hold up," Dylan called out, waving away Josh's attempt to turn the conversation. "Did you just say that you don't care if I fuck your girl?"

"Not as long as I get to fuck her too." Now that really was as blunt as he could make it. "Now, if you could focus on the reason we're here, I got news to report."

"Ah, the mystery of the burnt barn." Dylan sighed, his expression tightening into a look of grim acceptance. "Okay, hit me with it. What you got?"

"Not much," Josh admitted grimly. "There isn't much in the police report but the initial witness statements and the fire investigator's report of arson."

Josh picked up the stack of printouts he'd made and tossed them across the desk for Dylan to start leafing through as he went over what few details there were.

"Apparently the fire was started along the outside wall with gasoline being used as the fuel…and that's about it." Josh shrugged at Dylan as his brother glanced up at him with a clear expectation of more. "I'm sorry. It doesn't look like the local sheriff or any of his deputies even bothered to interview more than the people at the scene."

"Well, that's odd." Dylan scowled as he returned his attention to report in his hands. "Either the sheriff is completely incompetent or—"

"—he already knows who did it," Josh cut in, picking up another couple sheets of paper he'd stapled together. "And I got a feeling this might have something to do with the matter."

"What's this?" Stretching forward to take the two-page incident report from Josh, Dylan's scowl grew deeper as he scanned it. "A kid was picked up on a dirt bike with an empty gas can not two miles away? Well, that's certainly suspicious."

"So is the fact that most of the information is redacted." That's what bothered Josh the most, but it didn't appear to faze Dylan, who simply shrugged.

"That's par for the course when it comes to minors."

"When it comes to releasing information about minors," Josh corrected. "That report was…"

"Stolen?" Dylan supplied, his smile reappearing for a moment. "Don't go too far out on that limb, baby brother. I'm not sure I have the connections to save you if you fall."

"Don't worry, I do," Josh assured him dourly, irritated at Dylan's insistence in treating him like the little kid brother when he was only twenty minutes behind Dylan.

It was a long-standing argument, one that he knew he would never win. Maybe it was because of that that Josh always bristled at the reminder.

"Aren't you a big shot?" Dylan retorted as he tossed the report back on the desk. "You know so much, why don't you tell me where to find this kid? I think I might like to have a few words with him."

Josh held his hands up in defeat. "Sorry. That's something you might need to ask the sheriff because I can't find any paper trail left online between his office and the courts or child welfare services. Whatever happened to the kid, he didn't get put into the system."

"Or maybe he got hidden within it," Dylan suggested. "You know when we get kids witnessing crimes that we fear might be retaliated against, child services will…lose the paperwork until we can assure the kid's safety."

"You think the kid is a witness, then?" That was possible, but it hadn't been Josh's first thought, and neither, apparently, was it Dylan's.

"Nope, but I do think the Davis brothers have the kind of power in this community to wreck a kid's life, even if they never lay a hand on him."

That suggestion had Josh's stomach turning. He wasn't interested in helping anybody persecute a child. Then again, he had a hard time imagining Slade being so callous. "You think they would?"

"I think you don't want to mess with their woman." Dylan slapped his hands against the sides of his seat and shoved out of the chair. "I also think that Casey likes to have her nipples twisted, but if I don't get back down to the fair in time for the auction, it'll be somebody else tuning those knobs."

Josh blinked, watching Dylan walk away as his mind tried to sort out that farewell. It couldn't. It just kept coming up with one impossible conclusion. Casey was here…but that couldn't be right.

Chapter 10

The butterflies in Casey's stomach were having a kegger. They were in a full, drunken riot, making her quiver in her stilettos. The five-inch heels were hell to balance on, and having shaking knees didn't help. Neither did standing at the end of a line of drop-dead gorgeous, naked women.

There were tall ones, short ones, round ones, thin ones, dark-skinned ones, pale as paper-white ones, along with every shade in between, and then there was her freckled ass. She'd go strutting down the catwalk last, after every other woman had been bought and all the men were broke.

She could hope only that someone had enough dough left to afford her. If not, then her fears of ending up going for an embarrassingly low price would come true. Casey would know if she ended up being cheap.

As she stood there watching one woman after another fetch impossibly sounding high prices, she'd silently been calculating the average closing bid, which was somewhere around thirteen thousand buckles, the currency of the club.

That wasn't all Casey had taken note of. She'd also been keeping a mental track of who went for what and come to some conclusions. Fuller-figured women demanded a high price. So did the more outrageous and excited women. Frowners, on the other hand, went for a lot less.

The men seemed to favor tits, large asses, and big smiles. Three things Casey actually had, not to mention her custom-fitted teddy, which made her the true envy of all the other women, and yet still, by the time she was finally standing at the bottom of the steps leading up to the catwalk, Casey was all but ready to turn tail and run.

She couldn't do this. She couldn't parade around a bonfire naked while men bid on the right to keep her as some kind of sex slave. What the hell was she thinking?

"Breathe." Lana appeared at her side to offer Casey that bit of calm advice. "It's going to be all right."

That assurance brought a rueful smile to Casey's lips as she felt the butterflies finally take a breath and give her a moment. "Do I look that scared?"

"Petrified and one second away from fleeing," Lana admitted bluntly. "But that's okay. Everybody is nervous for their first auction, which is just why I thought you might like to have company."

Lana held up the leash in her hand in an offer that Casey was hard-pressed to resist. She really didn't want to be up there alone.

"Fine." Casey nodded her acceptance as the auctioneer closed the bidding on the blonde at eleven thousand, bringing back her worry that the men had gone broke.

She made a mention of that to Lana, earning a laugh from the other woman as she snapped the leash onto Casey's collar. Lana assured her that the men had been holding out, waiting for her, but Casey was too nervous to believe her. It wasn't until the crowd went wild as she crawled out onto the catwalk behind Lana that Casey finally relaxed and began to enjoy herself.

* * * *

"Oh my God," Josh whispered, his mouth falling open as his eyes went wide.

Dylan would have laughed at his brother's comical expression. Josh's response to seeing Casey crawl out on all fours and dressed in a barely-there teddy was classic. He stared up at the catwalk, not seeming to be able to make sense out of what he was seeing. So he stuttered and repeated himself.

"Oh my God."

"I told you so," Dylan reminded him smugly as he smiled, watching the redhead wiggling her way down the stage. She really was a sexy, playful little pixie, and he was ready to play with her.

"Oh my God. That's Casey!"

"I know!"

"She's tattooed!"

"And you should see where they lead."

"I can see her tits!"

So could Dylan and every other man there, thanks to the lack of actual cups in the lace teddy that looked as if it was painted on. He could have believed it was, too, if not for the wires hidden in the corset that shoved her breasts up and out, making them look full and round.

The dark lines of the henna swirled around those sweet mounds, highlighting the pink, puckered nipples that looked like ripe berries begging to be sucked. That apparently wasn't the only thing begging to be played with. As they reached the end of the stage, Casey reared back onto her knees before splitting her legs wide and showing off the glistening folds of her cunt.

The swollen lips of her pussy peeked through the slit in her crotchless teddy, leaving her open not only for the ogling but also for the teasing stroke of her own fingers. Like a sultry goddess intent on driving every man around her crazy, she reached down to run a finger through her folds before lifting her cream-coated tip to her lips and sucking it dry.

The crowd around Dylan went crazy as Josh's knees gave out and he fell back into one of the plastic chairs arranged around the stage.

"Oh God," he groaned.

"Look how *wet* she is," Dylan pointed out, all but panting and drooling. "I'll tell you what, our little firecracker not only likes to show off she also likes to get licked clean."

"Please," Josh begged, holding up a hand as he closed his eyes, blocking out the erotic sight before him, but Dylan wasn't going to let him hide from the truth.

"Oh, stop whining," Dylan snapped. "Our Casey is a pervert. *A pervert.* It's a gift from God, and you're supposed to say thank you."

Actually, they were supposed to express their gratitude. Dylan was planning to do that on his knees…or maybe he'd put Casey on hers. The possibilities were endless, and just the thought of them all was enough to enflame the need boiling in his balls.

Dylan's dick flushed and swelled so fast it damn near burst through his zipper. The hard, cold metal teeth bit into his sensitive length, but he barely felt the pinch. He was still stuck on the reality unfolding around him.

Captivated by the sight of Casey petting herself, Dylan smiled as he stared up at her in wonder. She was a sensual goddess, a wet dream begging to be fucked, and he was aching to give it to her. All the dreams, the hidden fantasies of dark, wicked acts that he'd harbored for so long flooded through Dylan along with the certainty that he'd just found the woman he would never tire of indulging in.

All he needed to do was buy her.

The auctioneer warned the audience that the Firecracker was wilder than most men could keep up with. The fast-talking man whipped through the litany of Casey's many skills and virtues, assuring every man there she was willing to try just about anything once. Now the question was, would there be a man willing to take that challenge? With that bold taunt, he opened up the bidding.

"Bidding?" Josh shot out of his seat as if it had just dawned on him in that second that they were at an auction.

"Don't worry," Dylan shot over his shoulder with a smile. "I got eighteen thousand buckles, and these guys got to be running low. I'll get—*What?*"

Dylan's assurance cut off with a dramatic gasp as the bid jumped from two thousand to twenty in less than that many seconds. It didn't stop there, either, but went skyrocketing toward the high fifties and then right on into the sixties.

"No. No!" Dylan shook his head. having trouble coping with the realization that he couldn't afford Casey. "This isn't right. They're supposed to be broke!"

"Who the hell cares?" Josh snapped furiously. "Now where the hell do you get these buckles, and how much do they cost?"

"They don't *cost* anything. You have to earn them."

"Then what the hell are we supposed to do?"

"We'll have to kidnap her," Dylan declared as he fought to think rationally through the panic starting to rip through him.

"Kidnap?" Josh repeated, sounding as though he didn't even understand the definition of that word. Dylan ignored him, focusing on his plan as he developed it on the spot.

"We'll take her back to Atlanta."

"Taking a hostage across state lines is a *federal* offense," Josh stressed as if that mattered.

"Do I look like I care?" Dylan roared. "We're going to kidnap her—"

"Can't we just ask the Davis brothers to help out?" Josh interjected, irritating Dylan with his logical, reasonable response. It was time to panic, not negotiate.

"We're going to *kidnap* her—"

"You just want to tie her up, don't you?"

"Trust me, she likes to be tied up," Dylan snapped. "She likes to be tied up, blindfolded, and put on display while some stranger whips her pussy and then eats her out, but before that stranger gets a chance, *we're going to kidnap her—*"

"Eighty thousand!"

A new but familiar voice boomed through the crowd, cutting Dylan off and unleashing a wave of silence that rolled across the field until every eye had turned on Chase Davis. He strutted forward like Moses parting the sea. The crowd melted out of his way until he came face to face with Dylan.

Dylan didn't have to be a mind reader to know what the hell had his old friend looking all sour-faced. More importantly, he didn't care. Chase could get all huffy if he wanted to. Dylan wanted only Casey, and he wasn't backing down.

"Eighty-five thousand."

That drew both their attention to the man who'd dared to interrupt their silent glaring competition. Dylan recognized him instantly as the man who Lana had screwed over at the pussy eating competition earlier that day. He also remembered her warning about how the guys would react to Dylan hogging Casey's time.

Apparently, she hadn't been wrong. She'd just forgotten that Dylan had a friend with deep pockets. That didn't unnerve the other guy. He stepped forward to confront Chase as Chase turned on him.

A sudden tension gripped the crowd as the two men slowly walked up on each other like gunslingers about ready to draw, but Dylan wasn't concerned that Chase wouldn't come out the winner. He was older, wiser, and, most importantly, a club owner. As for the other guy…

"Who the hell is that?" Josh asked in a whisper, not daring to break the silence that seemed to grip the crowd along with the heavy weight of anticipation.

"I don't know his name," Dylan muttered back. "But I know he wants Casey."

"Yeah? Well, he can't have her." Josh paused before finally coming around. "We'll kidnap her first."

Dylan snorted over a chuckle and shook his head as Chase upped the ante.

"A hundred thousand."

"A hundred and ten thousand," the younger man instantly countered before Chase doubled down on his challenge.

"Two hundred."

"Three."

"Five."

"Why are you even here, man?" Clearly flustered, the other man glared up at Chase, who just smirked.

"You ain't got five, do you?"

"You know I don't." Now officially the loser, the guy stepped back to pin Chase with a look of a puppy trying to play at being a pit bull. "But now you know I'll get revenge."

"First rule, puppy, don't make promises," Chase warned him with a cold smile. "Just take revenge. Lana?"

Dismissing the younger guy, Chase turned toward the stage to call out to the woman still holding Casey's leash. He ordered his "gift" to be wrapped up and put in a cube before he turned to pin Dylan and Josh with a hard look.

"And you two, I think it's time we had a talk." Chase nodded up toward the gardens in the glow of the buildings beyond. "Let's get a drink."

* * * *

"I think I need a drink." Of course, Casey already felt a little sick so maybe liquor wasn't the right answer. There was another one she needed though. "Am I mistaken, or was I just bought by the club's very owner?"

"His name is Chase," Lana supplied. "Chase Davis, and he is one of the co-owners."

"I see," Casey answered carefully, knowing that she was supposed to ignorant when it came to the Davis brothers but fearing they'd already figured out that she wasn't and that this could be a trap.

Even if it was, what was the worst thing they could do to her? Throw her out?

"Here." Lana handed Casey a shot of something clear along with a little advice. "Relax. Chase has got his own woman. You're more like a gift."

A gift to the Davis brothers' friend, and maybe her future Mr. Right. Casey told herself not to think like that. She hadn't come here to find anything more than a release from the sexual tension that had been building up within her. After all, she'd already found love with the wrong man...and his brother.

Maybe that was just her, though. Maybe she was just destined to fall for the wrong guys. Or, maybe, she really was a typical woman who found a need to infuse love into every sexual relationship...

Nah. Casey shook her head. That wasn't it.

She'd slept with enough losers to know that there actually was something special going on between her and her mystery lover. It was just there in the air, a strange tension filled with excitement and hunger. Surely her mystery lover had sensed it. Why else had he pursued her so insistently?

She could only hope.

"Drink," Lana commanded. "And stop worrying. Your mystery lover will take good care of you."

"Here is hoping that he knows how," Casey responded, all too aware of the camera hidden somewhere in the room as she lifted her glass up in salute.

"Trust me, he does," Lana assured her with a twinkle in her eye. "So don't worry, your education is only just beginning."

There was something about Lana's smile that had Casey's guard rising anew as she tread cautiously forward, glancing about the big glass room she'd found herself in. It was impressive. Throwing back the shot Lana had given her, Casey handed the glass back before starting to wander around.

"So? Are you going to unravel the mystery now?"

She'd meant about her admirer, but Lana either didn't understand or didn't want to. Either way she chose to interpret Casey's comment as being about the room and gave her the full tour of the glass cube that was simply known as a cube.

It had a hangout area, a gaming area, and a serious bondage zone that came complete with its own examination chair and a whole wall full of toys. If that wasn't enough to unnerve a woman, there was a courtyard right outside the window that made it clear whoever was in that chair was on display. The very idea of which had Casey growing warm.

That wasn't all that was tucked beneath the thatched roof. There were actually two more rooms hidden in back, a small bedroom and of course a luxurious spa-like bathroom. While the toilet came in its own private stall, the shower tucked in the corner had all glass walls and another courtyard where lookie-loos could gather to ogle whoever had the courage to bathe there.

Not that Casey was intimidated. She knew she looked good naked and better wet. Those were two things she already was, besides also being impatient. Everything looked like fun, and she wanted to play or, at least, get played with.

Beyond that, she was just plain anxious to finally meet and see her mystery lover, but apparently the man wanted to maintain his mystery. That became clear after Lana answered the phone that rang as they stepped back into the main part of the cube.

She answered it and spoke briefly to whoever was on the other end. Casey easily surmised that Lana was talking to a man thanks to all of Lana's "yes, sir"s. The rest became clear only after she hung up and turned to announce that the deal had been struck and that Chase had traded her to a new master.

"You are to obey him without hesitation and in all things. Is that understood?"

"And am I to assume you are speaking for him now?" Casey asked, knowing she was risking a punishment by not answering directly, but there was nobody around except for Lana.

She didn't think the other woman would rat her out. It wouldn't have shocked her, on the other hand, if Lana hadn't corrected her, but the other woman just smiled and answered as if she could read Casey's very thoughts.

"I think it would be best now to inform you that your master is watching us…and can hear everything that is said."

That was good to know. It also had Casey's eyes darting around the room as she looked for the camera. Wherever it was, it was well hidden because she couldn't find it. Lana gave her a moment to try before escorting Casey back over toward the examination chair.

There were markers painted on the floor, and she directed Casey to the dot that was centered beneath the bar hanging down from the ceiling. She obeyed, finding herself unnerved by the gathering crowd outside the window. It was different now that she could see the men with their women.

There were a lot more women than Casey had expected, most of whom were being put to good use. That explained why she wasn't hated out at the harem. She was revving up the engines they were getting to ride. She was the one getting screwed or, as technically was the case, not.

"You know, it's not that I have anything against women," Casey spoke up as Lana approached her, a blindfold dangling from her fingers, "but I really did come here for the dick."

"Don't worry." Lana came to a stop in front of Casey and offered her a smile that set the butterflies in her stomach fluttering. "You're going to get it."

Chapter 11

Josh prayed that none of the other guys noticed how badly his hands were shaking as he looked into the cube at the woman being bound before him. That was Casey dangling there. Casey. His Casey, and she was naked.

Naked!

His gaze raked down the length of her perfect body all flushed with her excitement and outlined with the sexiest tattoos he'd ever seen. Her breasts were bigger than Josh ever imagined and tipped with large, rosy nipples that made him ache to take a taste. Hell, he wanted to lay her down and lick her all over, tracing every single one of the dark trails of henna that twirled around her body. The intricate tattoos that graced her curves made Casey look all the more soft and sweet, pink and pale, like strawberries and cream.

That had always been his favorite desert, but now Josh might have to reconsider the matter because he saw something that he'd rather get a chance to devour. The swollen, glistening lips of Casey's cunt drew his gaze and held him hypnotized as his balls began to boil with an ache that went deep enough that he couldn't draw a breath without wanting her.

"You'll be getting as much dick as you can stand," Lana assured Casey, echoing Josh's own thoughts as she wrapped the blindfold around Casey's eyes.

"Promise?" Casey purred, and the husky tremor of want echoing in her voice stroked over Josh's throbbing cock as he imagined she was speaking directly to him.

Silently, he answered. He promised. He was going to give her all the dick she could stand, and she was going to love every single inch. Just the thought of Casey moaning beneath him as he bent her over and packed her full had Josh's dick pulsing painfully as it threatened to outgrow the waistband of his jeans.

He'd never been this big before, or this hard.

"Well, like everything at this club, it depends." Lana answered Casey's question as she lowered the cuffs down from the ceiling and bound Casey with them. "You have to earn your dick here, and your master has one last challenge for you to meet before he decides whether you've earned a reward."

"Now that sounds like both a threat and a promise." Casey giggled, clearly enjoying the moment.

Her enthusiasm was electric. More than that, it was contagious, addictive, mesmerizing, intoxicating—

"Wake up, baby brother!" Dylan's voice cut straight through Josh's ear thanks to the receiver plugged into it. "The ladies are waiting on you, so if you could wipe the drool off your chin…"

That earned Dylan a quick shot of his middle finger before Josh jerked forward, nodding at Lana to continue.

"Bend over."

That sharp demand whipped out of Lana, making even Josh start as he shot the woman a quick look of surprise. He hadn't known she had that kind of *oomph* in her and had to admit he was a little impressed. Casey…not so much.

"Aren't you a little light in the loafers to be making that demand?"

"Now!"

"Fine!"

Bending at the waist, Casey spread her legs and shook her ass, flaunting both the rounded cheeks of her rump and the plush folds of her pussy all at once. The sight was just too irresistible, and Josh gave into impulse, cracking a hand across her ass as Lana rushed to catch up his spontaneous spanking.

"Be still!" She barked that command, but it might have been too late.

Casey froze, appearing to scent the air as her nose lifted up, and Josh could all but sense her trying to figure out if the big hand that had just branded the pale curve of her rear with a searing imprint could actually belong to Lana. He helped her catch a clue and gave her other a cheek a matching mark, eliciting a squeal and a giggle from Casey as her cunt creamed hard enough for him to see the proof of her arousal thickening on her pink folds.

The sight nearly undid him.

The hunger and desire that he'd suppressed for so long rose up in a feral wave of need that would not be denied any longer. By the time Josh turned to take the lube from Lana's hands, there was no more mercy or hesitation left in him. There was just the naked want he could no longer disguise.

Neither could Josh hid his excitement as Lana commanded Casey to spread her ass cheeks wide. Then it was his turn to touch. With trembling fingers, he squeezed out some of the cool gel from the tube Lana had handed him, but when he should have reached for Casey, Josh hesitated. He'd never done anything like this and suddenly felt uncertain of just what to do.

Thankfully, Dylan was there, whispering in his ear as he instructed Josh to allow just the tip of one finger to trace down the sweet crease dividing the firm-looking mounds of her ass. He teased her with the cool feel of the gel coating the tip of the finger, and then he lodged it against the tight ring of muscles guarding the puckered entrance to her ass.

He pressed slowly inward, amazed as her muscles clenched around him and sucked him deeper, showing off a skill Josh had never suspected a woman could possess. Casey knew, too, that she had him hypnotized once again just as Dylan had warned him she would try to do.

According to his brother, Casey blatantly fueled the fires of passion in a blatant attempt to overwhelm her lover with lust. That was how she took control, and Josh would have eagerly given it to her if Dylan hadn't started barking at him to plunge his finger deep and fuck her into submission.

That sounded like fun, and he might just do that...once Casey was done fucking him into submission. Convulsing around his finger, her ass pulled it deeper into her tight channel, making Josh's dick pound and weep in desperation to be free to take that ass for a ride.

He might have given into that urge if Lana hadn't pointedly cleared her throat, drawing Josh's attention not only back to her but also back to the sound of Dylan yelling in his ear. His brother was panicked. He thought Josh was losing control. He just might be.

God, her ass was tight...and so were his balls. They were sweating with the most delicious pain. Josh savored the ache, wanting to make this moment last. So he gave in to it, pumping his finger in and out of her ass as he added a second and third one. He stretched her muscles wide, reveling in the panted gasps that fell from Casey's lips as she begged for more.

That was just what was on the menu.

Taking the glass plug that Lana held out to him, Josh fitted the head to her entrance and pounded it in with one deep thrust that had Casey crying out as she took two quick steps forward before coming to the end of her binds. She was still breathing heavy as Lana warned her not to let the plug drop.

"Now what, baby brother?" Dylan's amused voice sang in Josh's ear, drawing his dark gaze toward the camera as he shot his brother a dirty look for that taunt. "You need some suggestions?"

Actually, he could have done with some. Josh was well aware that he was the focus of everybody's attention as he moved off to study the wall of toys as he considered his options. Ignoring Dylan's repeated demands for Josh to listen to him, he settled on a pair of clamps that came with a chain and a plan that he was certain would impress this club full of perverts.

It was time to enjoy his treat and take a little taste. That wicked whisper echoed through his head as Josh knelt down before his pink and glowing goddess. That's what Casey was to him, and he planned on worshiping her for the rest of his life.

"You're not my mystery lover."

The certainty in that quiet statement had Josh stilling as his eyes shot up toward Casey's. The blindfold covered more than half her face, but still, he couldn't help but wonder if she'd somehow caught a glimpse of him.

"He likes to talk dirty," Casey explained as if sensing the question in Josh's silence, but, then again, she had always been good at reading his moods. "And he has calluses in different places on his hands."

"Damn," Dylan muttered, a hint of pride tinting his voice. "She's good."

So was Josh. "I'm the one who commands you tonight, got me?"

"Very nice," Dylan approved with a hint of pride.

"Yes, sir," Casey answered as her spine straightened and her chin tipped into the air, but her suddenly obedient attitude couldn't hide the smile tugging at the edge of her lips.

"Don't buy into that good girl act," Dylan cautioned him. "She's just buttering you up. Trust me, the pixie is plotting, and we got to keep her off center if we want to win this war."

Josh wasn't sure what war Dylan was talking about, but he didn't bother to argue with his brother. He knew him well enough to know that he enjoyed twisting everything into a challenge, not that it was hard this time to make that stretch.

"A new master, hmm…" Casey pursed her lips as she appeared to consider the matter. "Well, I hope you're as *meaty* as the last one, or I might just have to object."

That taunt elicited a roar of laughter from the guys back in the main room, not to mention the chuckleheads watching outside the window. Even Dylan snorted over a laugh.

"I told you she was sassy." Dylan tried to sound stern, but there was no masking the approval thickening in his tone. "Now take those clamps from Lana and get to work making her realize that the quiet men are the dirty ones."

Quiet men might be dirty, but vixens were known to drive men crazy, and that's just how Josh felt in that moment as the heady scent of Casey's arousal filled his every breath. The spicy musk intoxicated him and lured him into temptation.

Really, she had to be punished for that.

Soon, very soon, he'd have a taste of that cunt, but as Lana handed him the first clamp, Josh's gaze shifted upward to the heaving mounds of Casey's breasts. Tanned and oiled, they glistened like a ripe treat topped with rosy red berries all puckered and pointy, begging for attention.

Fitting the clamp between his lips, Josh leaned slightly forward to nuzzle his cheek between the rounded curves of her breasts. He hesitated for a long second as he allowed the velvety heat of her body to slowly envelop him before teasing her with the rough slide of his unshaven cheek down the soft, plush side of one generous globe.

Josh allowed the cold, hard edge of the clamp to trail along and could feel Casey suck in a hard breath. She tensed, going completely still as Dylan's voice whispered into his ear.

"Nice move, baby brother…uh-oh. She's moving."

Josh didn't need Dylan to tell him that. He was the one she was rubbing a leg up against. Like a cat in heat, Casey mewed and arched, stroking up against him in a demand that left no doubt what she wanted. It was a siren's call, and if Dylan hadn't barked a harsh command at him, Josh would have given in.

"Don't you dare crumble now, baby brother. Clamp that tit!"

Josh obeyed without thought.

Using his teeth to spring open the clamp, he settled his mouth over the pebbled tip of her breast and let loose. Casey's response was instantaneous. She squealed and danced backward as far as the cuffs dangling from the ceiling would let her. Josh watched the glorious sight of those breasts bounce and jiggle.

Oh, yeah.

Josh didn't know if he spoke the words, but they rolled around his head as he heard the men chanting in the background for him to do it again. He couldn't argue with that demand. Fortunately, Lana had the next clamp ready, and this time, Josh didn't give Casey any forewarning. Instead, he captured her nipple and sucked it straight into the unforgiving clasp of the toy's metal teeth before letting them snap shut.

Casey let out another startled shriek, flushing a delightful pink as she danced around once again, clearly enjoying herself. So was everybody watching her, Josh included. He could hear the men arguing behind Dylan about whether or not she'd earned a punishment.

Punishment. That was Josh's verdict.

"I think you forgot something, quiet boy, or aren't you planning on connecting these two with some kind of chain?" Casey dared to match that question with a shake of her boobs, flaunting her clipped tits at him and making the crowd go wild.

"Go on, quiet boy," Dylan hollered with a hoot. "Show that firecracker what comes next."

It wasn't Dylan's command so much as Casey's smile that had Josh growling and reaching for her. Wrapping his hands around her soft, resilient thighs, he jerked her forward even as he forced her legs wide open in one smooth move. He didn't stop there but buried his face in the sweet folds of her cunt, losing himself almost instantly in the heady scent of her arousal.

Josh's breath caught as, without thought, his tongue licked over her swollen folds, lapping up the addictive cream clinging to her pussy's lips. Ambrosia, the mythical drink of the gods—he'd found it, and he'd never let it go.

Never.

That thought hammered through him like a nail being secured into place, but instead of confining him, that truth freed him. Growling like an animal in heat, Josh shed the last remnants of domestication and gave into the feral need driving him to devour her cunt. Forcing the plump lips of her pussy apart, he claimed the intimate flesh hidden beneath as his own, making Casey cry out with pleasure even as Dylan began barking in his ear.

"Don't start getting distracted now, baby brother, or I'm going to have to come in there and tap you out," Dylan warned him before dropping his voice to offer a quick explanation. "We can't have you ruining the family name in front of all these guys, or we might not get invited back."

Josh wasn't concerned about that. He didn't need the club. He needed Casey, and he wasn't about to lose her to Dylan. That bastard really would come and tap him out or, at least, try. They'd probably end up in a fight.

It had been a long time since he'd gone fist to fist with his twin. While Dylan had experience on his side, Josh had over ten years of karate on his. The last time they'd gone at it, it had been a lose-lose situation for both of them. They'd both ended up broken and sore for days. Josh didn't have days to waste right then, so he made the intelligent decision to heed his brother's commands and focused on the mission.

Josh snaked his tongue back out of Casey's clinging sheath, and it took all of his fortitude not to give in to the pulsing demands of her cunt and fuck his way back into the delicious heaven he'd discovered between her legs. Another time, another day, he was going to strap her down to a bed and eat his fill, but not today.

Today, he reached for the clamp Lana handed to him and turned back to Casey's weeping folds and the small bundle of nerves peeking through. He'd never clamped a clit before. Hell, he'd never clamped a tit before, but at least he'd seen it done in the movies he'd kept hidden from Maria, movies he was certain Casey would enjoy watching with him.

In fact, he was betting she'd let him make a movie out of her. If she did, Josh would definitely recreate this moment. He savored it as he reached out to spread the lips of her slit wide open. With his thumbs, he brushed over her clit, plumping the little bud up as it swelled with its delight.

Above him, Casey mewed and arched her hips, silently begging for more. He indulged her, working her gasping breaths into a frenzy that ended with a squeal pitched high enough to damn near break glass as he fitted the clamp between his lips and leaned in to nuzzle her clit with the hard teeth before he released them.

They snapped down and lit her up as Casey jerked hard, dancing around in the tight circle her cuffs forced her to maintain as she continued to whimper and pant. Josh would have worried that it was too much for her but for the smile spreading across her face. All too soon, Casey's heated sounds of passion mingled with stray giggles as her motions grew more pointed and less frantic.

She clenched her thighs tight together, and her hips swayed and wiggled as she, no doubt, teased herself with the feel of the clamp. Casey was having fun. If Josh couldn't tell that by the rosy glow of her flushed skin, he could certainly hear it in the laughter lurking in her tone.

"Well, that was unexpected, quiet boy." Casey all but moaned over her words as she continued to writhe with self-pleasure before him. "You got any more surprises to delight me with?"

She was challenging him and absolutely mesmerizing as she danced before him, naked and bound with those damn clamps winking at him. Those little glints of metal fueled a feral need that demanded she be punished for tempting him so. Of course, the idea of punishing her tempted him more than anything, so perhaps Casey was getting just what she wanted when Josh accepted the flogger that Lana slapped into his hand.

He rose up to his feet as his fingers curled around the leather handle. It felt good there in his fist, as though it belonged there. With a snap of his wrist that Josh savored with a smile, he set the velvety tassels arcing through the air to lick straight across Casey's ass, making her squeal and laugh again.

Her plush curves bounced and jiggled in a mouthwatering display that left Josh hurting even worse. If he didn't get to fuck her soon, he was going to humiliate himself by coming in his pants, especially when she begged for another as he cracked the tassels across her tits.

"You do not speak unless spoken to," Josh snapped, finding his tone came out naturally deeper and rougher than normal, a natural disguise that fit his new persona. "And you don't tease yourself without permission, understood?"

"Yes, sir," Casey all but purred as she cast a blind smile back toward him that left little doubt that he had turned her on.

That realization had Josh's mind exploding with all sorts of possibilities. It was time to get creative. He was going to need the chain for that.

"What are you doing?" Dylan demanded to know, clearly alarmed as Josh reached for the gold links dangling from Lana's fingers. "Dude, you don't have the skill to pull this off."

He didn't bother to answer his brother, just sank back to his knees before his goddess. Dylan's warning echoed in his ear as Josh threaded the chain between his lips, but he didn't pay his brother any mind. Instead, he reached for Casey with every intention of threading the chain through all three clamps using nothing but his lips and tongue.

If it took a while…all the better.

Chapter 12

Dylan didn't know what had gotten into Josh, but he liked it. His brother was finally thinking like a man. He'd been afraid that Maria had neutered Josh, but thankfully, it had been only a temporary condition, one Casey was curing with every giggle and panted sigh.

She was having fun. That just made the whole show hotter, as if it wasn't already more than he could have ever dreamed. Dylan had a lot of dreams. He really should start a bucket list.

Oh, the things he was going to put on it.

Dylan sighed as he took his own heavy erection in hand as he watched Josh sink to his knees and bury his face between Casey's sweet thighs. She squirmed and moaned, clearly enjoying his brother's attention.

So, too, was Josh enjoying himself. With one hand clamped around Casey's waist to hold her still, the other wrapped around his own erection as Josh began stroking his dick. Dylan knew just how his brother felt.

He'd been forced to take himself in hand as well. It was either that or avail himself of the bevy of beauties surrounding him, but none of them tempted Dylan in the slightest. He had eyes for only one woman…his little pixie.

Dylan's breath caught as Lana retrieved two massive silver balls from the shelves of unopened toys at Josh's direction. She brought them back to him, handing them off as, one by one, he inserted them deep into Casey's cunt, using only his lips and tongue. Casey flushed and panted, giggling now as she jiggled her hips.

That had the men going crazy as Casey flushed with a sexy sheen of sweat. The moisture had the tail ends of her red curls clumping and curling, highlighting the curves that Dylan ached to touch. Soon, very soon, but right then, he didn't have the strength to stand, much less walk.

More importantly, he didn't dare miss a minute of the show that Josh was making out of Casey, especially not when he rose back up to his feet and picked the flogger back up. This time he didn't stop with just a few licks, and neither did he aim only for the tight, rounded curves of Casey's ass.

Instead, Josh wielded the flogger like a pro, snapping the velvet tassels over Casey's breasts and dancing them across her stomach before licking over the pink, plump folds of her cunt. Casey cried out, her hips arching as her legs opened wider in a blatant invitation that damn near had Dylan coming right then and there all over his fist.

He managed to control himself, but Casey didn't. She came in a hard, glorious screaming fit that had her blushing bright red as every muscle in her body strained before convulsing. Then she would have collapsed, but the cuffs held her limp form upright as Josh finally stepped back.

"That was fucking beautiful, man." Dylan heaved a deep sigh. "Absolutely fucking beautiful."

"Yeah?" Josh smirked, glancing up at the camera as he shot Dylan a look that he recognized well from his own mirror. "Watch this."

* * * *

Casey breathed out a sigh of satisfaction, feeling ready for a nap. It had been a long day filled with more excitement than she was used to. Now, after that little nightcap, she was feeling good, satiated and lip. Unfortunately, she was still bound, still forced to stand, and something told Casey there were no timeouts in this game.

Her prediction came true not but seconds later when an all-too-familiar set of rough hands gripped her thighs. The quiet boy wasn't done, and he was far surpassing the fantasies of Josh she'd always entertained. She knew Josh well enough to know what kind of lover he'd be, all "please, may I, and thank you."

Not exactly an exciting fantasy but definitely a sweet one. There wasn't anything sweet about her quiet boy, though. Ravenous, that better described the man whose heated, heavy breath tickled over the lips of her pussy. She was still smarting from the sting of the flogger, and the soothing caress of the mouth breaking over her cunt had Casey sighing.

As if reading her very thoughts and determined to prove her wrong at every turn, the quiet boy gently rubbed his cheek over her mound, nearly undoing her. She wanted to sink down and curl into the hard strength of the body she could feel pressing between her legs. That wasn't all she could feel.

There was no mistaking the hard, hot length of his cock bumping against her calf as he knelt there between her legs. He was big and thick, thicker than almost any other man she'd ever taken. Almost any except for the one she'd had earlier that day, and suddenly the thought of being taken by both her mystery lover and the quiet boy had Casey's cunt weeping with a rush of lust.

She'd have tackled the man at her feet and taken what she wanted if it hadn't been for those damn cuffs. They forced her to remain standing, and more importantly, they kept her at the mercy of the quiet boy, who was clearly intent on taking his time.

The gentle caress of the blunt tips of his fingers through her still-weeping folds had Casey whimpering and twisting within his hold. She didn't want it soft. She didn't want it sweet, but she didn't have any control. That was in the hands of a man who clearly showed no mercy as he began to lick her cunt clean.

Casey's breath caught as her heart seized and her body sparkled to life with a ticklish sensation that soon had every one of her muscles contracting as her whole body arched forward in anticipation for when that slowly lapping tongue would finally reach her clit.

Her poor, sensitive bud continued to throb within the tight clasp of the clamp. The pounding pulse beating outward grew to a delight almost too intense to bear as his tongue curled around her clit. Casey's stomach clenched as the blood in her veins began to boil hotter and hotter.

There was no controlling the heat or the sensation. All she could do was endure it as the need began to thicken once again within her. It wound tighter and tighter until he again brought her to the breathless edge of another explosion. He held her there as his tongue finally dipped down to circle the sensitive opening of her sheath.

In the blinding seconds that followed, Casey knew the pain of pure, undiluted ecstasy as he fucked his tongue deep into her cunt, bouncing those damn balls on the tip of his tongue. They rolled across her sensitive wall, their heavy weight pressing down on the plug still filling her ass and making her muscles clench and spasm.

It was too much, and yet only the beginning.

With a hungry growl, her quiet lover snapped the reins of his restraint and began to ravage her pussy with a mercilessness that sent her flying over the edge once again. Casey barely recognized herself as the pleasure mushroomed through her, tearing away any inhibition or insecurity she might possess and reforming her into a creature of pure sensuality that craved nothing but the wicked bite of carnal bliss.

Despite all the games she'd played before, Casey had never allowed anybody this kind of control. She'd never trusted anybody that much, but here she did. Here she was free to dream…dream of Josh because it was his kiss she ached for, even though Casey knew he'd never clamp a girl's clit…at least, she didn't think so, but one never knew about the quiet ones.

They were the dangerous ones. The man kneeling at her feet proved that with every lick. He didn't give her a chance to catch her breath, much less recover from the rapture still pounding through her veins.

Instead, he forced her higher, making her cunt cream harder as he continued to suck the proof of her never-ending release right off the shuddering walls of her sheath. Casey's breasts heaved as she gasped and panted for breath as his tongue continued to twirl over her sensitive flesh with increasingly frantic strokes.

Like a crazed animal, starving and unable to quench his need, he devoured her cunt as he drove Casey right to the edge of her sanity. Then he stole it, along with the tattered remains of her self-restraint as he reached behind her to grab the knotted end of the butt plug. Almost immediately, he began to pump it back and forth.

It was too much. She couldn't take it.

Her ass was on fire, her sheath a living flame, and the heat mushrooming out of her pelvis too intense to bear. Giving in to the forbidden ecstasy, Casey let go and allowed the inferno to consume her. She came in a screaming fit that seemed to echo around her, only it didn't die down, even as her cries did.

For long, thundering minutes she barely took note of the distant murmur, but as her breaths shortened and her heart rate began slowing back down, Casey couldn't help but focus on the strange sound. It reminded her of TV, one blaring, but at a distance. That didn't make any sense, not at first. Slowly, though, the fog cleared from her mind and the obvious explanation finally dawned on her.

"You're very good at that." She sighed. "I'd tip ya, but as you can see, I haven't got anything hidden on me anywhere. That, and one doesn't tip the puppet. Isn't that right, Pinocchio? Tell me what the deal is. If you do me right, do you get to be a real Cattleman? Because I kind of like the wood, especially when it's long and hard."

Casey didn't need eyes to know how that comment had been taken. She could hear the eruption of noise and sense it in the man kneeling before her. He was shocked, thrown off guard. She intended to keep him that way as she upped the ante and twirled to shake her butt at him.

"Especially when it's in the ass."

* * * *

Josh could hear Dylan yelling at him but couldn't make out his words through the ringing in his ears. The sound echoed, along with Casey's giggled confession. She liked it in the ass. She wanted him to give it to her, wanted him to bend her over and claim that forbidden channel, and God, he ached to do just that.

Her words unleashed a dark fantasy within him, one that called out to him and lured him further down the path of temptation. He knew instinctively that there would never be any going back.

That thought brought a smile to Josh's lips.

He didn't want to go back. Not ever. Not if it meant letting go of Casey and the pleasure of having her bound before him. Rising up to his feet, Josh raked a possessive gaze down Casey's naked length. He was hard, aching, his balls on fire, but he couldn't give in to those urges. Not yet. Not until he'd taught Casey a lesson about the dangers of teasing him, as she so recklessly did.

He considered just what he wanted to do to her first as he circled around Casey, his gaze lingering on the tight cheeks of her ass before lifting to survey the shelves stocked full of unopened toys lining the far wall.

Josh knew he had Casey's full attention, knew she'd tracked his motions and could see the tension gathering in her muscles as she waited for him to make his move. The way she licked her lips assured him that she was eager for whatever move he did make, only she didn't have a clue about the thoughts racing through his mind.

Lana did. She was quick to respond to his silent nod as he gestured at just what he wanted. Casey was just as quick, too, to respond to his demands, assuming she was about to get what she wanted. Leaning down until his lips brushed against the delicate curve of her ear, Josh watched Casey's lips curl into a satisfied smirk as he commanded her to bend over.

She obeyed without hesitation but with all the attitude he'd come to expect. Bending over at the waist, she backed up slightly with the motion as the cuffs kept her from lowering her arms. The cuffs, however, had nothing to do with her need to rub her ass against him.

That was just pure flaunting on her part.

Two could play that role, though. Josh proved that point as he reached out to palm the firm globes of her ass before splitting her cheeks wide open. He taunted her with the thought that she might actually get what she demanded as he pulled the plug slowly from her ass and dared to replace it with the sticky tip of his own flared cockhead.

Instead of pushing in, though, Josh pushed up, grinding the full length of his erection along the heated crease dividing her ass. Casey moaned, flexing backward to grind against him in a move meant to entice. Josh couldn't deny that he was tempted, but he managed to hold off as Lana approached with the harness he'd requested dangling from her fingers.

Everything was lubed and prepped. All that was needed was for him to gather his strength and brace himself for the agony of pulling free of the heated press of her body. Josh grimaced at the instant streak of pain that shot down the length of his erection as the cool night air engulfed his enflamed flesh. His cock throbbed as the hunger boiling in his balls grew more intense.

The ache only thickened as Casey murmured her own incoherent objection and shook her ass once again at him. The woman was all but begging for it. While Josh might have been able to hold back the urge to bury himself in her tight hot body, he couldn't do what was necessary.

It was time to take the balls out of Casey's cunt. It was like a game with only one rule—no hands allowed. It took him a good five minutes of fucking his tongue deep into Casey's spasming sheath and corralling the balls back to where he could suck them free. All the while she squirmed and bucked, moaning and pleading, only to end up whimpering when he managed to get the second one out of her and stepped back, leaving her weeping flesh cooling in the evening air.

He knew how much that sucked, but it wouldn't last for long.

Stepping back, Josh took the harness from Lana. It snapped open on either side, allowing him to tuck one of the built-in dildos against the weeping opening of Casey's pussy and slide it in before folding the back around her ass and fitting the rounded knob of the second dildo against the dark opening that eagerly ate up every inch he fed her.

"Oh," Casey breathed out a deep sigh of delight as she wiggled her hips. "That feels *so* good."

"That's the point," Josh warned her as he snapped either side of the rubberized panties that basically made up the harness back together.

"Yeah?" Casey smiled as she tipped her chin to gaze blindly over her shoulder at him. "Now what, quiet boy? A spanking? Because, you know, I've been a *baaad* girl."

"That you have," Josh easily agreed as Lana lowered the chains that would snap into the hooks sewn in to either side of the harness.

The chains were linked into a motorize pulley system. Though Josh wasn't sure what it did, he could take a pretty good guess. Clearly he and Lana were thinking along the same lines, which just went to prove that, while great minds thought alike, perverted ones worked in perfect harmony.

"And you know what happens to bad girls?" Josh asked, watching as Lana cranked the chains back upward until Casey's feet floated inches off the floor.

The sudden lift up had Casey squealing as her weight sank her deeper down onto the matching dildos stretching her wide. Clearly bereft of the ability to answer, she still managed to gasp out a series of "no"s as Josh stepped up to push her higher like a child on a swing. He held her aloft as he offered her up a compromise.

"I can see you need some time to consider your answer, so how about I give you an hour or two?"

"Wha—no, wait!"

But Josh was through waiting. He stepped to the side and released Casey, letting her swing back through the air and ride those dildos into a screaming fit. She fought her cuffs, cursing at him as her breath grew into short pants that quickly turned into full-on gasps as Lana followed Josh back toward the door. He paused there to glance back at the sight of Casey not only bound and clamped but also penetrated and sweating.

God but she was beautiful, and he needed to zip his pants up before he did something stupid.

Speaking of stupid... He caught sight of Dylan racing down the path as Lana hesitated just outside the door. She waited there to the side as he jogged right past her toward Josh, who crossed his arms and intentionally blocked Dylan's path.

That didn't stop his brother from all but running into him. Josh, though, was braced for the impact and managed to hold steady while Dylan stumbled backward.

"Dude," Dylan yelped in outrage. "What are you doing? And what did you do to Casey?"

Dylan's eyes widened with that question as he caught sight of her through the glass wall, clearly having missed the last few minutes of the show. He probably had panicked the second Josh had nodded toward the harness.

"Holy crap!" Dylan spat as he gaped at the window and Casey swinging on the other side of it. "What did you do?"

"Punished Casey," Josh answered succinctly. "And I'd thank you not to interfere."

"Well, look who suddenly thinks he's king of the hill." Dylan snorted as he glanced over at Lana. "You headed out?"

"I've got to go meet a friend." Lana smiled as she cast an appreciative look back at Josh. "Besides I think your brother's got it covered…just don't forget you have to get those clamps off in the next ten minutes."

"Like he's going to last two more." Dylan snorted at that.

"I can last," Josh objected instantly. "And I don't need *any* assistance."

"Is that right?" Dylan cocked a brow before obnoxiously mimicking Josh's position and crossing his arms over his chest. "And do I need to remind you that you're only here because of me?"

"No, but all that makes you is in charge of the investigation. Casey is mine." Josh couldn't make it clearer than that.

Equally clear was the glint that darkened in Dylan's gaze and deepened his tone as he instinctively rallied to that bold challenge. "She's *ours*."

"Whatever you say, man." Josh waved away that correction, playing indifferent, despite the fact that he was secretly pleased. "So…you wanna go whip her with the flogger?"

Chapter 13

Casey didn't know how long she hung there strapped in the harness at the mercy of the two men who seemed intent on driving her insane. Her mystery lover had joined the party, and, unlike the quiet boy, he didn't keep his comments to himself.

Just the opposite, he grunted out encouragements as he drove the lust consuming her higher and hotter with every snap of his flogger. He was as ruthless as he had been earlier that day, making Casey dance backward and straight into the quiet man's clutches. He didn't say a word, just pushed her back into the rain of velvety tassels and making her squirm on those damn dildos.

The hard plastic cocks were just thick enough to tease and far from filling enough to please. They certainly didn't compare to the fantasies she'd been harboring for the past four years. Casey knew what would—the thick meat of her mystery lover and his sidekick, the quiet boy.

She wanted them. She needed them. She begged for them, but they denied her, forcing Casey to endure the pleasure of being played with until every second became thickened with a new delight that quickly pooled into a sea of bliss.

She was drowning in the rapture that was both blindingly intense and yet still not enough to release her from the pressure winding through her muscles. It didn't matter how much she pleaded, demanded, or threatened. They didn't pause or hesitate.

This really was punishment, and it didn't stop until she was left incoherent and incapable of doing anything other than moaning out agreements to whatever her mystery lover demanded.

Only then did he give her a moment to catch her breath. That moment grew as long and labored as her breathing as the silence thickened with the same tension beginning to twist through her stomach. Casey could sense them circling her and felt very much like bait strung up in a shark tank, waiting for the first strike, but it didn't come.

Instead, they held back, and she could sense the dare in their hesitation. They were waiting for her to say or do something that would earn her another round of punishment, but Casey wasn't going to give it to them.

Remaining still and silent, she bit down on her lower lip to hold back her moans as her mystery lover stepped up behind her. She recognized him instantly. His scent, his touch, the very feel of the air that surrounded him, they were all familiar to her now, familiar and comforting while, at the very same time, eliciting a thrill of excitement through her.

That flicker flared into a full flame that licked up her back as her mystery lover reached out to settle his hands on her waist and pull her back against his heated length. Almost instantly, the tantalizing scent of man and leather, of wind and a storm ready to break free, infused her every breath, drugging her with its intoxicating heady aroma.

"Well, Firecracker? You ready to submit?"

"No," Casey breathed out, daring to defy him, even as she relaxed into his hold. "Do it again."

"You don't demand," her mystery lover whispered back as he reached a hand around to grasp her still-throbbing nipple within his rough grasp. "You beg."

With that growled command, he snapped the clamp pinched around the tip of her breast free and allowed the blood to rush in. Pure, molten pleasure blossomed through her chest, making her beg and whimper when her mystery lover captured her tit in between his fingers and twisted.

"Oh…oh…*please!*" Casey panted out, writhing with the motions of his fingers as he rolled her puckered tip with a mastery that distracted her long enough not to remember exactly what she was begging for.

It didn't matter. He remembered, and so did his sidekick, who answered her cry by snapping the second clamp free and sending another searing rush of pleasure washing through her. Casey squirmed and squealed as every nerve ending she possessed popped and fizzled with the frantic sensation.

Even as the tide of delight rolled back, it left her buzzing with a bliss that had her murmuring that it was too much, not that her lovers cared. Casey's quiet boy stepped up to capture both her breasts in his large hands. Her mystery lover released her swollen and flushed flesh to him, allowing his own hand to slide down to her hips and the hooks linked into the chain holding her aloft. He snapped the first one free, even as the heated wash of his breath whispered across the curve of her breast.

"Oh, yeah," Casey moaned, pressing her hips back against her mystery lover and her breasts toward the lips brushing softly over the puckered tip of her nipple.

Back and forth, he teased her with the barest of touches, distracting her as his partner in crime snapped the other hook free. She'd have fallen to her feet if quiet boy hadn't stepped up to capture her breast deep in his mouth while he pinned her back against the naked length of her mystery lover.

Using his lips, teeth, and tongue, he tormented her, making her squirm back against the slender dildo filling her ass even as she felt the thick, heat of a real erection pressing against the side of her cheek. That's what she wanted.

"Please," she whined. "I need you, both of you. So thick and hard…I wanna feel you rough…fast, deep…*any* way you want to give it to me. Just undo the harness and *take me.*"

The frustration thickening in her words had her plea ending in a demand that was instantly punished as her mystery lover wrapped the chain still connected to the last clamp holding her clit in a tight fist and gave it a little tug, making her mew and moan as her quiet boy continued ravaging her breasts.

He sucked, licked, and nibbled his way from one pebbled peak to the other, making her twist and whimper for more. It didn't even dawn on her that she was back to demanding, but Casey couldn't help herself. It felt too good not to insist on more.

That's what she wanted—more, more of everything, more of those maddening kisses making her breasts throb, more of the wicked tug and pull of that damn clamp that kept her cunt weeping, and definitely more meat on the thin shafts teasing her with a hint of what it might feel like to take two men at once.

That's really what she wanted. She wanted to get fucked, to get double-stuffed. She wanted to ridden—raw and wild because that is just how she'd always imagined it would be like to be taken by both Dylan and Josh at the same time.

If pleading didn't buy her that fantasy and demanding didn't work, then maybe taunting would.

"You're both so thick and hard," Casey murmured as seductively as she could, given the ragged pant of her breath. "But if you're having trouble with the rough, fast, and deep part, then don't worry. I can do the work...and I'm always available for practice."

Casey's offer ended in a squeal as her mystery lover tugged hard on her clit's chain, making the sensitive bundle of nerves explode with frothy, fizzy delight that left her panting for breath as her cunt clenched down around the dildo teasing the sensitive walls of her cunt. They rippled and pulsed, desperate for something meatier to cling to.

There was nothing. The sparkly explosion that held her in its thrall quickly imploded back into a need that had her moaning out her approval as her mystery lover's hands finally curled around the latches binding her in the harness. Quiet boy's hands joined him, and they both stepped back, allowing her to slide down onto her own feet.

Casey's knees shook and threatened to buckle as the snap of the latches echoed loudly in the heavy silence. Then they were peeling back the flexible plastic and making her whimper as the skinny dildos began sliding free of her body. Not thick enough to satisfy, both cocks were nonetheless solid enough to make her whimper as they rolled down the sensitive walls of her sheath and ass. The delicious sensations ignited a ripple of excitement as she tensed, ready for the real meat.

The harness finally fell free, and her two lovers stepped back up to pin her between their equally hard and thick erections. Behind her, Casey's mystery lover pressed his cock between the rounded globes of her ass, teasing her with the heated feel of his cock. With a slow roll of his hips, he began to pump that big dick up and down, a silent reminder of just how he'd taken her earlier that day.

"Oh, yeah," Casey breathed with a sigh as he taunted her with the tantalizing press of his deliciously engorged cockhead against the sensitive ring of muscles guarding her ass.

"You like that, my little firecracker?"

Those words, soft and filled with a husky warmth, rolled over Casey, making her twist with a primitive reflex as she answered him with the flex of her own hips, grinding her ass back against the velvety heat of his erection. The sensual motion pulled a feral growl from the man behind her.

It rumbled out of his chest in a warning that was more than familiar, but she was too lost to heed the voice whispering through her head. In that moment all that mattered was the feel of a second meaty erection pressing down over her mound to slide right between the splayed and swollen folds of her pussy. With his mouth still ravaging her breasts, her quiet boy's hands tightened on her hips, forcing her to arch toward him as he pumped his thick dick over the still-clamped and pulsing bud of her clit.

That sensitive bundle of nerves throbbed with a deep ache that had Casey whimpering once again. "Please…"

"Hush now, Firecracker," the quiet boy murmured, lifting his chin to brush soft, gentle kisses across her lips. With a tenderness that beguiled her, he lapped up the tears of frustration that had begun to roll down her cheeks. "We're going to take good care of you."

Another warning rolled through her, but Casey barely had a second to take note of it before she was being pressed forward, forced to bend over at the waist by the big hands of her mystery lover as he controlled her motions. She eagerly obeyed the silent command, her breath catching as his callused fingers slid down her back to dig into the fleshy cheeks of her ass and part them.

She remembered how good he felt before when he'd taken her there and couldn't resist pressing back on the rounded, bulbous head of his cock as it pressed a sticky kiss against the entrance to her forbidden channel. Only nothing was forbidden. Not here. Not now. Not when she ached to feel him stretching her wide and pumping her full of cock.

That's just what her mystery lover treated her to, a hard pounding stroke that fucked his latex-covered dick all the way into the tight clench of her ass. There was no hesitation in his motions, no gentleness to temper the searing burn of his penetration, no stopping until he'd seated his full length deep inside her, and no difference between him and her dreams of Dylan because this was exactly how she'd always imagined him taking her, how she'd always imagined how he'd make her feel—deliciously full.

Casey panted over the sensation, unable to help her body's instinctive response as her muscles pulsed and contracted around the heavy cock stretching her wide. Neither could she control the urge to wiggle and make him growl as her cunt melted and wept, eager for a taste of what her ass was getting.

Her chances appeared good as her mystery lover's fingers slid around her hips and over her tummy to press in on the quivering muscles and direct her back upright. Casey didn't wait to be told before spreading her legs wide and opening her pussy up, a silent offering to her quiet boy.

For a moment she thought he was going to take her up on the invitation, but instead of the hard feel of his cock sliding over her folds, Casey felt the blunt tips of his fingers part her lips and the heated wash of his breath over the creamy folds of her cunt. In that moment she knew just what he planned and couldn't help but whimper as she squirmed backward onto the cock keeping her pinned in place.

There was no escaping the lips boldly closing over her clit, though. They popped the clamp free from her clit, sending an echoing boom of rapture through her body. The searing flash of delight was too much, and it ignited a release that had her crying out as she bucked under the force of her climax.

The ecstasy that pounded through her and drove her to a pinnacle of pleasure condensed quickly, imploding into a whirling pool of agonized need that grew only stronger as the man kneeling before her began to devour her cunt. Like a living flame, his tongue danced over her molten flesh, fucking itself deep into her cunt and tickling over the spasming walls of her sheath.

He drove her damn near mad in a matter of seconds. What little sanity she clung to was shredded as her mystery lover began to sway behind her, offering her small little pumps of his cock that teased her with a friction that was just enough to bring her to the quivering edge of another release.

She just needed a little more and she would be flying free once again, but instead, she sank back to earth as her lover denied her. Together they slowed their motions until Casey was writhing blindly in a frantic protest that had her trying to take what she wanted, what she needed.

Her mystery lover was stronger, though, and he easily managed to force her still, holding her steady as she sensed her quiet boy lifting back up to his feet.

What they intended became clear only a second later as her wrists were freed from their cuffs and a hand fisted hard in her hair. It dragged her steadily down until her lips were brushing against the sticky head of a cock, all swollen and hot. The heady scent of male arousal filled her senses as a need to taste overwhelmed the rules that demanded she wait for direction, or at least permission.

With blind hunger, she let her tongue lick out and around the flared head before she caught it between her lips and sucked him straight in, taking him as far and deep as she could before she began pumping her cheeks and making the quiet boy squirm.

This was going to be fun.

Casey was about to claim her revenge.

* * * *

This was perfection...Dylan hadn't lied. Josh had never known such need, such hunger, or such intense pleasure. Nothing in his life had ever felt as good as Casey's velvety lips engulfing him and a moist, suckling heat that had his muscles clenching down tight as he fought to hold out.

She didn't make it easy. She pumped her cheeks around him, and her tongue twirled and swirled over his length as she managed to suck in damn near every single inch of his erection. The sensitive head of his cock hit the back of her throat and then bent down it as the moist heat convulsed around his length in a rippling tide that had him panting just as hard as his brother.

Josh cracked an eye open and gazed across Casey's back at the sight of Dylan pounding into her ass as he rode her just like she wanted—rough, hard, and fast. Casey, clearly, didn't regret those words. There was no denying the excited whimpers falling from her lips, even as she greedily slurped over Josh's cock.

She was having fun, enjoying it both ways. That realization damn near had him coming right then and there, but he fought back, struggling to hold out and make the moment last a little longer. It was a pointless battle, and he could feel the strings of his self-control snapping one by one until he could finally hold on no more.

The searing hot bliss boiling in his balls erupted as he roared with a primitive sense of victory. In that moment, Josh felt like the conquering hero, one that was adored by his servant, by Casey. Like a well-trained mistress, she sucked down every last drop of his release, happily nursing his strength straight out of his dick until Josh was ready to collapse at her feet.

He didn't dare, though, not about to embarrass himself in front of Dylan or the rest of the guys. Not that he worried he would. Even as the ecstasy flooding through his body made the world shimmer and twist before his eyes, Josh's cock remained hard and ready for a second round.

It was a miracle.

It was also a nightmare.

He still hurt. He still hungered. Josh feared it could take years, if not a whole lifetime, to satiate the need still boiling in his balls. While he had a ring, a house, and the right woman this time, it remained to be seen whether or not things actually worked out.

Right then wasn't the time to worry about it.

Chanting out endless praises to the lord, Dylan heaved like a racehorse coming down the final stretch. That was just about how savagely he was fucking Casey. She met him stroke for stroke, her hips pumping back to meet every one of Dylan's thrusts, which just went to prove that she really did like it in the ass.

Josh couldn't wait to give it to her. In fact, he didn't see any reason to wait. He was hard. He was capable, and Dylan had already gotten his turn. That thought had him jerking forward as he snatched a

condom out of the pile Lana had left out for them. He had his erection
sheathed and ready within seconds.

Without thought of consequences or how his brother might
retaliate, Josh laid a hand on Dylan's chest and shoved him straight
back. He caught Dylan by surprise, and his brother stumbled over his
own feet, falling to the ground. Josh stepped over him and grabbed
onto the flushed, bouncing globes of Casey's ass. She was on the
move, trying to turn as she called out in confusion.

That cry ended in a squealed gasp as Josh split open the plush
cheeks of her ass and gave into the feral lusts that had simmered for
too long in his veins. He didn't even hesitate before he slammed into
her, fucking a moan of delight right out of Casey as she began to
instantly pump her hips back, meeting *him* thrust for thrust now.

"What the *fuck*, man?" Dylan scrambled to his feet, casting that
idiotic question at Josh, along with an outraged look.

Considering that it was clear what he was doing, Josh didn't
bother to answer. Instead, he shot a smug look back over his shoulder
at his brother without missing a beat as his hips flexed, driven by
more than simple longing. This was need—pure and raw. He couldn't
stop as he fucked the throbbing length of his erection back into the
tight, sweet heaven of Casey's ass.

She felt good. Better than. She was making all his dreams come
true and then some. Her muscles clamped down and pulsed in a
motion he knew she controlled, and she knew that it was driving him
crazy. Knew it and giggled over it.

"You like that, quiet boy?" Casey teased him, earning an answer
from Dylan, who was in the process of yanking off one condom and
rolling on another.

"You know he does."

Moving around to the front of her, Dylan fisted a hand in her hair,
but instead of guiding her pouted lips to his latex-covered cock, he
forced her back up, bringing Josh's motions to a slow roll even as

Casey's features furled into a delicate frown. It was a warning sign. One Dylan didn't seem to notice.

"And I know what little pixies like."

Dylan snarled over his words, and they came out with a soft threat that stood in stark contrast to his rough motions as he released her hair and wrapped his hands around her thighs. He jerked Casey right off her feet, dragging her legs up around his hips as he stepped forward to press the thick head of his cock up against the opening of her cunt.

Josh could feel him there, a heavy weight pressing back on his own dick, a threat and a promise of the pleasure to come. He knew what Dylan planned but didn't know if he had the ability to withstand the coming pleasure. He wanted to find out, though, and he wasn't afraid to lose. Not at this game, but Dylan just had to have one more word.

"They like to get double-stuffed," Dylan assured her, an arrogant satisfaction tinting his tone.

"D-Dylan?...Is that *you*?"

Chapter 14

That one hesitant question sent a trickle of freezing dread racing down Dylan's spine. She knew. She was about to lose it on them, accuse them of all sorts of wicked, horrible things, and how could he deny them when he was on the verge of burying the hard length of his erection balls-deep within the molten well of her cunt?

Dylan's cock pulsed, throbbing happily away as that thought—the one that warned him this was wrong—only added to the forbidden delight that flowed through his veins. The potent mixture of pleasure and anticipation had him tensing as he waited for the inevitable explosion. Only it didn't arrive.

Instead, Casey hung there staring blindly up at him, her legs clinging tightly to his hips, her cunt weeping over the flared head of his cock, her lips quivering as she waited for his response. It took him a moment, though, to gather his wits enough to speak, and this time he remembered to disguise his voice.

"You can call me whatever you want, Firecracker."

The smug arrogance in his tone drew a customary snort from Casey, who responded immediately to that challenge with one of her own.

"I'll only call you by the name you earned, and if you were Dylan, then you wouldn't be hesitating to fuck your big, thick, dick deep into me while you attempted to prove that your loving was addictive enough to be illegal."

She did know!

She knew and was still begging for her fucking, begging *him* to fuck her. Dylan's gaze collided with Josh's, and he could feel the bolt of energized awareness that shot through both of them and changed the moment into something much deeper than simply the dirty fun it had felt like second ago.

This wasn't just about sex anymore. This was now a claiming, a mastering. It was about finally putting Casey in her place, right where she belonged between him and Josh.

With a nod to his brother, Dylan pressed forward, slowly sinking into the velvety sheath that rippled and pulsed in welcome around him. Casey was tight, her muscles gripping and rippling around the sensitive length of his dick, making his cock pulse and swell with a fresh rush of need fueled by the molten ecstasy that thickened once again along his spine. The sensation was a delicacy he savored.

Dylan knew he was going insane, but he didn't care. He didn't care if he went dumb, bald, or broke. All that mattered was the sound of Casey's breath catching on a moan of delight as she pleaded with him by name.

"And if that's you, Dylan, you better make this as good as all my dreams. Otherwise, I'm going to tell everybody you are a braggart with a three-inch boner."

She wasn't begging any more. Casey was back to threatening, and she knew better than to challenge him like that. Better than to challenge *them*, Dylan corrected himself as Josh slid his hands up around her breasts and used them to press her back against him while he all but growled in her ear.

"And what about me?" Josh demanded to know before teasing Casey with a hint of his own identity. "You're not going to rat me out to my neighbor, are you? After all, she thinks I'm the *quiet* one."

Dylan cringed and then smirked at the emphasis Josh placed on that one word. He wasn't lying. He was the quiet one, which was just why Casey couldn't be faulted for her doubts.

"*That* I'm going to need to see to believe," Casey retorted with a snort that all but dared them to remove her blindfold. There was only one way Dylan ever responded to a challenge.

"Well, then, you better have yourself a look," he advised her as he pulled the tail of sash wrapped around her eyes.

The heavy cloth slid away to reveal the delicate perfection of Casey's features. From the graceful bow of her lips to her adorable nose and elegantly arched brow, she was more than beautiful. She was captivating.

All too frequently Dylan had found himself hypnotized by the shifting sea of angry blues and greens that tended to swirl through her gaze whenever she was arguing with him. Tonight, though, the storms had quieted into a brilliant crystalline green that reflected back the clarity of her emotions.

She wanted him. There was nothing but welcome in Casey's smile, nothing but acceptance and longing in her eyes. Dylan's heart froze, going painfully still as an emotion he didn't recognize flooded through him. It was deep and warm and dangerous.

That probably should have scared the crap out of him, but it didn't. He hadn't come here to find contentment, but he had. Now Dylan knew only that he had no intention of letting it go. He sealed that vow with a kiss before Casey could say anything and ruin the moment.

He could see it coming in the twinkle in her gaze. Casey was getting ready to taunt him because she'd won, and they both knew it. This was supposed to be his moment, his claiming, but as Casey's lips parted beneath his, Dylan realized he had it all backward.

He was the one being claimed. Actually, more like enslaved because that was just what he was—a servant to her passion. His fate was sealed at the first sweet taste of Casey's lips.

In all the years he'd envisioned fucking the pout right off her mouth, Dylan had never wasted a second imagining how good something as simple as kissing her could be, not that she allowed him to savor the moment. Her tongue was as wild as the wind, whipping around his with teasingly light agility that had Dylan growling as he tried to capture hers, but it was him who ended up caught between Casey's lips.

She showed no mercy, tightening her mouth down around him and sucking hard. The maddening pull had his dick pulsing and weeping as a quick rush of seed escaped his balls, a silent threat of more to come if he didn't get control of the situation.

Hell, even then he wasn't going to make the fucking Casey had coming last long enough to suit his pride. He wanted to make this good for her. He needed to. He needed to be good enough that she never felt the need to leave. Dylan didn't question why that was important, and neither did he worry that he wouldn't succeed. In fact, he was certain he would, even more certain as Casey released his tongue to lean back and smile up at him.

"I *knew* it was you," she gloated, clearly impressed with her powers of deduction.

"It took you all day." Dylan snickered, unable to break the habit of teasing her at every turn. That shot earned him a dirty look, though the sparkle remained in her eyes as she responded in kind.

"I knew it from the beginning," Casey scoffed. "I was just waiting to see if you were man enough to reveal the truth…that is, before you fucked me. Now I guess I have my answer, huh? You really are a naughty, naughty boy."

"And what about me?" Josh asked, his harsh tone drawing a purely evil smile to Casey's lips as she glanced back at him.

"Don't worry, I'll still think you're a nice guy…that is, if you do me a little favor and get a move on it." Casey's gaze shifted back to Dylan as he snorted, and she smirked. "So what are you two waiting for? An invitation…or instructions?"

"Instructions?" Dylan chuckled over that, his gaze locking with Josh's as they shared the moment of amusement. "What do you think, baby brother? You think the little pixie has anything to teach us?"

"No, but there is something I'd surely like to show her." Josh leaned in close to nibble on Casey neck, making her giggle and squirm so delightfully Dylan thought he might pass out from the pleasure.

"Really?" Casey was back to purring like a little sex kitten as she cast another glance over her shoulder before giving her ass a little shake, making Josh's grin tighten. "And just what was that?"

"A little humility."

With that, Dylan jerked back, dragging the throbbing length of his dick down the rippling walls of her sheath before he hammered that promise home with a powerful stroke. He fucked a gasp right out of her and a groan out of Josh.

His brother snarled as his gaze flashed with a dangerously feral look Dylan had never seen before. Not that it mattered. The only thing that mattered in that moment was the pure, white-hot rapture rushing straight up his spine while every drop of his blood pounded downward, making his balls swell painfully tight.

That's just what Casey was—wondrously, deliriously tight. Tight, wet, and milking every single inch of his dick, her cunt pulsing around him as Dylan pounded into her in an alternating rhythm with his brother. They held that tempo, knowing that it drove Casey completely insane.

She begged. She pleaded. She demanded. All the while she was twisting, flexing, fucking them back, and making them pay for denying her because they were also denying themselves. That grew harder and harder to do.

Dylan's breath heaved in with labored pants as the sweat began to build up along his spine. The slick slap of their bodies filled the air, along with the rich scent of sex, an intoxicating aroma that threatened to weaken his defenses.

He couldn't focus. His control was slipping, the need for a release becoming overwhelming, and his reasons for holding back got lost somewhere in the fog of lust thickening in his head. All that mattered in that moment was Casey.

Casey threw her head back into Josh's chest, and her eyes closed as her swollen, pouty lips parted on another whimper. Lost in her passion, she looked like a goddess, a creature of pure sensuality made for fucking. She certainly had the strength to keep up. Casey had locked her ankles together, pressing them into the small of his back, giving her leverage to keep up with them thrust for thrust. That was just downright sexy.

In that moment, as he gazed down at Casey's flushed features, all the other nameless, faceless women who had come before were washed away, and all that was left was the certain knowledge that here was the woman who could fulfill all his needs, no matter how dark or dirty they were.

Right then, though, the only thought filling Dylan's head was the desperate need to come. His balls were on fire, the sensitive length of his cock tingling with a rush he couldn't help but give in to.

Jerking out of the steady rhythm the three of them had set, Dylan switched beats to match the heavy pound of his brother's strokes. He could feel the hard press of his brother's cock as they pounded into Casey's tight body at the same time. There was barely enough room, and the silken walls of her cunt clung to him as tight and hot as the latex keeping him from feeling her ripple against him skin to skin.

He knew he wasn't the only one holding on by a thread. Panting and cursing, Josh sounded as though he was strangling on every breath he managed to get out.

"Oh shit. Oh…shit! *Oh shit!*"

Dylan would've laughed at his brother's desperate sounding pleas if he hadn't been silently echoing them. He managed, though, to keep his own cries to himself, fucking himself deep into Casey's body with snorted grunts that matched her own sexy pants. Her gasps grew shorter and shorter as her nails dug deeper and deeper into his shoulders.

She clung to him as her motions grew more and more frantic. Dylan knew she was close to a release that would surely be stronger than any she'd known before. That's what he wanted, to permanently mark her as his in such a way that she could never even imagine herself with another man.

He knew he'd won that battle when she finally cried out with her release and it was his name falling from her lips.

* * * *

Casey had never felt so good in her entire life as she did right then. She was packed full and being ridden hard, but the ecstasy sweeping through her was sweetened not only by the sheer eroticism of being caught between two hard, hot male bodies or even being used so savagely by them but in knowing that it was Dylan and Josh.

Her heart exploded with her body as she called out to them, needing an end to the agonizing torment of rapture winding through her. It pushed her to the edge of a pinnacle so high she was almost afraid of what would come next, but there was no stopping the rising tide.

It hit her with a glorious brilliance that sent her soul flying high enough to touch the stars, even as her body collapsed, convulsing with a firestorm of rapture that left her whole body buzzing with endless ripples of delight. Still Josh and Dylan continued to pound into her, causing the shudders to condense into another mind-altering wave of ecstasy.

Casey cursed as her worn and sore muscles contracted yet again, forced once more to strain and stretch for release that would surely be the end of her. Then it hit, leaving her clutching at Dylan as her legs clamped tight around his hips as he roared with his own release.

The sound echoed back from behind her as Josh joined them, his dick pulsing as he continued to mindlessly pump it into her ass. It took over a minute for him to wind down. Even then, he wasn't the slightest bit soft, despite the fact that he was clearly worn out.

Josh should have been satiated. So should his brother. Dylan had come all damn day long, but apparently he hadn't lied when he'd bragged all those times about his stamina. Not only was he hard but he still had the strength to hold her close as Josh seemed to lean in on both of them.

She let him catch his breath as she leaned back to offer Dylan a satisfied smile, along with a rare compliment. "I guess you weren't lying. You really can go all night."

Dylan didn't take the opportunity she offered him to gloat, which would not only have been his right but also very much like him. More worrisome than his lack of response was the scowl he beamed down at her. He looked so serious that, for the first time ever, he reminded her of Josh.

"And what about you, quiet boy? Never figured you for being an ass man."

"You're my first," he admitted, not sounding particularly happy about that fact, though he certainly felt it.

He might not have the strength to stand on his own, but his cock was just as hard and swollen as it had been minutes ago. Neither did his tone soften as he grumbled over his complaint.

"But I wasn't *your* first, was I?"

Jealousy tinged Josh's tone, sending another thrill racing up her spine. As wickedly delightful as that prickle of sensation was, Casey didn't have any interest in stoking it, especially not if it meant hurting Josh. So she tried for diplomacy with just a touch of honesty.

"No, but you were one of the best."

That might not have come out sounding as sincere as it should have, but it was hard to fake a serious tone when she was feeling so damn good. Hell, she was feeling better than good. She was feeling ready for a nap.

"Casey, we need to talk."

"What?" Alarmed by that simple statement and shocked that it had come from Dylan, Casey blinked and shook her head. "Oh, no. No. No. No."

"Yes," Dylan insisted, seeming intent on ruining the moment.

"No." Casey wouldn't let him ruin it. She was feeling too damn good right then to get all serious.

"Casey—"

"*No!* We don't. Not about this. Not now." Casey paused before adding on, "Not ever."

It could just be what it was, and then there wouldn't be any need for consequences. That was the theory. The reality was that she was stuck, quite literally, and there wasn't much she could do about that fact but whine…or yell.

"Casey—"

"No!"

"That's—"

"No!"

"Damn it, let me—"

"No!"

"Enough!" Josh interjected, lifting a hand to clamp it around her mouth. "Dylan has something he wants to say, and you're going to listen."

She was not. Casey let that be known by taking a nip at Josh's palm, which bought her freedom and a few curses. She ignored those and spoke fast, knowing just what to say to put an end to this uncomfortable conversation.

"I came here for one reason and one reason only, so you two can either put out or get out, got me?"

Chapter 15

Casey issued that ultimatum, knowing just what choice both brothers would make. At least, she thought she did. Her confidence, however, faded slightly at Dylan's dour look. He should have been smiling and bragging and all too eager to do it again.

Instead, he stepped back, pulling free and clear of the clinging depths of her pussy. Casey whimpered as his heavy weight dragged over the sensitive walls of her sheath. Her cunt wept over the loss, clinging to the last delightful shivers racing up through as her ass clenched around the cock still buried deep in it.

Her hope that Dylan would pound himself back inside of her and teach her a lesson for daring to challenge him died, though, as Dylan turned and simply walked away. He headed toward the back bedroom and, no doubt, the bathroom beyond, leaving Casey quite literally at Josh's mercy.

She couldn't help but wonder if he planned on giving her a lecture. After all, he was known for them, but Josh didn't say a word as he lifted her straight off his dick and dumped her back onto her own feet. Casey's legs trembled, and her breath caught as she waited to see if he followed his brother out the room, and in that second, Casey realized the magnitude of what had just happened.

Dylan was probably done with her. Whatever her feelings, she knew where she stood with him—alongside a lot of other women who didn't mean anything to him. Sex was like any other hunger to him, and Dylan liked a different meal every night. While that thought cut deep, she knew there was no fighting it.

Josh was different. He was her friend. Her good friend, and she didn't want to lose that, didn't want to lose him. Casey had reason to hope she wouldn't and that they could possibly just expand on their current relationship.

That seemed to be his very thought as he reached down to pull the used condom off and flicked it at the trashcan before snatching up another. Casey's gaze followed his motion, her eyes rounding on the large pile of condoms at the ready. There had to be over two dozen, and she couldn't go that long. Neither was Casey convinced that both brothers could, but they could trade off.

That thought hit just as Josh settled back onto the exam chair. He beckoned her forward with a nod and an invitation that sent a dark curl of need unfurling through her.

"Come on, Firecracker, let's see what you got."

The challenge was there in his tone and in the hard look he shot her. Casey recognized that glint in his eyes. Josh was enjoying himself. Unlike his brother, he seemed completely content with the current situation.

That thought sent a shiver through Casey as she climbed up onto his lap, aware of his gaze tracking the swing of her breasts before he tipped his head to the side to catch a glimpse of her cunt. She was more than willing to let him have a look but was torn about whether she should let him have a ride or a taste.

Both ideas left her wet. Her clit tingled with a shivery ache for the feel of his tongue lapping at her sensitive bud while her cunt clenched at the very sight the large, oversized cock standing proud as a flagpole between his legs. She'd never have thought he'd be such a big man.

She'd known, however, that he was well cut and liked to work out. Knowing, though, was different than feeling the heat of his corded muscles pressing against the moist folds of her cunt as she settled down over his stomach, careful to avoid the erection sheathed in the flesh-colored condom.

It was a shame he'd gotten all dressed up. Casey would have liked to take a taste. That thought renewed her confidence as she remembered one important point. When it came to sex, she was the pervert and Josh was as close to a virgin as she'd ever gotten. Hell, he'd already confessed to being at least *one* type of virgin.

Casey bet there were all sorts of things Josh hadn't tried before. All sorts of things she could be his first for. That thought warmed her through as she smiled down at him. He didn't return the gesture.

He couldn't, not without unclenching his jaw. That's when Casey realized that Josh was drawn tense and tight, braced for whatever she planned next. He knew. He was going down.

With that intent in mind, she bent down to rub her smooth cheek across the stubbled length of his, allowing the tips of her breast to tease the heated flesh of his chest as she captured his lips in a kiss meant to prove just who was in command of this moment. He didn't fight her but opened his mouth to the invasion of her tongue.

It was a trap, but Casey realized that too late. Already she was drunk and addicted to the warm honey and beer taste of his kiss. The sweet and heady flavor intoxicated her, making her forget for a moment everything at stake.

Instead, she lost herself in the pleasure thickening in her veins as his tongue rallied to challenge hers. They dueled, a wicked and fierce battle that had Casey melting into Josh's embrace as his arms closed around her. He held her tight as if afraid to let go, or, perhaps, that was her own fear.

That thought sank through her right along with the fear itself. Things were moving too fast. They were too intense. She stood to lose too much if she didn't get a hold of herself. Pulling back, she gasped, straining for breath and sanity as she desperately tried to remember the point of all this—to enslave Josh with lust.

With defenses fortified and her determination renewed, Casey twisted to capture his big, thick dick in her fist. Gazing down at him as she watched his reaction, Casey squeezed and pumped his rigid flesh, learning just how he liked to be stroked, which turned out to be any and all ways.

With a growl, he reached back to cover her fist with his own while the other buried itself in her hair to drag her back down to meet his kiss. This time he took command, but there was no controlling the wild flare of passion that ignited from the still-smoldering embers of a hunger that that hadn't been completely satiated by their recent release.

All too quickly the need that had been there, burning beneath the surface for years, raged back out of control. Fueled by a lust that demanded action, Casey was all too eager to assist when Josh's fingers tightened around hers, but instead of forcing her into a faster rhythm, he ripped her hand away from his engorged flesh as his other hand dropped back to her waist. It took both hands, though, for him to lift her up and bring her back down over the flared head of his cock.

He hesitated there to growl up at her. "Look at me!"

Casey's eyes fluttered open as her gaze locked on his. He held her captive with the dark hunger swirling in his eyes as he forced her down his thick length even as his hips flexed upward, sheathing his long, hard cock deep within her, driving the intensity of the moment ever higher.

He wasn't just penetrating her body. He was branding her as his. She could feel his claim searing through her as his thick dick stretched her wide as she sank all the way down over his heated length. This was so much more than simply sex, and as Casey felt Josh shift beneath her, pumping that thick cock of his deep within her, she knew that she was being claimed in some primal, feral way.

A part of her craved his ownership, his domination. He was hard, hot, and strong, each thrust proving that he was more than man enough to keep her happy for the rest of her days…if only they could have those days. That thought whispered through Casey as she gave her body over to the ecstasy, making her arch and cry out as she met him thrust for thrust.

Her soul, though, she clung to, trying desperately to protect it and her heart. It was a futile effort. In that moment, there was no him, no her. There was only them. They were as one, moving in perfect rhythm. Together they reached the same pinnacle and hurtled off of it.

Knowing that Josh shared in the ecstasy flooding through her made it all the more intense, and Casey cried out his name as she collapsed on top of Josh, her hips still flexing and fucking with an instinctive urge to chase after the delight cascading through her until she'd worn herself completely out.

Sighing with a soul-deep sense of satisfaction, Casey smiled as she snuggled into Josh's chest, enjoying being just being held by him. He smelled so good…and felt even better. God, she'd never had it better, except maybe for his brother.

That dirty, wicked thought had a giggle bubbling up to her lips. She was half tempted to share it with Josh, but he beat her to the punch and spoke up first.

"Now, you were about to explain to me why you are here."

She should have known. There was no way that Dylan wanted to talk and Josh didn't. The only difference between the two brothers was how they went about getting what they wanted. That didn't change the fact that the best way to handle both of them, given the situation, was to make sure things didn't grow too intense.

"What do you think?" she murmured as she feathered little teasing kisses across his chest in a blatant attempt to distract him. "I'm here for the same reason you are, stud, to have a little fun…or a whole lot of it," Casey corrected herself, tossing him a wink as she rolled her hips, unleashing a shower of sparkly delight that had her moaning as she tried to repeat the move, but Josh held her steady, refusing to allow her to even have a hint of fun. Her moan turned to a groan as her smile dipped upside down.

"Don't be a killjoy, Josh." Casey wiggled pointedly in his hold. "I'm not sitting here because I'm in the mood for some deep conversation."

"Casey—"

"Come on, quiet boy," Casey cajoled him with a sexy smile as she teased both him and herself with a gentle rub of the hardened tips of her breasts against his chest in a provocative gesture that she matched with a sultry purr. "There is no need to talk when you can just show me what you want."

* * * *

What Josh wanted was Casey, and not just for a week, but that wasn't what she was offering him. She was offering him this moment, and he would be a fool not to take it. He might have only a week, but he would use that time to enslave Casey to the pleasure only he and Dylan could give her.

When the week ended, hopefully she wouldn't have the ability to walk away. Hell, she wouldn't have the ability to walk if he gave in to all the needs burning through him. He knew Casey thought she was the pervert, but he had a whole lot to show her.

Four years' worth of fantasies, to be precise, with even more springing to mind by the second. They'd get to them all, but first he had to fuck the need swelling in his balls back to a low simmer. He couldn't help but wonder how many times he was going to have to come to finally reach a state where he felt anywhere near rational.

It wasn't going to be any time soon, not with Casey sitting there perched on his cock with her soft, velvety sheath squeezing him tight in a creamy, heated vise that assured him she was far from tired. Instead, she was hot, wet, and grinning down at him with a lecherous gleam in her eyes.

"That is, of course, if you are willing to give me equal measure?"

Casey already had that kind of power over him, but Josh wasn't crazy enough to admit it. He'd known her long enough to know just how she'd abuse that sort of power. While he was sure he'd enjoy the torture, Josh wanted to enjoy a different treat right then.

"Give you?" Josh smirked as he loosened his hold on her hips. "I only got one thing to give you, Firecracker, and you're already sitting on it."

That earned him a laugh as Casey shook her head at him. "Have I ever told you how cute you are when you lose an argument?"

"Who said anything about losing?"

In fact, Josh was planning on claiming victory in a few short seconds. Casey might have known that if she'd bothered to take note of Dylan sneaking back into the room. Josh didn't know what the hell his brother had been up to, but he knew what he was planning right then, especially when he picked up the flogger.

"Well, let me be the first to tell you that you are cute when you're bossy, adorable when you think you're about to win, and downright fuckable when you talk dirty, so go on and say something nasty to me, quiet boy," Casey teased him with a giggle. "Go on and tell me how much you like sucking on my cunt...or haven't you had a taste?"

"Yeah," Josh drew out that word with slow satisfaction as he recalled just how much fun that had been. "You are addictive, but your ass..."

"That was so much more fun, huh?" Casey smiled smugly, enjoying the memory herself.

"Nope." Josh shook his head as he relaxed back on the seat, getting comfortable for the coming show as Dylan came to a stop directly behind Casey. "But it is about to glow red."

"Wha—"

Casey's question ended in a scream before she could even finish asking it as Dylan snapped the leather tassels across her ass. She jerked upward with the blow, those big beautiful tits of hers bouncing while her cunt slid up over Josh's shaft before milking its way back down.

It took all of his effort not to let his eyes roll back behind his suddenly heavy lids as the pleasure of being ridden flooded through his veins, but Josh fought back against the need to come, not wanting to miss a moment of what came next.

* * * *

Casey was on fire. The flames licking over her were being driven higher and higher by the velvet tassels cracking across her ass and driving her to pump her hips and fuck herself up and down Josh's thick length while he sat there watching her with a smile. He looked so damn sexy, and felt even better.

It was almost more than she could take, but it was barely a drop of what she could give. If they wanted to make a show out of her, then she would give them both one. Twisting at the waist, she turned to snatch the tassels flying toward her right out of the air in one hand while the other came to cup her breast and lift it upward.

"You know that's really not necessary," Casey stated in a voice clear enough to impress even her.

She definitely managed to get Dylan's attention. Their gazes collided and locked. She could easily read the hunger darkening in his as she dipped her chin to bury it in the soft, plump curve of her breast and allowed her tongue to lick out over her nipple. Casey kissed the pebbled bud, letting the pleasure of her own tasting soak through her before daring to tempt Dylan by releasing his whip.

"Besides, I'm sure there are better things you could be doing to my ass." Casey turned back to confront Josh, leaving Dylan to smolder behind her as she taunted his brother. "And you, quiet boy, give me your hand."

She held hers out expectantly, ignoring Josh's raised brow and his amused smirk, certain that he would obey. He was too curious of a man not to. He also happened to be a man who knew what to do with the challenge, just like Dylan.

After a moment Josh laid his hand in hers. Casey didn't hesitate to bring those blunt fingers to rest over the curve of her mound before issuing a challenge she knew she might live to regret.

"This is a pussy. You pet it," she informed him as she stretched over him to dangle the tips of her breast right over his lips. "And these are tits. You suck them…and this is an ass." She wiggled her butt, lifting it up into the air before casting a pointed glance back at Dylan. "You fuck it. Any questions?"

Dylan laughed at that, the deep rumble of his chuckles growing enticingly closer. "I don't think you could have been any clearer, Firecracker, though I should warn you that I do enjoy spanking asses almost as much as I enjoy fucking."

"You can spank it later, stud. Right now, it's time to take it for a ride."

"You heard the woman," Josh chipped in as he slid a finger down between the swollen lips of her pussy to pin her clit beneath its heavy, callused weight. "It's time to mount up like a man and give the lady what she wants."

"How about what she deserves, baby brother?" Dylan laughed as Josh's smile dipped into a frown.

"You've got twenty minutes on me," Josh shot back, taking up an argument Casey had been listening to for the past several years.

It wasn't the only argument she knew by heart. In fact, they'd turned disagreeing into a pastime, one that they both clearly enjoyed. Casey, on the other hand, was not in the mood to listen to the two of them try to one-up each other for the next hour, though she might be in the mood to *feel* them try.

"Twenty minutes and a good inch." Dylan smirked.

"Then why don't you—" Casey had been about to tell him to put that good inch to work, but Josh cut her off as though he didn't even notice her there sitting on his cock.

"Please," Josh snorted. "I got two on you all day long."

"Two? That's all you got?" Dylan snickered dismissively. "Well then, you might want to consider getting a strap-on because I'm sure Casey's used to a lot more than two inches."

"Okay, that's it!" Josh snapped, grasping Casey by her hips and lifting her right off him to dump her on her feet.

Gaping in outrage, she watched as both brothers ignored her to take up the ridiculous argument.

"We're getting a ruler."

"Fine!" Dylan retorted as he crossed his arms over his naked chest and took his stand with his cock bobbing straight out as if trying to prove his point. "But it better be a long one because I need something that goes *past* twelve inches."

"In your dreams."

"I'm twelve when I'm soft."

"You're an inch and a half if you're a day old."

"Where is that damn ruler?"

Casey stared in disbelief at the brothers faced off before Dylan turned with that question and stormed off. Josh followed him as they continued to bicker and harass one another, leaving Casey standing there all alone watching them walk way.

She really shouldn't be surprised. This is what happened when a woman was dumb enough to fall for two hardheaded brothers. That didn't mean she was just going to stand there and take it.

Chapter 16

Lana shook her head at the blonde-haired beauty grinning like a damn clown back at her. She knew that grin, knew that it only ever led to trouble. That's just what Angie lived for, which was a good thing because trouble followed her around like a shadow. That might have something to do with her propensity to stick her nose where it didn't belong.

"I can't believe that you're still fighting this battle." Angie sighed as she glanced around the jungle-themed garden she'd found Lana lounging in.

Actually Lana had been about to join the rest of the revelers playing in the pool that had been made to look like a perfectly blue lagoon. It even had its own waterfall, which was just perfect for washing off the sweat on a muggy night like this one.

"I mean really, honey, you could sell your stake in this club back to those bozos and end up rich, and you're already hot...what else could a woman want?"

That was Angie, not shallow but definitely superficial in a lot of ways. She was also blunt, opinionated, loyal, big-hearted and a lot of fun to hang out with.

"First off, I'm already rich," Lana corrected her with a smirk. "And what I want *can't* be bought."

"Oh, please," Angie groaned as she shot Lana a frown that still, nonetheless, held a hint of mirth to it. "Chase Davis isn't even worth the two cents Patton paid for him. Neither is that little brother of his, Devin. Now Slade…"

"You got a thing for the nerdy ones, huh?"

"I got a thing for a man who knows how to take care of a woman," Angie corrected her, her Spanish lineage coming through in that moment as she smiled smugly, or maybe it was her Italian lineage.

It was hard to tell with Angie which half of her overly passionate family history was motivating her in that moment. Of course, there was also the Irish influence. Given all that, though, Angie was as American as they came with her violently pink, barely alcoholic girl-drink sitting in front of her.

"And I'm not just talking about in bed," Angie qualified as she swizzled a too-cute, tiny umbrella through her barely touched drink.

"That's because you don't know anything about '*in bed*,' virgin," Lana retorted. "Trust me, those two idiots you've been chasing after for the past decade are only known to be good at *one* thing…though I think the bed is considered optional."

"That may be," Angie allowed. "But that's why they need me, to teach them how to be real men."

Lana snorted at that. "Good luck."

"Now, see, that's your problem," Angie informed her as she straightened up on her stool. "You—"

"Hey, Angie." Dean Carver appeared by her side with a sly smile and a gaze that dipped pointedly downward. "It's good to see you again."

"I would say the same, but since you so *rudely* interrupted my conversation, I'd be lying," Angie shot back with clear disdain before reaching out one lone finger to tip Dean's chin back up. "And my *eyes* are up here."

Angelina was the only woman who would strut around naked and actually expect men to look her in the face. Hell, she demanded it, which was one of the reasons that she was considered a real catch among the Cattlemen. That and the fact that she was a virgin, a haughty, hot, snotty virgin that every man there wanted to teach a lesson.

There was a price on Angelina's ass, and they were all vying to pop that cherry for her. They didn't dare press the issue, though, because Angie was the faucet that kept the women coming. Without Angelina's connection as a travel agent, all those hungry, lonely women would have ended up on singles cruises instead of playing servants to the Cattlemen's desires.

It was that business association that had grown into a real friendship between Lana and Angie, a minor miracle really, given that Angie was one of Patton's good friends. Of course, Patton didn't know that Lana considered Angie the same—a good friend, and she didn't have many of those

"I guess that it was my mistake then," Dean shot back coolly as he straightened away from the bar Lana and Angie were seated at. "Pardon me, *ladies*."

He managed to make that last word sound like an insult and left no doubt that's just what he was—insulted. Angie didn't care. Heaving her own aggrieved sigh, she rolled her eyes and shook her head as her gaze shifted back toward Lana.

"I really don't know how you put up with these men. They're all a bunch of prima donnas if you ask me."

"And is that what you tell your clients when you sell them on their weekend passes to paradise?"

"No. I tell them the men know how to make a woman purr." Angie's smile returned as she snickered. "Of course, I only have your word to go on that."

"You don't have to take my word for it," Lana assured her. "You can ask any woman here…in fact, you can ask them now because I've got to take this."

Picking up the phone that had started to vibrate on the bar top, Lana frowned at the number flashing on the screen. The call was coming in from one of the cubes, and she knew exactly who was on the other end.

* * * *

"Three-eighths of an inch! Ha!" Dylan raised his arms and pumped his fist in victory as Josh scowled and tried to snatch the tape measure out of his hand.

"Oh, shut up," he snapped. "And give me that."

Pumping and stroking his dick back to full length, Josh stretched the tape measure out down the length of his erection and frowned. "I need Casey. She's the one who knows how to make the wood really grow."

"Yeah…Casey." Dylan stilled, his grin dipping as he caught Josh's gaze. They shared a moment of heavy silence as it dawned on both of them just how they'd left her… "She's going to be pissed."

That was an understatement as far as Josh was concerned, but in their defense, she knew how they could be when it came to settling their arguments. Neither twin liked to be wrong and tended to become consumed with proving themselves right, which was just what had happened that night.

The real problem wasn't the argument. It had been finding a measuring tape. That had required putting on pants and abandoning her in the cube. They shouldn't have done that, or, at least, they shouldn't have left her unleashed.

"Shit!" Josh echoed Dylan's sentiment exactly as both brothers began rushing to right their pants.

"We are in so much trouble," Dylan warned Josh as they both tried to fit through the bathroom door at the same time.

They popped out into the club's main hall, only to stumble over each other as both brothers came to a quick halt. Their gazes, along with everybody else's in the large room, locked on the screen still reflecting the events unfolding in Casey's cube.

She wasn't alone anymore.

Neither was she naked. Not really. Dressed in almost all leather, with a whip in her hand, Casey lorded over the three naked women writhing at her feet. Josh barely took note of the orgy she was clearly conducting. Instead, his gaze remained fixated on Casey and how good she looked in her cute, little outfit.

It was comprised of a cupless corset that pushed her plump breasts upward in a mouthwatering display of tits and cleavage and a skirt too short to leave much to the imagination. Best of all, though, were the five-inch-stiletto boots that laced all the way up to her knees.

"I think I can beat that three-eights now," Josh whispered. Hell, he was certain of it.

"Yeah?" Dylan nodded toward the clock now counting down over the projector. "You notice the scoreboard?"

He hadn't, not until then. On one side it read, *Girls,* on the other, *Boys.* They were at zero while the girls were at eight, which turned to nine as one of the women let out a scream and convulsed with an obvious release.

"We are in so much trouble," Josh whispered, agreeing with Dylan's earlier sentiment because he was beginning to get a picture of what was going on. From the glares they were getting, Josh knew, too, that they were about to lose control of more than just Casey.

"Come on," Josh nudged Dylan, breaking him out of his own stupor. "Let's go join the show before somebody else starts racking up our points."

"And you better hurry," Lana spoke up from behind them, catching both Josh's and Dylan's attention as she shook her head at them. "You two...you know your girl has all but started the third world war—the one of the sexes?"

"How? What did she do?" Josh wasn't certain what Lana was talking about, but he had a sick feeling it had something to do with the scoreboard.

"She publicly declared that women didn't need men because they were better at giving it to each other than men were, and as you can see"—Lana nodded toward the screen—"you're proving her right with every second she sits there smugly doing her nails. Would you like to know what Chase has to say about that?"

"No." Dylan scowled, clearly irritated at being threatened. "We're going, and trust me, we can drive Casey to nine orgasms like that!" Dylan snapped his fingers at Lana before sticking his chin in the air and strutting off, full of confidence.

He hollered back at Josh, interrupting him before he could offer Lana a more sincere assurance. "You coming, Mr. Three-Eighths Short?"

"You want to re-measure now?" Josh demanded to know, taking instant offense as he took off after Dylan. "Because I'm ready to go."

"I bet you are, but you know what?" Dylan paused at the exit to turn and meet Josh's glare. "So am I, only I'd rather put that extra inch to better use."

With that, Dylan stepped back, using his butt to push open the door. After a second's hesitation, Josh stepped past him and out into the night with a mutter.

"Fine, but I call cunt."

Issuing that claim, Josh started to storm down the grassy path that was being well trod that night. He left Dylan to argue with himself, not that his brother wasted any time following him. Besides, getting stuck with the ass wasn't such a bad deal.

"You know, we really probably should come up with a plan before we get back to the cube," Dylan suggested, jogging up alongside Josh to fall in step with him. "Because Casey, no doubt, has one."

"I think we've already *seen* her plan," Josh retorted, silently thinking of everything else they'd gotten to see of hers. Hell, there weren't any secrets left between them.

"That's not what I meant," Dylan muttered. "Trust me, I know the criminal mind—"

"Casey is not a criminal," Josh reminded him, already knowing the direction this paranoid conversation was going.

"She's up to no good and, no doubt, has a phase two to her scheme."

"And what is this great scheme? To make us fuck her? Because I'm willing to concede that point and be happy to be called a loser."

"What if it's to make *us* beg? Or to see how many times she can make us come?"

"Still, not seeing the problem here, old man." Josh really wasn't. Alarming tone aside, Dylan didn't seem to have much of an argument. "But let's just say there is one…what do you suggest we do?"

"I don't know." Dylan shrugged and shot Josh an expectant look. "You're the strategy guy. I'd think you'd have some clue as to what to do."

"I do. Fuck her."

"That's it? Fuck her?"

"Mmm-hmm." Josh nodded. "Fuck her, long and often."

Josh's flippant attitude didn't seem to sit well with Dylan, but what didn't sit well with Josh was the number of men gathered around the courtyard of their cube. They were watching and cheering on the show the three women were putting on while Casey had moved on to flipping through a magazine.

"You want a plan?" Josh turned on his brother, who was eyeing the crowd with the same distaste as him. "Then here it is. We keep Casey happy and occupied until the end of the week. Then we take her home and keep her."

"We can't just take her and keep her." Dylan snorted. "There is no way she'd let us get away with that."

"Yes, there is," Josh contradicted, certain of his own conclusions. "Casey's in love with us. She's just afraid to admit it."

"Casey? Afraid?" Dylan sounded bewildered by the very idea. "I don't think that's possible."

"Sure it is, and she has every reason to be. After all, we've spent the last four years rejecting her," Josh pointed out. "We can't exactly blame her for not trusting us now, can we?"

Dylan opened his mouth to disagree but snapped it close when Josh shot him a pointed look. He knew better than to argue because there was no point in even trying to deny the obvious. They'd both been waiting for the other to figure out the truth, to realize that not only were they both in love with Casey but that she wanted them both as well.

* * * *

Dylan didn't bother to answer Josh but turned and headed inside. Shedding his pants as he went, he strutted right up to where Casey was sitting, reading some article in her girlie magazine. He plucked her off her seat and ignored her startled shriek as he ripped the clothes clean off her body and spun her around to bend her right over.

He hesitated only long enough to roll on a condom, and then he was fisting a hand in Casey's copper-toned curls as he shoved a leg between hers and forced her to open up the pink folds of her pussy and expose her wet flesh to the blunt invasion of his hard shaft. Casey giggled and wiggled back as she cast a look over her shoulder at him that assured Dylan she was claiming her victory, even if he was claiming her body.

"It certainly took you long enough to return."

He answered that with a smooth thrust of his hips as he fucked the painfully throbbing length of his cock past the soft caress of her lips and into the tight, velvety heaven of Casey's body. The sheer bliss of driving himself deep into the velvety clench of her body was only amplified when she bent all the way over to reach between her legs and capture his balls in her cool fingers.

She worked him with a skill that only fueled the primitively possessive fires raging within him as she rolled and tugged on his balls, making him sweat and feeding the frantic rhythm of his hips as he pounded into Casey with hard, relentless thrusts. He fucked the giggles right out of her.

The bubbly sounds quickly turned to moans of need and want before being smothered into the wet, slurpy noises of a devouring that had Dylan cracking open his heavy lids that had fallen shut with his first stroke into paradise.

Josh had stepped up in front of Casey and put her pouty lips to good use. She didn't seem to mind. She nursed Josh's cock with a greedy abandon that had Dylan's brother sweating and cursing within a matter of seconds.

Dylan smiled and allowed his eyes to drift back closed. This was perfection. There was no other word to describe the searing hot rapture that erupted out of his balls as he felt Casey's cunt tighten around him. The walls of her sheath rippled and spasmed with the beginning quivers of her release.

He could have lived there in that moment forever. Only Dylan couldn't hold on, or hold back, as the rising tide of pleasure began to swamp through him. His consolation was that Josh came first. With a roar, his brother gave it up, his whole body arching and straining as he pumped the seed of his release deep into Casey's throat.

Dylan followed, shouting out his own victory as his release claimed him. Glancing down, he admired the bouncing globes of Casey's ass as he fucked her with hard, rough strokes, milking every last drop out of the rapture pounding through him as the pleasure stole the very strength from his body. He could have collapsed right then and there, dying a happy man, but Dylan knew there was a scoreboard, and they were running far behind.

That was just the first one.

That was why he never stopped fucking Casey. He rode her right through one release and pumped her toward a second, receiving a little help as Josh forced her back upright. The shift in positions left even less room in her tight channel for the big cock he pounded her full of, and Casey's cries twisted into high-pitched squeals as she demanded he do her even harder and faster as she sailed toward another climax.

"Open up, Firecracker," Josh commanded, his tone coming out as rough as gravel and full of want as he reached for her thighs and jerked Casey right off her feet. "You want to make a show out of our loving then we better make sure it's a good one."

The dare was there in his words, and there was no hint of hesitation in Casey's easy response. "Saddle up then, quiet boy, and let's see what kind of stamina you really got."

"It looks like you're going to have to move to the back seat, old man."

Dylan could have taken exception to that, but instead, he caught the condom Josh tossed at him, liking the sound of the back seat. He liked it a lot, enough to suffer the pain of pulling free of her clinging pussy and the frustration of having to swap out the old condom for the new, but soon enough, he was wrapping his palms around the smooth, velvety curves of Casey's plump ass cheeks.

He split them open and burrowed his aching length between her soft curves to press his engorged head against the sweetly shadowed entrance to her ass. He watched her clenched muscles part as he pressed inward. Better than watching, though, was feeling as he claimed that entrance, forcing the tight walls of her channel wide.

If Dylan had any doubt about Casey's eagerness for what came next, she laid it to rest with a giggle. The bubbly, joyous sound matched the enthusiastic wiggle of her hips as his ball sac nestled against the soft, velvety curve of her as she tossed a saucy smile up at Josh.

"I'm still waiting."

That had Josh growling and stepping up to grip Casey's hips and slam her back down on Dylan's dick. His strength damn near crumbled as the tight walls of her channel constricted around him like a vise. The pleasure grew so intense it bordered on painful. That was still nothing compared to the feel of his brother tilting her hips and forcing his thick length into the hot depths of Casey's cunt.

Dylan could feel Casey's liquid response to Josh's invasion. The heated proof of her desire dripped down between the swollen folds of her pussy's lips to bathe his burning balls in a molten tide of creamy arousal. The seed inside his tender sac churned, demanding release, but Dylan held back.

With his muscles corded and his self-control strained to the very feathered edges, he fought the delight searing out of his dick as Josh began to fuck one moan out of Casey after another, each stroke forcing her to flex up and down his own cock in a erotic massage made all the more intense by the knowledge that this was Casey.

His Casey…and three hot women going at it over her shoulder. It figured that despite his best attempts to imagine the most outlandish ways in which he could have taken her, she still managed to out-crazy him. That thought lit Dylan with a kind of joy he'd never imagined existed. She was going to drive him crazy, and he was going to love the ride.

Hell, he already was.

He was sweating and quivering, fighting to hold back his release as Casey fought her own. It was a struggle of wills, and sadly, he was weaker. It was too much. He couldn't take anymore. With a snarl, the reins of his restraint snapped. Dylan's hips spun out of control, pounding with savageness that matched the merciless thrusts of Josh's own hips.

The ecstasy started to peak within him as Casey twisted and bucked, laughing as she taunted him to come with her now, as though she was in charge. Bristling under that thought, Dylan reached out to grab onto his brother's sides and force him to slow back down, refusing to allow Casey her release.

After all, they were never going to catch up with the women, but that didn't mean they couldn't outdo them. He didn't even need to say a word. Josh understood. Throwing off Dylan's hold, he leaned in to whisper menacingly against Casey's ear.

"How many times do you think we can deny you, Firecracker? Hmm?" Josh leaned back to cast a glance at the writhing puddle of shapely limbs on the floor before casting a smirk back at Casey. "How about every time one of them comes...we start over?"

"Wh..." Casey's question was cut off by the obvious shriek of a woman coming hard.

Dylan knew just what that meant. Sliding his hands around her sides to cup Casey's breasts in his fists, he lifted them up toward his brother in a silent offering that had Josh licking his lips.

"You just don't think you can keep up with a bunch of women," Casey dared to taunt them, but Dylan could hear the quiver in her voice. It held the truth. She was afraid. She should be because they'd only just started.

Again and again, they played with her, alternately teasing her with slow and gentle caresses that always sped up into a frantic fucking that came to a sudden abrupt end as the women behind them reached peak after peak. They didn't allow Casey to reach even one.

It didn't matter how much she demanded, threatened, or begged. It didn't even matter how painfully hard it grew to hold back. Dylan's balls were burning, his muscles trembling beneath the strain and sweat rolling down his back. The only thing that had helped him to hold on was the absolute compulsion to win.

That was something he shared with his brother.

They didn't quit, not until Casey had grown incoherent and loud, thanks to the silence that filled the room. The women were done. The men had outlasted them...even if it had cost Dylan his sanity, which he had because he'd completely forgotten that by winning his own silent battle, he'd lost the real competition.

He didn't care. Not right then. Not when the need twisting through him still demanded appeasement. Dylan gave into it, allowing the lust and want boiling in his veins to infuse his strength. His hips began to flex and pump with a damn near inhuman speed as he fucked Casey with all the finesse of a caveman gone wild.

Each stroke drove the sensitive length of his erection past the clenched constriction of her muscles, making his whole dick throb with a pleasure that pulsed outward through his whole body until Dylan could feel nothing but the heated rush of rapture flooding out of his balls and straight into Casey's body.

The scorching tide left him wrecked and barely able to stand as both Josh and Casey joined, riding the same wave with matching screams that assured every single man watching that she had found more than simple satisfaction in Josh and his arms. Dylan knew he'd found more.

The pleasure searing through him carried with it a tide of a bliss so pure and clear it filled him with a sense of peace, and he knew in that second that he'd found where he belonged. Then, just as quickly, he realized that it wasn't where but to whom...to Casey.

Dylan would always be hers. He'd always do whatever it took to make her smile and laugh and welcome him into her arms. Even as Dylan laid down that silent vow, he could feel his legs beginning to quake as his balls finally began to run dry and the delight began to retract fast enough for him to feel the impending darkness. He managed to utter a single curse before collapsing and taking Casey and Josh with him all the way down to the floor.

Chapter 17

Josh gazed up at the ceiling and wondered how he'd ended up here, sprawled out on a cold cement floor with naked women all around him. This wasn't his style. Even if it had been fun teaching Casey a lesson, it was time to put the toys away and snuggle up with the woman of his dreams.

First, though, he had to muster up the energy to get off the floor. That actually took a few minutes, and even then, his motions were slow and his limbs felt heavy. Leaving Dylan and Casey spooned-up together, he lumbered over to click off the camera after waving goodbye to the crowd dispersing out in the courtyard and closing the curtains.

Next he headed toward the bathroom, where it took him several minutes to prep everything. Then it was time to wake the women and escort them to the door. All three made it clear that they'd had fun, that they liked Casey, and that if Josh ever wanted to invite them back…

He smiled and didn't fill in their pointed attempts to score an invitation.

Josh wasn't sharing Casey. Not with anybody but Dylan. Definitely not with any women who might convince her to give up men all together. Something told him he was going to have enough troubles coming his way in the near future.

That thought brought a small frown to Josh's brow as he considered how chaotic his life would become if he actually spent the rest of it with Casey. He liked order, structure, and normally needed time to contemplate all the consequences of an action before he committed himself to it.

Casey was just the opposite. She tended to act first and simply deal with the consequences later. That was just how she lived her life and ran her business—taking big risks and daring to dream even larger. Just as he felt about Dylan, Josh couldn't imagine his life without her. He needed them both, just in different ways.

Like right then, he was hard and hurting and in need of a little attention from Casey and a little time alone with her from his brother. With that in mind, Josh turned back to pull Casey free from Dylan's arms. He left his brother snoring on the floor as he scooped her up and carted her off toward the bathroom.

Josh knew he'd awakened her, even if her eyes remained closed. They'd fluttered slightly when he pulled her free of Dylan's cock, bringing a smile to her lips as she curled deeper into Josh's arms with a satisfied sigh.

Casey might have been satiated, but that didn't mean she was done. With lazy intent, she wiggled and shifted, looking for the perfect fit as her lips began to brush back and forth over the sensitive curve where Josh's neck met his shoulder. The softly whispered kisses quickly grew as she roused with a hunger that had her nibbling and sucking her way toward his mouth.

Josh didn't deny her as Casey's tongue swept along the seam of his lips but opened himself for her invasion, enjoying her aggressiveness and allowing her to control the kiss until it grew hot enough that he couldn't contain his urge to dominate. Then he pushed back, his tongue mating with hers as it dueled its way into the sweet, succulent depths of her mouth.

The intoxicating taste of her kiss had Josh forgetting for a moment the mission he was on, and he stumbled into the side of the tub, almost dropping Casey into the fragrant, sudsy depths of the bath he'd drawn. He managed to save the moment, though, stepping over the edge and into the swirling, heated waters without ever even loosening his hold on her.

Casey remained innocently oblivious to the danger as he settled them both down into the bubbling waters that smelled of jasmine and midnight, a scent that did not go unnoticed by her. Breaking free of his kiss, she glanced around for a quick second before her gaze settled back on him, a smile tugging at the edges of her lips.

"Well, this is an awfully romantic setting. Who knew you had it in you, quiet boy?" she teased him.

"How long are you going to continue to call me that?" Josh asked, hoping she didn't intend to make it a permanent moniker.

"I don't know." Casey shrugged, her smile growing wider as the twinkle in her eyes began to glimmer with all wicked amusement. "What else would you have me call you?"

"Josh."

That got him an instant laugh as Casey shook her head at him. Twisting in his arms, she settled down to straddle him, curling her legs around his hips and grinding up against him like a well-paid stripper. Josh couldn't help but wonder where she'd learned her moves, or perhaps she came by them naturally.

Either way, he wasn't complaining, especially not when she reached for one of the condoms piled on the nightstand. She held his gaze as she ripped open the metal foil with her teeth and a second later she was running her hands down the hard length of his cock.

"You know, this is supposed to be a fantasy," Casey murmured as she pumped her hips against his thigh, allowing Josh to feel the heated want weeping from her cunt and reminding him now was not the time to argue.

"In that case, you can call me Ricardo," Josh instructed her, sliding his hands up the soft, silky curve of her thighs to grip her hips and lift her high enough to guide her straight down onto the hard length of his erection. "And don't worry, my intentions are just as lecherous as Maria's, apparently, always suspected they were."

"Is that a fact?" Casey gasped as she pumped her hips, fucking him with slow, smooth strokes as his hands directed her motions.

"It is without a doubt," he assured her, relaxing back against the tub's smooth wall to enjoy the sight of Casey riding him like the sexy vixen he always knew her to be.

She was a thing of beauty, like a goddess rising up and over him as her hair curled through the water. The ends clung to the plump, flushed globes of her breasts and drew his attention to the hard, puckered tips as she rose in and out of the water's foaming bubbles. Josh couldn't help but touch. Abandoning her hips, his hands freed Casey to take him as she wanted as he did the same, sliding his fingers up to cup her softness and test the resilience of her flesh.

Casey moaned, arching into Josh's touch and offering up her breasts for his pleasure. That was an invitation he couldn't deny. Dipping his head, he caught one hardened tip between his lips as his thumb swept out to tease her other puckered nipple. He rolled and sucked, nibbling and pinching until Casey was moaning over him, her fingers threading through his hair to hold him tight against her breasts as her cunt creamed and spasmed around his cock, assuring him that she was enjoying everything he was doing to her.

That wasn't good enough. Josh wanted more. He wanted to hear Casey scream his name again, to feel her pussy pulse and milk the seed straight from his balls. This time he was going to bathe her womb in his seed, a primal marking that would lay his claim. A claim he'd never made before with any other woman.

Until that night he'd never gone in bare-skinned, but as Josh felt Casey's velvety walls contract around his swollen flesh and the heated glide of her arousal down his length, he knew he would never be able to have her any other way, just as he knew he'd never want a woman the way he did Casey. The pleasure she gave him was special, and Josh wanted to treat her as such.

So he loved her with a tender care. Treating her to every trick he knew to send her screaming into one orgasm after another, refusing to claim his own satisfaction until the tears rolled down her cheeks and she sobbed, swearing she could bear no more. Only then did Josh give in to the rapture tearing through him, clutching Casey as he held her tight through the storm.

The tempestuous winds receded, leaving only a blissful satisfaction in their wake. Still Josh couldn't let Casey go. She was so soft, so his, and he couldn't control the urge to run his hands over her body in endless strokes. With gentle care, he washed the sweat from her limbs and kissed the whimpers from her lips.

Casey let him, trusted him enough to let Josh bathe her without complaint. She barely even bothered to open her eyes even when he lifted her out of the water, though her breathing hitched as he wrapped an arm around her waist, pinning her hips tight against him and assuring his cock remained buried in the sweet heaven he'd so recently ravaged.

Josh knew she was sore, knew that she wasn't used to being taken so ruthlessly or so often, but he also knew she'd loved every second. He had the scars to prove it. Casey dug fresh ones into his shoulders with her nails as she clung to him, her breath beginning to pant out on her as he took that first big step over the edge of the tub. By the time he reached the bed, she was shivering and moaning, her cunt tightening down around his dick just as her thighs gripped his hips in an unshakable hold.

Josh didn't try to dislodge her. He liked her just the way she was. All that needed improvement was his position. Taking Casey with him as he dropped onto the mattress, he rolled her beneath him, perfecting the moment as he reared up onto his arms to get better leverage as he pumped his hips in a steady, constant rhythm that had them both sweating again within seconds.

This time he drew out the pleasure, fanning the passionate fires with slow, steady strokes. All the while his hands stroked over her, his lips raining kisses all over her as he whispered all sorts of outrageous compliments. Casey laughed and teased him back, her hands running just as wild as his, her lips just as ravenous.

It didn't take long before things spun back out of control and the bed was pounding against the wall. Only this time Josh came so hard he got lightheaded, and then he collapsed right down on Casey, blacking out for the first time in his life.

* * * *

That's just how Dylan found them several hours later when he woke up uncomfortable and a little sore on the hard, cold cement floor. Despite his aches, he had to smile, impressed that his brother actually had it in him to steal a woman right out of Dylan's arms. That wasn't all Josh had the balls to do.

He also managed to pass out with his dick still stuck in Casey, not that she appeared to mind. Drawn into a gentle smile, her features were relaxed, reflecting her clear enjoyment of holding Josh close in her arms, or perhaps it was the feel of him beneath her hands that had her glowing.

Dylan's skin prickled with a longing he'd never tasted before as he watched Casey's hands slide gently up and down Josh's back. He wanted to be held like that, to be wanted and enjoyed like that. Something told him he could be, that he could be the other man who made Casey smile like that.

It wasn't just arrogance on his part, either, though there was a touch of that, but the truth had always been obvious. They were drawn to each other. They were too much alike not to be.

In that moment Dylan felt like he had when he'd left home all those years ago. Back then, he'd been lured by the call of the wind, wanting to find an adventure that took him far from his small town and the narrow life he'd known. Back then, he'd been filled with the thrill of endless possibilities, and that was just how he felt standing there watching Josh and Casey.

The future unfolded before him like an endless sea of unbound possibilities. There would be laughter and fights and sex so wild that they ended up with a whole brood of kids. There would be sons to teach to be men and daughters whose boyfriends he would get to harass. There would be tree houses to build and bikes to assemble and family vacations to fill all the weekends for the rest of his life.

One thing Dylan knew was he wouldn't be getting a whole lot of sleep. So he might want to start loading up on some extra Z's while he had the chance...or he could just have wild, monkey sex and start loading up on some of that.

Chapter 18

Tuesday, May 27ᵗʰ

"So that is your plan?" Dylan asked, staring over his forkful of egg at his brother in disbelief. Josh didn't flinch, though, or shy away from his answer.

"Yes."

"That is a stupid plan."

Dylan knew that was harsh, but he couldn't keep the thought to himself. He was that honestly shocked by Josh's suggestion. His brother was the master of strategy and yet...

"Hell, that's *not even* a plan." Dylan just couldn't let the matter drop.

"Yeah? Then what is your great idea?" Josh shot back. "That we go kiss Casey's ass and beg her to be our girlfriend?"

"No!" Dylan stiffened up indignantly at the condescension in Josh's tone, but his brother wasn't completely wrong. He'd been with enough women to know how they liked to talk. He also knew that the best thing was to be honest.

"I'm just suggesting that we have an open"—Dylan hesitated before forcing himself to say it—"*heartfelt* discussion with her. After all, solid relationships are built on honesty, and don't you want a solid relationship?"

"Who the hell are you?" Josh reared back as if he'd smelled something he didn't like. "You're not my brother. My brother did not just suggest—"

"Never mind," Dylan muttered, not interested in putting up with his brother's teasing, especially not when the subject was so serious. "But let me remind you, taking somebody else's stuff is *robbery* and taking them is considered *kidnapping*."

"Don't worry." Josh waved that consideration aside. "I got connections."

"Well, I hope they're better than me because—"

"Oh, they are," Josh assured Dylan, cutting him off with a pointed smirk.

"Fine." Dylan caved with ill grace. "We'll try it your way, even though you *don't* have a lot of experience with women, but if it doesn't work…"

"Yeah. Yeah. Yeah. I know." Josh heaved an aggrieved sigh as he rolled his eyes. "Then you'll go beg and plead until she agrees out of pity."

Josh was being difficult and rude, and Dylan knew why. He was afraid, and he had every reason to be, given what Maria had done to him. While she might not have broken his heart, she'd done something far worse. She'd destroyed Josh's plans.

Dylan knew just how important plans were to his brother. Josh didn't do anything without a plan, or hadn't until now. Now he was simply trying to avoid the problem in the most logical way possible by having no plan.

That wouldn't last. After all, Casey wasn't Maria. If one really planned on taming a vixen, it was probably best to have a plan. Hopefully Josh would remember that before this new carefree attitude went too far.

That's where Dylan came in. He didn't care what kind of fancy connections Josh might have. Josh was his brother, and Dylan would always be there to make sure Josh didn't get into any trouble or screw himself out of the best thing that ever happened to him.

That went for Casey as well.

Dylan was there to protect both of them, and the more he considered the matter, the more he realized just how pivotal he was to Josh and Casey's relationship. They were from two different worlds. Dylan should know because he and Casey came from the same planet, whereas Josh was kind of like a weird, nerdy alien who spoke some strange language.

Fortunately, Dylan was bilingual.

* * * *

Casey woke up to the heady aroma of coffee and bacon. The delicious scent pulled her from the rumpled bedding and had her stumbling across the blanket and pillows that were strewn across the floor, along with the bed sheets. Things had gotten a little wild last night...and that morning.

Without any concern for her nudity,she staggered into the bathroom and managed to find a whole basket full of supplies. There were unopened toothbrushes and tubes of paste along with facial scrub and lotion. There were even drops for her bloodshot eyes, along with a hairbrush so she could at least beat back the knots that were as tangled as the sheets.

Even with all of that, she still looked like a woman who had spent most of the past night being ridden hard, which she had been and hoped to be again soon. That is, right after she got some breakfast because Casey was starved and the air smelled good enough to eat.

Wrapping herself up in one of the plush, oversized towels stacked near the tub, she headed back through the bedroom, only to come to a stop in the shadowed depths of the doorway as she spied Josh and Dylan hunched together and clearly plotting.

They were up to something. She could sense it, not that it took a great deal of intuition to figure that out. Anybody who knew Josh knew he had to have his plans. God only knew what his bullet list looked like this morning.

That thought drew a snicker to Casey's lips as she considered it probably went something like, "Step one: lick pussy. Step two: suck clit," and so on until he got to step forty-seven and finally fucked her. That thought gave her pause as she wondered just how many steps it would actually take him to get finally to penetration and how many she could make him skip.

Casey smiled as she studied the two men hunched over the coffee table centered between the two leather couches in the far corner of the room. With their voices kept low, they already looked guilty. They acted it too, falling suspiciously silent as she finally came out of the bedroom.

Watching her as though she was some kind of experiment, both brothers eyed her with open curiosity as she settled down beside the coffee table to help herself to a plate. Neither man offered her any kind of greeting, and Casey played along, enjoying the game almost as much as she was enjoying the delicious spread laid out before her.

There was crisp bacon, mounds of fluffy-looking eggs, and monstrously-sized biscuits with a slab of butter sitting on a dish beside them that looked as if it probably weighed a whole damn pound. Casey left the butter alone and built herself a biscuit filled with so much stuff it was way too big to fit into her mouth. She was set to try, though, when Dylan finally spoke up.

"What's with the towel?" He waved a finger at the crisp white terry cloth she'd wrapped around herself. "Don't tell me you've forgotten the rules."

"The floor is cold." Casey shrugged.

That wasn't completely true. They were actually kind of warm, but that excuse sounded better than admitting that in the bright light of day she'd been a little intimidated at the idea of walking across the completely open room naked, especially when Dylan and Josh were both fully clothed and looking so sexy.

Of course, they looked good to her no matter what. That's what made it so damn hard for her to resist when Dylan patted his knee and beckoned her forward.

"But Daddy's lap isn't," he assured her with a lecherous grin. "So why don't you come on over here and have a seat?"

"That's disgusting." Casey wrinkled her nose as she shot him a dirty look. "Please don't call yourself that."

"Call me what you want, Firecracker. I'm still waiting," Dylan informed her, unperturbed by her rejection and making it clear that she was going to have to be more specific.

"And you can keep on waiting because I'm eating breakfast. I need my strength, especially if you are planning on ravaging me again."

"Oh, Firecracker, I'm planning on doing a whole lot worse than that." Dylan snickered, his smirk crumbling into a wicked-sounding chuckle that had Casey flushing with a thrilling warmth.

It would be so easy to give in to that passion again, but they needed to come to some kind of understanding because there were certain things she wouldn't be able to tolerate. Other things she knew she must.

"Well, in that case, I think we should lay down some ground rules." Casey took a deep breath and braced herself for the coming conversation, though she should have known Dylan wouldn't make it easy for her.

"What? I thought you were all, 'no, no, no, no talking'," he shot back, the laughter still lingering in his tone.

"Yeah? Well, now that I don't have dick shoved up in me, I'm ready to talk."

"Hey, you *liked* that dick. In fact, you *begged* for it," Dylan taunted her, doing a little dance in his seat that Casey recognized instantly.

"Oh God no! Don't do the victory dance!" she pleaded, but it was too late.

Dylan's ass lifted out of his seat, shaking from side to side as he wiggled about in such an awkward motion that Casey was embarrassed for him. She couldn't even watch. It was that bad. Worse, the victory dance came with a song.

"Casey sitting on me. F-U-C-K-I-N-G! First came missionary then came doggy then came Josh and double-stuffed!"

"Oh God," Casey groaned again as her head hung down with a mixture of embarrassment and hidden amusement.

She managed to quell that quiver and scrunch her features into a disgusted frown that she turned on Josh, who was just sitting there watching his brother and sipping his coffee.

"Can you make him stop?"

That question drew his blank gaze in her direction, and he blinked as he stared at her for a moment in apparent confusion. Then, quite deliberately, he set his cup down on the coffee table and rose up. Dylan stilled, watching his brother with the same expectant look that Casey knew was mirrored on her own features.

"First off," Josh began somberly, "Casey was sitting on *me!*"

"Oh God no!"

Casey hit her head against the coffee table as Josh began dancing around, joining Dylan in making up all sorts of graphically lewd lines. Some of their ideas were both gross and some intriguing, but still, she had to object to the general tone of their song. So, Casey cleared her throat and pointedly interrupted.

"Unless you want me to start making up rhymes about the twin teeny-tiny penises, you best both shut up and sit down," Casey commanded, managing to be heard over their chanting.

She doubted it was her threat that had them falling silent, especially not when they shot each other identically smug grins before pointedly taking their seats and turning to stare expectantly at her. Neither brother spoke. Instead, they allowed their silence to speak for them in an obnoxious gesture that Casey had the good sense to ignore.

"As I was saying, we need rules."

"We already have rules," Josh pointed out instantly, not giving Casey a chance to explain what she meant. "We command. You obey. No more rules needed. Isn't that right, old man?" Josh tossed that question at Dylan, who nodded as if on cue.

"Right you are, baby brother."

"And I do believe we told her that as long as she was in this cube she was to be naked with her legs spread so we could admire that pretty pink pussy of hers, but do you see any pussy, old man?"

"No, I do not."

"I want to see some pussy, pixie." Josh turned his attention back on her, matching that crude command with a smile that she'd only ever seen Dylan wear before.

That wasn't the only thing Josh had stolen from his brother. The attitude was pure Dylan, too, which left her both wet and concerned because, as much kinky fun as it might be to play with two Dylans, it would be a nightmare to manage both of them...or maybe not.

"Fine," Casey caved with ill grace and a forced smile that was all an act. "We'll do it your way."

With stiff motions, she shrugged out of her towel and shifted to kneel back on her heels. Then she spread her knees, opening her cunt up wide as she sucked on her finger. Wetting the tip, she reached down to roll her clit, taking both brothers' gazes with her. She had them hypnotized in a second. That's when she started laying down her own rules.

"You can admire this pussy. You can lick it, suck it, fuck it, finger it, spank it, and pack it full of whatever you want...as long as it's the only pussy you're playing with," Casey stated firmly, bringing her motions to a stop and the pleasure that had started to flood through her to a simmering halt as she waited for their response.

She'd expected one to come quickly, but what she got instead was another silent stare that unnerved the crap out of her. They appeared to be waiting for more, but Casey had nothing to give. Or, maybe, it was Josh and Dylan who had nothing to give, no assurances at all. Now what was she supposed to do?

* * * *

Josh watched the doubts darken Casey's gaze and could almost read her thoughts but didn't make a single attempt to reassure her that her fears were unfounded. He shouldn't have to. Casey should trust him, if not Dylan.

If she didn't, then she might end up like Maria, and Josh couldn't take that. Maria's betrayal had only damaged his pride. Casey...she would shred his heart. He wouldn't survive, so Josh needed to know that Casey trusted them.

Dylan, on the other hand, had always been a sucker when it came to the ladies. All it normally took was some doe-eyed look and his brother crumbled. With Casey, it took even less, and suddenly, Dylan was sliding down onto his knees and all but swearing allegiance to the woman.

"Don't you worry, Firecracker," Dylan drawled, his accent thickening as he crawled toward her. "I only ache to taste the sweetest of cunts, so why don't you spread them legs a little wider and we'll start at the top of your list and let me have a little lick?"

"There ain't nothing little about you, old man," Casey all but purred back as she rose upward, lifting the swollen lips of her pussy until they brushed against Dylan's lips.

He smiled, growling out one last warning against the smooth curve of her mound. "I'll show you old."

"I hate to interrupt your romantic moment," Josh said, speaking up before his brother could follow up that cheesy line with any kind of action. "But don't you have a list of possible suspects to go interview?"

He asked that pointed question, drawing a dark look from both Dylan and Casey, but only one was annoyed. The other was confused.

As usual, Casey didn't bother to mask her suspicions or temper her curiosity.

"And just what does that mean?"

"It means baby brother wants some time alone with you," Dylan grumbled as he shoved back up to his feet. "All he had to do was ask. He didn't need to go find work for me to do."

"I'm not the one who hooked us up with this case," Josh reminded him.

"What case?"

"No, but you are the one who came up with an overly long list to keep me pointedly busy," Dylan accused him with a sullen pout, but Josh could see through his brother's act.

Dylan didn't want to get to work because he didn't want to leave Casey, but she wasn't technically theirs. She was "on loan" from Chase, who had made it clear that if he wasn't happy with their progress, then Casey wouldn't be available to make them happy. A fact Josh quickly reminded his brother of.

"I was thorough, just as Chase made it clear you should be."

"I'm always thorough," Dylan retorted, a husky note of perversion invading not only his tone but his smile as he cast a gaze back down to Casey, who frowned back.

"You're friends with Chase Davis," she spoke slowly, appearing to be working something out. "And he's an owner?"

"Yep." Dylan's chest puffed up. "A personal friend, actually."

"And you're working a case for him? What kind of case?" Casey's knees started to drift closed.

Either she'd already forgotten the rules, or she was using her pussy as leverage, but Josh could sense an ulterior motive. She was up to something. He could just sense it, and after years of battling it out with her in the virtual world of video games, he'd learned to trust his instincts. Dylan clearly had none, which was kind of odd given his job.

"It's just a little matter of arson, nothing for you to worry over," Dylan assured her as he dropped a quick kiss onto Casey's upturned lips and stepped around her. "But Egg-head is right. I got work to do, so put that pussy on ice and I'll reheat it later."

Dylan shot that command at Josh with a waggle of his eyebrows that brought a smile to Josh's lips. His brother was actually kind of amusing, and so were his ideas, but he didn't have anything on the perverts at this club. They actually employed an ice sculptor to make them all sorts of toys, two of which were resting in the freezer over in the wet bar.

Oh, the fun they were going to have with Casey.

The fun *he* was going to have because he was living life Dylan-style—no plans, no worries. For the first time ever Josh intended to give into the moment and abandon the safety net of his plans. As his brother had pointed out, he had no real plan when it came to Casey, and he wasn't terrified at all.

Chapter 19

Saturday, May 31ˢᵗ

Dylan didn't know what the hell he was doing. It had been six of the best days of his life, and he should have been back at the club enjoying what was left of Casey's vacation. Instead, though, he was at some dippy diner, tracking down the legendary George Davis, who was better known as GD.

Scanning the small dining room, Dylan's gaze landed on the Hulk-sized He-Man trying to look as inconspicuous as possible in a booth tucked way in the back. It was a futile attempt. From his height to the amount of muscles padding his frame, the last thing GD would ever go was unnoticed.

The same could be said of the blonde fatale seated at the bar, doing her dead-level best to ignore the big man glaring at her from the shadows. Years on the police force had honed his instincts, and Dylan could sense that he'd walked in on some kind of silent battle between the two, but he didn't really care.

What he did care about was back at the club being taken advantage of by his brother, who had really lightened up this week. For the first time ever, Josh appeared to be simply relaxing and enjoying the moment...sort of. Actually, he was still quite controlling, but that only made him a natural dominant. Casey, on the other hand, was not exactly an obedient submissive, but that just made things all the more entertaining.

What was not entertaining was trying to hunt down the Davis brothers' arsonist. In fact, that simple goal was turning into a nightmare. There were no witnesses, no evidence, and way too many rumors about people who might have motive while almost all of them turned out to have alibis. Those that didn't turned out not to need them, which left Dylan exactly where he was six days ago—next to nothing.

Fortunately, he could work with that because nothing meant at least one thing. There was somebody hiding something, and it was time to put the screws on the pressure points and find out who snapped first. GD didn't look like the type to break easily, but Dylan knew that looks could be deceiving.

The glint in the big man's eyes as they settled on him didn't lie, though. GD was neither dumb nor weak, and that was going to make Dylan's task a whole lot harder. He sighed over that bit of misfortune as he sauntered up to the edge of GD's booth. He didn't take it personally. They eyed each other for a long moment, each taking the other's measure, before GD finally broke the silence.

"Lana wasn't lying when she said you were a pretty boy." Just like his body, GD's tone held a depth that resonated with a sense of strength and a touch of amusement. He was testing Dylan, waiting to see how he took that comment.

"And she told me that you were the best private investigator in these parts," Dylan returned politely, knowing how often compliments actually did work…just not on GD.

That earned him a snort and a smirk. "I bet she did because every woman knows I'm the best at all things."

He said that loud enough to assure the blonde at the bar heard him. As if Dylan had any doubt who he was talking to or what he was talking about, the pointed look GD shot the woman made it clear just who those words were intended for, not that the blonde appeared impressed. She sniffed dismissively and pointedly turned the page on the book she was reading.

"Lana also mentioned that you were on a case," Dylan commented, drawing GD's gaze back to his as Dylan shot the blonde a pointed look. "I'm not interrupting, am I?"

"Nothing important," GD assured him, though Dylan suspected that was a lie. He let it go as the big man nodded toward the opposite side of the booth. "Have a seat and tell me what it is I can do for you."

"I'm looking into the Davis brothers' barn fire," Dylan began as he slid onto the vinyl cushion that crackled beneath him. "I understand I'm not the first person they turned to for answers."

"Nope." GD's eyes darted back to the blonde. "But they still haven't got any answers, do they? That should tell you something, don't you think?"

"I certainly do," Dylan drawled out slowly, sensing GD's lack of attention was more an act for his benefit than the fatale, who had drawn more than one admirer's attention.

GD frowned at the man moving in on the blonde, appearing distracted, but his answers were sharp and quick when Dylan pressed him.

"Still, I'd still like to take a peek at your notes—"

"Don't have any," GD cut in before offering Dylan an overly sweet grin and pointing to his head. "It's all up here."

"So then maybe you'd care to share?"

"Sorry, man, there is nothing up there." GD shrugged, his gaze cutting back over to the man the blonde had just shot down and eyeing him the way a dog did a rabbit. "After all, you've been all over the place interviewing everybody…you got anything?"

"I got an almost completely redacted police report about a kid picked up with a gas tank not but a few miles away," Dylan stated pointedly enough to have GD's gaze shifting back toward him to give Dylan another once-over before the big man offered him another shrug.

"Kid's not guilty."

"Really?" Honestly caught off guard by the certainty in GD's tone, he couldn't help but come to the obvious conclusion. "If you know the kid's not in on it, then you got to know who did set the fire."

"I have an opinion," GD allowed. "But then so does everybody else in this town."

"Well then, it's my opinion that it's the kid." It wasn't really, but Dylan sensed that GD would try to protect the kid. That gave him leverage. Right then, Dylan needed some of that.

"Look," GD leaned across the table as he dropped his voice down low. "I'm not saying anything, but I did notice that you didn't bother to interview Lana or those idiot brothers of hers."

"Lana's brothers?" Dylan grimaced, hating even the thought of putting up with them. They were like Tweedle Dee and Tweedle Dum but in supersized, more violent-prone versions.

"Yeah, Lana talked Chase into giving them some part-time work, and idiot that he is, he didn't fire them when he changed over to his new bedmate."

Dylan didn't need GD to tell him how the rest of the story went, or how it was going to end when Chase found out. After all, Chase was a little prone to violence himself.

"What a mess," he sighed.

"You're telling me," GD grumbled as he heaved an aggrieved sigh and slouched back into his seat. "Ever since Patton came back to town, my life has been nothing but a headache. That girl causes more trouble than Pig-Pen did messes. It's a good thing she's a hell of a lot better-looking than that kid."

"Hell, she must be downright gorgeous to beat out Lana." He knew it wasn't right or fair, but Dylan was loyal, and he was Team Lana all the way.

"You haven't met Patton, have you?"

"She never seems to come by the club." And Dylan didn't have much interest in leaving it.

"Yeah, like those boys would let her anywhere near the club." Just the idea seemed to make the other man pale. "The less Patton knows about the club, the safer we *all* are."

Dylan didn't think any of them were particularly safe right then. When Chase found out about Lana's brothers, there would be blood spilled and all kinds of accusations. This was the worst possible outcome, and he couldn't very well rat out her brothers without giving her a warning.

That's how he came to find himself sitting a half-hour later in Lana's office. She greeted him warmly enough, but her mood soured quickly as Dylan got to the point of his visit. He took his time, explaining how he'd gone through the whole list and interviewed everybody, but her brothers.

Dylan hesitated then, letting that sink in before he pressed Lana just as he had GD. "They're last on my list…and, from what I understand, without an alibi."

"I really don't have any idea what he is talking about," Lana assured him, but she wasn't half the actor GD was, even if she was more motivated to hide her lies.

"Lana—"

"We're talking about my brothers, Dylan," Lana pleaded as she cut him off. "What would you do for Josh?"

That was a low blow because they both knew there wasn't anything he wouldn't do for his brother. Still, before he could help Josh, he'd have needed the truth from him. That's just what Dylan demanded of Lana.

"Did they set the fire?"

"They say they didn't." Lana crossed her hands over her desk and met Dylan's gaze. "And I believe them."

No she didn't. Lana was lying, and Dylan bet if he told her about the kid she'd fold. After all, she might love her brothers, but she didn't have it in her to sacrifice a child. The question was, did he?

"Fine." Dylan knew that what he was about to do would weigh on him for the rest of his life, but it would have no matter what he chose to do. "I'll leave it alone."

"Thank you." Lana offered him a sad smile. "You know, whatever they did or didn't do, it was only because they loved me, and I would feel very guilty if they suffered because of that."

"I know." Dylan rose out of his seat but hesitated to leave Lana looking so sad. "I'm sorry that Chase hurt you."

That had Lana's gaze dropping almost immediately as she tried to hide the flash of hurt that his words sent through her eyes. "Don't worry. I'll recover."

"I hope that you do because he's not worth this much pain."

"You don't think so?" Lana forced a smile that looked as brittle as her tone sounded.

"Not if he can't see how amazing you are or hasn't figured out how special. Only an idiot wouldn't be able to see that," Dylan smirked as he considered his own words. "And you know that I always did think Chase was a little slow when it came to things."

Lana wasn't as amused by Dylan's comments as he was, and he quickly left her to her brooding to go find the idiot himself. Dylan wanted this matter settled so he could return back to the cube and spend the last day with his firecracker uninterrupted by any other obligations.

His search for Chase led him all over the club, and he happened to pass through the dining hall at the same time the sheriff was seated by himself, wolfing down a late lunch. Dylan figured it would only be polite to give the man a warning of what he intended to do.

"Sheriff Alex Krane?" Dylan pulled up to a stop by the sheriff's table and offered the man his hand. "I'm Dylan Andrews."

"Nice to meet you." Alex shook his hand, returning the polite greeting before asking the obvious question. "Is there something I can do for you?"

"You can tell me about the kid."

"Pardon me?" The sheriff's brow lifted with polite confusion. "I seem to be lost here."

"I don't think you are." In fact Dylan knew he wasn't. Alex might be the best actor of them all, but Dylan still knew a lie when he heard it. "In fact, I think you know exactly what I'm talking about."

Without waiting for an invite or bothering to ask, Dylan pulled out the seat opposite of the sheriff and sat down before he continued on. "I'm talking about the kid, the gas can, the Davis brothers' barn fire. Any of that ring any bells?"

"So you're the detective that they brought in from out of town." Alex smiled, neatly avoiding Dylan's question, but he wouldn't be put off so easily.

"I'm also the man who knows about the kid and the fact that you didn't run any investigation."

"I don't know what you are talking about."

"You know, I'm getting really sick of everybody lying to me." Dylan heaved a sigh and shook his head. "And it doesn't even matter. You keep your secrets if you want. I'm just here to let you know that I'm telling the Davis brothers that *you* know who set the fire."

That was low. Dylan knew it, but that was the only way out that he could find. He owed Chase an answer. He couldn't betray Lana. He wasn't about to rat out a kid. The only thing that left for him to do was to force the sheriff to do his damn job.

That Dylan had no trouble doing.

"In fact, there's Chase now. I think I'll go have a word with him."

He shoved away from the table, aware that the sheriff did the same as he walked away. By the time he reached Chase, who had caught sight of him and turned in Dylan's direction, Alex had disappeared, a fact that didn't go unnoticed by Chase.

"Where the hell is Alex running off to?" he asked by way of greeting, tracking the sheriff's movements for a second before shifting his scowl in Dylan's direction. "You didn't happen to give him a lead, did you?"

"He already has one," Dylan retorted, knowing he was about to be a complete dick to two people while saving one heartbroken woman. "And yes, that means just what it sounds like. Your sheriff's been holding out on you, man."

To his credit, Chase didn't jump on that comment but seemed to weigh it silently in his head before offering up a response. "Maybe you better explain what you mean by that over a drink because something tells me I'm going to need one."

Dylan didn't expect him to make it through the whole glass, but Chase shocked him. Instead of running off after the sheriff, he hesitated, looking more upset than pissed as he stared down into his glass.

"Is something wrong?" Dylan sure as hell hoped not. He really didn't want to waste much more time on the matter, especially not since he had such little time left before Casey's vacation came to an end.

"No," Chase assured him before instantly contradicting himself. "It's just that I suspected Lana's brothers because…you know, of what happened with Patton and everything, and so I fired them."

Now it was Dylan's turn to feel a little guilty and a little sympathy for Chase, which Dylan was certain his friend hadn't gotten much of in the whole Lana mess. After all, Chase had ended up with the love of his life, and Lana had ended up alone.

"Look, man, I don't claim to know what is going on between you and Lana or…Patton." Dylan damn near choked on that name, having to fight hard to say it without laughing, but he didn't manage to pull it off, and Chase cut in to call him on it.

"What?" Stiffening up indignantly in his seat, Chase's scowl darkened dangerously. "Are you laughing at Patton's name?"

"No…yes, but seriously, your girl is named after a dude, and not an attractive one." Not that Dylan knew what Patton looked like, but he knew what Lana did. "Whereas Lana is built to rock any man's world."

"Trust me, so is Patton."

"If you say so."

"You don't believe me?"

"Of course I do." Dylan smiled, knowing he sounded as if he was lying, even though he was being honest. He knew Chase well enough to know what his friend's taste were, but that didn't mean he didn't enjoy watching the other man flush as he reached into his pocket for his phone.

"Fine. I'll prove it to you." It took him a second before he found what he was looking for, and then Chase thrust the phone at Dylan. "*That*'s Patton."

"Wow, she's—"

Dylan had meant to say "pretty" in a condescending enough tone to make another lie out of his words, but he got distracted by the picture glowing on the screen in front of him. He recognized that smile, and it didn't take him more than a second to figure out the rest. Patton wasn't the only one who attracted trouble like Pig-Pen.

Her best friend, Casey, was normally at her side.

Chapter 20

Josh massaged the flushed cheeks of Casey's ass, running his fingers over the slowly fading lines of the henna tattoos as he watched her perfectly rounded rump bounce up and down. He hung his head over her sweat-slickened shoulder, allowing her to do the hard work. Casey did so without complaint. Instead, she panted with sexy grunts as she pumped herself up and down the thick length of his swollen cock, riding him toward a release that had her arching back as her fingers dug into his shoulders.

Josh lifted his chin to capture the puckered tip of her breast as it rose upward in a tempting offer he couldn't resist. Sucking her pebbled tit past the hard ridge of his teeth, he lashed her sensitive nub with his tongue as he caught her other breast up in his fist. Without mercy, he tormented her nipple, pinning it beneath his thumb and rolling it as his tongue matched the motion, twirling over the hardened peak of her other breast.

Casey cried out, her cunt pulsing around him with endless waves of heated cream as she fucked him harder and faster. Her motions quickly spun out of control, becoming frantic as Josh slid his other hand down the crease between her ass cheeks to tease the clenched muscles guarding her forbidden entrance.

With her legs bent along his thighs, Casey's knees dug deeper into his sides as she begged him for more, even though she was the one in command, the one riding him as she worked herself into a lather. All Josh had to do was sit back and enjoy. That's just what he was doing, enjoying the show.

Casey was putting on a good one. Crying and carrying on as her sleek body flexed and arched, her curves wiggling and shaking, she was his every fantasy come true and more. He'd never come close to even beginning to fathom how tight and wet her little cunt was or how strong a grip her sheath could have as it tried desperately to milk the seed from his thick shaft.

Josh worked just as hard to deny the velvety flex of her rippling walls. Her pussy spasmed demandingly around him, and he knew he wouldn't be able to hold back for long, especially not with the feel of Casey's release raining down over his naked flesh. The heated waves of cream seared his sensitive flesh in direct violation of the Cattleman's Club condom policy.

The Cattlemen could kiss Josh's ass. He, Casey, and Dylan had talked it over. They were all clean, and she was protected from pregnancy by a shot, so there had been no reason to deny themselves the satisfaction of feeling each other skin-to-skin. Wicked and forbidden, the sensation excited Josh every time.

It was an erotic thrill that he'd never before indulged in. Not even with Maria. She'd been too afraid of ending up pregnant and having to interrupt her modeling career to have or deal with a baby. That had been fine with Josh. He hadn't wanted a baby to interfere with his career.

At least, he had thought he hadn't, but the idea of Casey pregnant was enough to make his balls boil and explode with a release so intense he bit his lip without even realizing it. All he knew in that moment was ecstasy, both physical and emotional, at the very idea of his seed bathing Casey's womb.

Just the thought filled him with a feral contentment that faded slightly along with the pleasure as Casey collapsed against him. Yeah, a kid would be nice but would probably interfere with the amount of time he got to spend naked and playing with the baby's mama. Right then, Josh would rather be making the babies than actually having to raise them.

The cell phone he'd dumped on the coffee table earlier cut into his wayward thoughts with its shrill ring. The sound drew Josh's gaze back toward the Scrabble board littered with letters and the phone sitting right beside it. He'd have liked to ignore it, but that was never really an option. The problem with running a business was that he never really got to take a true vacation.

Not that Casey could complain. She'd had to field her own business calls, which had been kind of amusing, given he and Dylan had done everything they could think of to distract her while she was handling whatever problems had cropped up with the store or their suppliers.

Josh had to give her points for being able to focus no matter what, but right then, it was his turn to force himself to do what was necessary, even as much as he hated to move. Sighing, he patted Casey on the ass and roused her from the nap she appeared ready to take.

"Sorry, Firecracker, but I got to get that."

With that apology, he lifted her up by the hips, grimacing against the torturous pleasure of feeling her sheath glide over his still-throbbing length. Her muscles clamped around him like a vise, making it all the harder for him not to slam her back down. The twitch of Casey's lips assured Josh that she not only knew about his inner struggle but had tempted him on purpose, no doubt to punish him for making her move.

He'd return the favor later, but, right then, Josh dropped Casey onto the couch beside him and quickly adjusted his jeans before he gave in to the renewed rush of lust pounding through his veins. Casey didn't like being denied. She made that clear with a scowl before rising up with a huff and storming haughtily off toward the bedroom.

Josh watched her go, eyeing the firm cheeks of her ass as they bounced with every slap of her bare feet against the floor. Firecracker—the guys had named her well because she sure was hot when she got all riled up, which was exactly what she was, though Josh knew it had nothing to do with the phone ringing.

Casey was more than understanding about the demands of business. On the other hand, she was a sore loser and pissed that he'd *crushed* her in Scrabble. As usual when he won, Josh claimed her cunt as a prize. Sometimes he had her feed it to him, other times he had her play with it, and more often than not, he had her mount up and take him for a ride.

He considered that a charitable attitude, given that Casey claimed more humiliating prizes, like having Dylan paint her toenails. That, actually, had been amusing to watch. Of course, she'd made Josh do a strip dance for her, with the curtains *open*. She and Dylan had a hell of a laugh over that one.

Then again, she and Dylan shared a lot of laughs these days. They were like two perverted peas in a pod. Josh kind of considered himself the pod, given, without him, the two little peas would probably roll around haphazardly and, no doubt, do a good bit of damage. Everybody should be so lucky to have a pod, Josh thought as Casey disappeared into the bedroom, allowing his attention to turn to the phone still ringing.

He picked up the small cell and glanced at the name flashing on the screen before answering. It was Dylan. Given he was supposed have returned over a half-hour ago, Josh could only assume he wasn't calling with good news

"Yeah? What's up, man?"

* * * *

Casey allowed herself to smile once she was sure that Josh couldn't see her anymore, or hear her, because all too quickly her grin turned into a cascade of giggles as she recalled the look on his face when he'd won. He'd been so cute, and even a little smug.

Of course, that was because Josh considered himself the smartest in the group. Technically he might have been. After all, he was the straight-A student who had graduated with honors and a full scholarship to college. She and Dylan, on the other hand, were blessed with a different type of smarts.

One of her special talents was actually her vocabulary. Her mother used to do crossword puzzles while in the bathroom, leaving a dictionary that Casey had read out of sheer boredom on more than one occasion. That meant she didn't lose in Scrabble unless, of course, she wanted to.

Normally Casey hated losing, but Dylan and Josh made it more tempting to throw a game than to win at it. After all, whoever won got to claim a prize. The guys almost always demanded a sexual favor, which always ended with her begging, pleading, and coming hard enough to leave her shaking. They were that good.

Good enough that she was not only a little sore but also kind of sensitive, enough so that even the spray of hot water from the shower's body jets felt like a sensual caress. It was as though she was in a constant state of arousal, and she wasn't alone.

Not in her need or in the shower.

Casey's smile took on a wicked curl as Josh stepped up behind her. He'd stripped down before joining her in the shower. As he pressed in against her, she could feel the heat and hardness of his muscles flexing against her. That wasn't all she felt.

Despite the fact that he had shot a full load not minutes ago, Josh's dick was once again swollen and ready for action. Casey could easily guess what kind of action he was looking for, too, given the way he ground the velvety length of his erection into the crease dividing the cheeks of her ass.

"I thought you already claimed your victory?" Casey murmured as she wiggled back against him, nestling the thick dick deeper between the swollen globes.

Josh didn't take her up on the invitation, though. Instead, his arm stretched around her side to reach out and grasp the washcloth clutched in her hand along with the bar of soap hidden in it. With slow, deliberate movements, he bathed her, tending to her with a tender care that had Casey melting back against his chest.

Letting her eyes drift closed, she gave her will over to him, allowing Josh to do as he pleased, even when his touch became more intimate. He brushed his hands over the generous curves of her breasts, massaging her heavy flesh with a gentle touch while the rough rasp of the washcloth teased the puckered peaks of her nipples.

The contrast had her moaning and arching into the delicious pleasure, but it almost immediately ended. Not that she could complain. Casey didn't have the breath to. Caught on a groan, she gasped silently as every muscle in her body tensed with anticipation when Josh's hand slid slowly down over the quivering muscles of her stomach to cup her mound in the broad heat of his palm.

Her cunt wept as her legs shifted, opening the pink, puffy lips of her pussy to the coarse invasion of the washrag wrapped around his fingertips. He took every care to clean every inch of her intimate flesh, inside and out. With each stroke of the terry cloth through her folds, another shimmer of delight twisted through her, fueling the need boiling inside her into an inferno that had Casey pumping her ass against the massive cock still lodged between her cheeks.

This time her insistent demand drew a response, as Josh dropped the rag to gather the thick cream coating her cunt up on his fingers. Then those magical tips slid back to tease the ring of muscles protecting the entrance to her ass once again. Unlike before, though, he didn't hesitate to press inward.

Casey whimpered and twisted, bending over at the waist as she offered herself up to the delicious ecstasy of being penetrated from behind. With slow, smooth strokes, Josh teased her with a taste of what was to come as he lubricated her tight channel up before replacing his fingers with the flared, bulbous head of his cock.

He held her steady as he slowly screwed the thick length of his dick all the way in. Stretching her muscles wide, Josh didn't stop until the heavy sac of his balls pressed against the weeping lips of her pussy. He treated her to a tantalizing pump that had Casey squealing with a rush of decadent delight. It flared with a hot, sparkly bolt that raced up her spine as the hands clutching her hips began to force her to rise back up.

The motion had her ass clenching down tight around the thick width of his erection as the bliss flooding her pelvis mushroomed outward in a bloom of bright rapture that had her whimpering once again. The sweet sensation sharpened, growing more intense as Josh reached back around her to kill the spray of hot water raining down over them.

Her knees went weak, her mind blank, and every nerve in her body popped and fizzled with a euphoric rush as Josh straightened again, giving her another little twist of his hips that had his cock grinding against the sensitive walls of her ass. He stroked those ecstatic flares as he rolled his hips in a constant motion that had her gasping and paying little attention as he captured her wrists and lifted her arms over her head.

She barely noticed as he bound her wrists in the cuffs that hung down from the ceiling. All Casey was aware of in that moment was the titillating pleasure blinding her to all else, including the sight of Dylan strutting fully clothed into the shower stall.

If she had noticed him, then she might have also taken note of the gleam in his eye. It warned of his dark intent, but Casey hung there, perched on Josh's cock, happily oblivious of anything but the hands curling around her thighs and lifting her right off her feet.

Little did she know how much trouble she was in.

* * * *

Dylan smiled, eyeing Casey as she dangled there helpless and flushed. Impaled on Josh's cock with her ass cheeks holding him tight, she wore a smile, a few sexy tattoos, and nothing else. That's just how he liked her. Hell, he more than liked her.

He was in love.

He wasn't alone. Dylan could read the truth in the dark depths of Casey's gaze. They shined with a light that assured him that he was not only welcome. He was wanted. If he had any doubt, all he had to do was glance down toward the pink, swollen folds of her pussy, weeping with a need that only he and Josh could satisfy.

Like an offering, Josh held her up as both he and Casey waited for Dylan to make his move. He hesitated, allowing the moment to thicken with a tense anticipation as he slowly took in Casey in all her naked glory. Her nipples were hard, the heavy mounds of her breasts heaving, and the muscles of her stomach quivering with visible shivers while her cunt was wet, the thick cream dripping down over the swollen balls tucked tight up against her ass.

"Is it time to double up?"

The husky invitation in Casey's tone licked over Dylan like a flame, sending tendrils of heat racing down his spine to flood his balls and swell through his cock until he was hard enough to feel each individual tooth of his zipper biting into his sensitive length.

He had more than three-eighths of an inch on Josh now. Dylan was certain of it but in no mood to go get the ruler. He had other plans in mind. So did Casey.

"Because, you know, that is my favorite afternoon treat."

Casey licked her lips as she eyed him hungrily, leaving no doubt of what she was looking to get a taste of. Neither did she bother to disguise the challenge in her tone, and Dylan wasn't one to back down from a dare, and neither was he one to threaten.

He liked to deliver.

That's just what he intended to do as he strode forward to kneel down before Casey's cunt, but he didn't give in to the temptation to lean forward and take a taste. Instead, he reached for the shower's handheld wand and clicked on the cold water.

"Hmm…" Casey purred as the twinkle in her beautiful eyes grew into a mischievous glint. "I think I'm going to like this even bett*eeeer*."

Her words ended in a squeal as her whole body jerked beneath the frigid blast of water he aimed at her open cunt. Almost instantly her shrieks turned into full gales of laughter as her toes curled and her legs bowed, lifting her whole body into the cold spray.

That wasn't the reaction he'd expected. It appeared as if the only person he'd punished was his brother. Josh's jaw clenched as he struggled to control Casey's motions. Dylan could easily imagine the strain his brother was under. He'd been there before, buried balls deep in Casey's ass while she wiggled and squirmed her way toward a release.

Dylan didn't take mercy on Josh, though. His brother would either hold strong or break, and that was his problem. Dylan's was getting Casey's attention. The cold water wasn't working, so he tried spanking her pussy. That only had her begging for more, proving just how hard it was to actually punish a little vixen like Casey.

Over the past few days, he and Josh had discovered that only one thing really worked—denial.

Chapter 21

Dylan let himself drown in Casey's intoxicating taste. The heady flavor of her arousal had him forgetting just what he was about for long minutes. It was only when her cunt clenched around his tongue, rippling with the beginning of her release as she thanked God that Dylan remembered he didn't want her that appreciative.

Resisting the wicked delight of fucking his tongue back into Casey's cunt, he fought the urge to lick his way back up her spasming walls. She was a hot, tasty treat and one that was pitching a full-on fit. Leaning back on his heels, Dylan watched as Josh tried to hold on as Casey fought both his hold and her cuffs.

She could squirm and cuss as much as she wanted. She wasn't going anywhere, and he wasn't going to let her come until he got his answers. That was that.

"You ready to listen to me now?" he asked, testing the waters and finding them bitter.

"You're a son of a bitch," Casey all but snarled, glaring down at him so prettily.

Dylan took her response for a no and sighed. He guessed he still had a point to prove. That's just what he did as he trapped the swollen clit under the heavy press of his thumb. Dylan gave the sensitive bundle of nerves a rough roll that brought her squeak back to a squeal.

"Let's get one thing straight," Dylan started again as he glanced up to catch Casey's gaze. "You are a naughty girl, and you are—"

"I am not!" Casey instantly interrupted to defend herself, managing to sound indignant despite her position. "I didn't do anything to deserve thi—"

This time when he spanked her open cunt, Casey had a more appropriate response. She gasped, a heavy sound of passion that matched the deep flush that flooded across her creamy folds. Dylan treated himself to another quick taste, drawing a whimper from Casey before he leaned back.

"As I was saying," he began again. "You are *naughty*, little girl, and you *are* going to answer all my questions honestly, or you will be punished. Understood?"

Casey's chin stuck out at a stubborn angle, and she remained mutinously silent, but that didn't last any longer than it took Dylan to spank another gasp out of her. Her pouty lips parted over her breathless answer as she finally caved.

"Yes."

He didn't believe her, but Dylan gave Casey a chance to save herself. even though he knew that she was about to lie to him again.

"Then let's start with something simple," he suggested. "Why don't you tell me why you're here?"

"I thought that was obvious. Because I wanted to get lai—"

Casey cried out as, this time, Dylan snapped a little jeweled clamp over her clit. Flushing a brilliant shade of red, her breathing dissolved into chaotic gasps that quickly thickened into heavy pants that assured him she'd caught enough of her breath to answer.

"*Why* are you here, Casey?"

"*Why* do you keep asking me the same—ah! Okay! Okay! I'll tell you," Casey hollered as she squirmed, desperately trying to avoid the frigid blast and making Josh sweat.

Dylan could tell his brother wasn't going to last much longer. Hopefully, he wouldn't have to. Holding on to a vain thread of hope that Casey might actually be ready to confess, he clicked the showerhead off and gave her another chance to come clean.

"We're waiting," Dylan pressed almost immediately, knowing the longer it took her to answer was simply more time she spent on figuring out a better lie.

"Yes, I know," Casey snapped, clearly irritated.

That was a dead giveaway that something was wrong. They'd been tormenting her for days, playing games a lot rougher than this, and she had laughed her way through them all. She should have been laughing right then, but instead, she looked worried.

"Just give me a moment," Casey pleaded, her tone betraying her anguish. "You know, this isn't easy."

Dylan could believe that. He was asking her to betray a friend, something he would never have done except for Casey. Asking for the same from her didn't seem as if he was asking too much.

"*What* isn't easy?" Dylan demanded to know.

Casey took a deep breath and appeared to center herself before meeting his gaze and answering with an honesty that was almost believable thanks to the blush racing across her cheeks. "Admitting that I...*followed* you here. You know, I've wanted you both for so long, and the thought of you with all these other women..."

"That's sweet." Dylan smiled as he caught his brother's eye. He knew exactly what Josh was thinking, just what he was aching to say. He put him out of his misery, by saying it for him. "The only problem with that theory is that you arrived the day before us."

"I saw your invitation," Casey responded with an agility most liars didn't have.

"Our invitation was verbal and given over a phone."

"Then I overheard you," Casey snapped as she dared to glare down at him. "Why do you have to be so damn difficult about this? It's a sex club. Why do most people come to one of those?"

"You're not most people." And Dylan was glad for it.

"What do you want to hear me say?" Casey asked in exasperation. "That I'm desperate? That I'm pathetic? That I haven't been laid in over a month? And that I was tired of wearing out the batteries of my favorite vibrator? I mean, really? Can't you let me have a little dignity?"

Dylan snorted at that impassioned plea. It was overacted just like the rest of Casey's monologue. This wasn't some cheap dinner theater production, and he wasn't going to waste his time asking her for the truth again, but she would give it to him.

Of that, he was certain.

* * * *

Casey's heart raced, sending blood pounding through her veins in a frantic pace that matched the rapid, heaving pants that escaped her lips as she desperately tried to draw in enough air to soothe the fires burning in her, but it was a futile task. One that neither Dylan nor Josh appeared willing to let her accomplish.

Between the two of them, they kept her stretched on the razor's edge of one release or another, torn between panic and anticipation. Somewhere deep inside of her, Casey knew she should rebel against their domination. They didn't have a right to force her to answer them, but that didn't matter.

Not to them and not to her.

Right then, all that mattered was the pleasure. That was fed by both their touch and their primitive display of power. They were proving a point, and she was loving their efforts. They were hard and demanding and full of male aggression. They made her feel so delicate and sexy, wanted like she'd never been wanted before.

It wasn't an act, either. Casey could feel the heat of passion in Josh's hard body flexing behind her. He ground his deliciously thick cock against the sensitive muscles of her ass, splitting it wide with the proof of just how much he really desired her. Dylan too, though, his passion was, as always, a little rougher but no less exciting.

Casey reveled in the hard slaps of his hand over her open cunt as much as she did in the intermittent laps of his tongue as he tried to drive her pleas toward a confession, but he was only demanding what he already knew.

Somehow, some way, Dylan had found out that Peyton was Patton. What he didn't know was that Casey had another secret, a bigger one. How could he? She'd only figured out the truth herself in the past few days.

Casey may have come to the club to help Patton and indulge her own sexual curiosity, but she'd stayed for them. For Dylan and Josh. If not for them, she probably would have left because this—the domination, the bondage, the sharing, the exhibition, all of it—only felt right because Dylan and Josh were there to share it with her.

That was the real secret she kept sealed behind her cries, but it grew harder and harder to hold it back as Josh and Dylan drove her back toward a point where desperation would force her to choose between her own secrets or Patton's.

It was an unfair choice, and she rebelled, even as the ecstasy began to wind into a tight, glorious release that was snatched right out of her hands every single time she reached for it. Without fail, Josh and Dylan seemed to know right when Casey was about to come. Every time they sensed her pending climax, they stole it from her with an arctic blast of cold water over the heated flesh weeping between her legs.

That's just what Casey wanted to do—weep. The intensity of the emotions building inside of her, the pressure growing within, it was all too much to bear, and it was only the beginning.

Casey bit down on her lower lip, trying to hold back her whimper as she watched Dylan set aside the hand-held showerhead. Every muscle in her body tightened in anticipation as he turned back to her, his hand settling on her thigh close enough to the folds of her pussy for Casey to feel the heat of his palm spread over her mound.

Dylan's hands were just as big and thick as Josh's, but where his brother's fingers tended to slide over her skin, teasing her with an almost ticklish touch, Dylan's bit in to her soft flesh with a savage strength that warned her his patience had come to an end. He didn't give her a chance to brace herself, though, before he yanked her free of Josh's hold, jerking her forward to drape her knees over his shoulders and bury his face in her pussy.

Casey's squeak of surprise turned into a squeal of delight as Josh's cock slid almost free of her ass while Dylan began devouring her cunt with the ravenous hunger of a starving man. His tongue whipped over her sensitive flesh, curling around her clit before dipping to plunge into her sheath at the exact moment Josh rammed his thick, swollen length back into her ass, pounding Casey down the length of his brother's tongue and fucking a scream right out of her.

They passed her back and forth, screwing Casey with a relentless rhythm meant only to torture her. They wanted the truth, and she knew it wouldn't be long before all of her defenses caved and she gave it to them. Still, Casey fought to make the moment last.

The carnal indulgences that had filled the past several days had taught her just how intense the bliss could be if all she did was hold on as long as she could, allowing the pleasure to bloom into unspeakable heights. She was almost there, mere breaths away from that beautiful sunrise, when Dylan and Josh came to yet another stop, plunging her back into the shadowed depths of a need that had her writhing in a futile attempt at rebellion.

"*No!*"

She lashed out with a bellow, unable to break their hold as she twisted and bucked. With her hands pinned high above her head, Casey could do little else but roar...roar, and answer their damn questions because they were clearly more stubborn than she.

"Yes," Josh contradicted her, the harsh wash of his whisper heating her neck as he growled over her shoulder and straight into her ear. "Tell us, Firecracker. Who sent you here?"

Casey hesitated, reluctant to her core to betray a friend, but then Dylan caught her clamped clit beneath his thumb and pumped the little bud, eliciting both a gasp and an answer, though she had enough sense to offer only half a truth. It wasn't her fault they saw it for the lie it was.

"Peyton."

"You mean *Patton*," Dylan corrected her almost instantly, proving that he knew way too much already.

"If you know the answer, then why do you ask the question?" Casey shot back, her fighter's spirit rallying with that pointed question. Almost immediately they punished her for her insolence.

Without wasting his time on reminding her who was in charge, Dylan, instead, unleashed the clamp, allowing the small bud to swell with a rush of sensation that shot her straight back toward the edge of a release that she needed so desperately that she would say or do anything for it.

"*Yes!*" Casey snapped, giving him all that he demanded—the full truth. "Yes! Okay? Patton! Patton is Peyton, but we didn't know you knew her men... This wasn't about you but finding out..."

"Finding out what?" Dylan pressed when Casey's words faded away. "Finding out of if her men were loyal?"

"No, never." Casey shook her head. Patton might be jealous, but she wasn't afraid of her men straying. "This isn't about them. It's about the club. They won't let her in and...she wants to know why."

"And have you figured out why?"

Casey blinked open eyes she'd clenched closed long minutes ago to meet the gaze of the man lingering near the bathroom door. Chase Davis stared back down at her, waiting for his answer. She didn't know how long he'd been there or when he'd arrived. All that Casey knew for certain was that Patton was in a whole lot of trouble.

"No."

She really hadn't. That's all Chase apparently needed to know. He shot a nod at Dylan before turning and disappearing into the bedroom. Casey didn't have a chance to wonder where he was headed. Her concentration remained completely focused on Dylan as he rose up to his feet.

In the next breath, he had her fully penetrated and stretched wide over the thick width of his erection. Casey caught one last glimpse of

Chase retreating before her eyes fluttered closed and she gave herself over to her two lovers as they began to fuck her with hard, sure strokes.

Caged within the strength and heat of Josh's and Dylan's arms, Casey felt both cherished and wanted as their hips began to pick up speed. All too soon, the lust and passion that sprang up whenever they came together spun out of control, and they were taking her with a ruthless desperation.

Two sets of hands clutched at her hips, forcing her to bounce back and forth between the two big cocks pounding into her in an alternating rhythm that had Casey begging for more. She needed it.

So did they.

Josh stretched her ass wide over his thick, heavy length before allowing her to be pulled back down over Dylan's massive dick. The brothers fought each other, their motions picking up speed until they were slamming into her at the very same time. The pressure was too much, and she clung to Dylan as she felt the pleasure boiling in her veins erupt into a magnificent release that stole the very soul from her body.

This wasn't just about sex…but that didn't mean it was going to come to an end.

That thought had her heart seizing painfully as it led to the reminder that this was her last day. Worse, this might possibly be the last time she got be held like this by them. They meant everything to her.

That thought sliced through her and then faded away, along with the rest of the world as her climax consumed her. All that remained was pure, undiluted bliss. Casey was cast adrift in a sea of splendor, and time meant nothing to her. All that mattered was the pleasure.

She was only dimly aware of Josh's and Dylan's shouts of fulfillment or the feel of their releases flooding into her body. Casey couldn't even be bothered to stand on her own two feet when the brothers finally pulled free of her body, but she moaned over the loss of their cocks, not caring for the empty feeling that plagued her almost immediately or the sense that she was suddenly free falling.

Josh and Dylan were there to catch her. Catch her, bathe her, and tuck her into bed. The two men, who had so mercilessly used her, tended to Casey with a gentleness and care that left her feeling loved as she curled onto her side. Loved and protected, there was no other way to describe the contentment that filled her as Dylan and Josh curled her between them, keeping her safe as she passed into complete oblivion.

Chapter 22

Sunday, June 1st

Casey woke up to the stroke of rough hands and the heated massage of moist lips as Josh and Dylan once again rallied her toward another sweaty release that hadn't even begun to fade before they began again, going all night long. Each peak she reached was higher than the last, driven in part by the heart-wrenching belief that this was the end until finally it was and there was nothing left to do but slip out of the bed.

She left Josh and Dylan snoring happily away, not daring to wake them and test the bonds of her self-control with an actual goodbye. Holding it together, Casey managed to make it all the way back to the harem, where she moved about in a daze, following Lana's instructions without a thought. She didn't dare to have one, fearing that any hesitation would bring about her total humiliation as she broke down in front of a woman as strong as Lana.

It became easier to hold back as she dressed for the first time that week. With each layer of clothing she pulled on, Casey felt as though another chink of armor was snapped into place until finally she looked in the mirror and saw her reflection staring back at her.

She looked tired but otherwise normal, which was a lie because she felt far from normal. That didn't mean she didn't know how to bullshit her way into appearing healthy, happy, and fine as she entered the same dank little office Lana had first showed her into to find the raven-haired beauty waiting there wearing nothing but a sad smile.

"I'd ask if you'd be interested in returning, but I'm guessing the answer is no," she murmured as she stepped up to give Casey a quick hug.

"I doubt the Davis brothers would let me come back." Casey returned the quick sign of affection before leaning back to assure Lana that she meant no harm. "I can imagine that they were a little upset, but really Patton was just curious…and so was I."

Casey wasn't so focused on the wretched knot growing in her stomach that she didn't noticed the flash of emotion that darkened Lana's eyes at the mention of Patton's name. As it was, Casey was too busy trying to get out the door before she broke down and ended up a sobbing puddle on the floor to care.

"Motives are irrelevant." Lana waved away her explanation. "The only thing that matters is that you had a good time."

"It was the best." That wasn't a lie.

"Good." Lana opened up the door that led back out toward where Casey's car was still parked. "Then our mission has been successful… Don't look so sad. I have a feeling your education in ecstasy is only just beginning."

Actually it was ending. If their mission had been to break Casey's heart and leave her with a burning need that she feared no man but Dylan or Josh would ever be able to appease, then the club had certainly served its purpose. Otherwise, the truth was she didn't really belong there.

It was just too bad that she'd figured that out too late.

Now everything had changed and would need to be changed because she couldn't go on living next to Dylan and Josh. The very thought of listening to Dylan brag about his conquests or, worse, seeing them as he dragged them into his apartment had her hands shaking as she clutched the steering wheel.

Then there was Josh. Their friendship would obviously never be the same. There was no going back. There was clearly no going forward either. If Josh had wanted that, then he would have mentioned it. After all, he wasn't the emotionally stunted one.

Josh was the upfront one. The honest one. The type of guy who said what he meant and meant what he said and didn't speak unless he had something to say. His silence was all Casey needed to hear. It was all she could bear.

If he'd even bothered to try and offer her some cheap reassurance, she probably would have broken down. As it was, she managed to fight the coming tide until she'd reached the Davis ranch. She could feel the control slipping away from her as she got out of her car. All it took was one look from Patton, who greeted her at the door with a smile that quickly darkened into a frown as Casey stumbled into her arms and broke down.

"What happened?" Patton pulled her into the house as she demanded answers without waiting for them. "What did those mean men do to you? You tell me who, and I promise I'll have the bastard strung up by his balls. Just give me a name."

"It's Dylan." Casey sniffled as she glanced up and spilled the one secret she'd been intending on keeping. "Dylan and Josh!"

* * * *

"You are a real son of a bitch, you know that?" Chase asked, not giving Dylan a chance to defend himself against that accusation before he continued on his indignant ranting.

"And they say I'm the asshole, but at least I never intentionally set out to make my woman cry, and I sure as hell didn't laugh when she did!"

"I'm not laughing," Dylan denied, though he was on the edge of it. "I'm just smiling."

"Uh-huh."

"I'm not!"

"Whatever you say, man." Chase waved away Dylan's outrage as if it were nothing. To him it probably was because there was only one thing that Chase really cared about. "That's between you and your woman. I'm concerned about my woman, and she's concerned about yours, so you see I now have to consider Casey under my official protection."

That sounded ominous, but Dylan didn't have a chance to press Chase on the matter before Josh came jogging up in a rush, which was just what he'd been in all morning.

"Hey, man, thanks for inviting us down. This place is awesome." He paused long enough to shoot Chase a nod before turning to pin Dylan with a pointed look. "We got a lot to get done and not much time to do it. So you ready to hit the road?"

"Yeah, I'll be there in a sec," Dylan assured him, waiting for Josh to take that hint and back off, giving Dylan a moment with Chase.

"Hey, look, man, I'm really sorry we didn't manage to catch your arsonist."

"Don't be," Chase cut him off, his scowl darkening with a sense of true tension. "That little shithead of a sheriff knows what is going on. You helped me figure that much out, and that's all I really need to know."

"Yeah," Dylan drew out that agreement as he eyed Chase with concern. "Well, just remember he's the sheriff, and I'm left with the impression that he will throw your ass into jail."

"Won't be the first time," Chase shot back, proving not only that he wasn't listening but that he wasn't interested in hearing any of Dylan's advice. "If you really wanted to help me, then you would get your ass out to my ranch and take Casey back home so that *I* can go back home without risking getting blamed for whatever it is you did to make her cry."

"I didn't do anything," Dylan defended himself, though he knew that was just the problem.

Casey had been waiting all week for some sign or little clue from Josh or him that they planned to continue the relationship once they returned home. Dylan didn't exactly see the wisdom in Josh's plan, but he managed to hold his tongue, despite the worries darkening in her gaze.

That didn't mean it hadn't been hard. Despite Chase's accusation, knowing that they'd made Casey cry did weigh on him, but she wouldn't be suffering for long. Besides, Dylan reasoned, she could have said something.

* * * *

"So, you just walked away without saying anything?" Patton blinked as if she were confused by her own words, which they both knew she wasn't, making the question all the more obnoxious.

"Me?" Casey responded in kind, going with a dramatic rebuttal as she straightened up in her seat, clinking her coffee down indignantly as she confronted her best friend as if Patton were one of the two men driving her nuts. "Why should I have to say anything?"

That earned her a snort and not a single ounce of respect as Patton smirked. "Because *you* are the one who felt something."

"Exactly!" Casey exploded, not understanding how Patton couldn't see the very point she'd just proved. "If they felt anything, they would've said something, so why should I be the only one who says anything?"

"Because this is Dylan and Josh, and you know how screwed up they are." Patton paused for a second as if measuring her own comment and finding it to be less than adequate.

"I mean *really* screwed up," Patton emphasized as if Casey didn't know what she meant. "Dylan is way too insecure to be the first to ever say anything, and Josh is way too dense to figure out when to say it, so that leaves you to be the sensible one and take control of the situation."

"Sensible one?" Casey wrinkled her nose at the very thought. The word just provoked an image of pigtails and saddle shoes in her mind, and that had never been Casey's thing...unless, of course, the outfit was matched with a skirt that barely covered her bottom and a brassiere top that had set of chains running down—

"You know me better than that." Casey shook off that thought before it could lead back to Josh and Dylan. "I'd be insulted to be considered sensible."

"And if you weren't sensible, I wouldn't have gone into business with you," Patton shot back just as the back door opened.

Casey got a glimpse of Slade Davis, who had been about to step into the kitchen, but at the sound of Patton's waspish rebuttal, he turned right back around and slipped out before Patton ever even noticed him trying to sneak in behind her. Casey noticed and couldn't help but smirk over the observation.

"I think your men are afraid of you."

"What?" It took Patton a moment to adjust to the switch in topics, but she caught up quickly. "Oh, please. There are three of them, all bigger, stronger, and—"

"Still intimidated by little-bitty you."

"I'm not little-bitty."

"And I'm not dumb enough to tell Dylan or Josh the truth."

"Fine." Patton heaved an aggrieved sigh. "You just sit there holding on to your secret little crush just like every other good girl—"

"Oh, please," Casey cut her off with a huff. "Don't even try that insulting tone on me."

"—ever did as they waited for their Prince Charming to come and sweep them off their feet."

"I like to keep my feet on the ground, thank you."

"Of course, he ain't never coming." Patton shrugged as her lips began to curl back into a smug little smile. "Because people like me got off our asses and went out there and seduced all the Prince Charmings into our beds."

Casey blinked at that, not even sure what to say to that prediction. That she was right? Eventually another woman would come along and take Dylan and Josh away? She feared that would happen no matter what she did.

"It's seduce or be forgotten," Patton declared, pinning Casey with a pointed look as she issued her an order. "Now stop crying over the matter and make your choice."

Casey sighed, sniffing back the last of the tears that still lingered in her eyes from her recent pity-fest and braced herself as she confronted her best friend.

"You are a pain in my ass."

"And I'm right."

"And you're right." Casey couldn't deny that Patton had a point.

If she went home right then to strip down and wait for the boys in their apartment, Casey knew exactly what they'd do. If she was there every day waiting, there wouldn't be any other room for another woman to come along. That still wasn't love, though.

The real question was whether or not it was enough.

Casey honestly didn't know.

"It's kind of odd, though," Patton murmured as her brow furled into a frown. "I mean you running into them there, at the club...it's like kismet."

"Yeah," Casey muttered, shifting guiltily in her seat. "About that..."

It had become apparent that Chase hadn't revealed what had happened yesterday to Patton, which left Casey in the uncomfortable position of having to rat herself out. As much as she didn't want to, she still had to.

"You know"—Casey cleared her throat and tried again to confess, but found she couldn't hold Patton's gaze while she did—"it turns that Dylan and Josh are actually friends with Chase and the rest of the brothers."

"Is that a fact?" Patton stilled, straightening slowly up. "Then it's not kismet…is it?"

"They were there to investigate the fire…and, yes, they figured out who you really are and what I was really doing there," Casey said, answering Patton's questions before she could ask them. "And yes, under *torture*, I confirmed some things."

"Oh, don't sweat it." Patton huffed. "I knew Chase was upset about something last night. Now I know about what."

"He's pissed, huh?"

"He keeps saying that I don't trust him, but I do," Patton insisted before hesitating. "Well, I mean, I did, but he keeps saying it, and so I got to wonder why he's so obsessed with me thinking he's guilty if he's not actually guilty, but I think there's no way he's guilty, so I don't know what it is that has him acting so guilty, if you get what I mean."

Casey didn't have a clue, but she was saved from that admission by the ring of the doorbell and then damned by it not a minute later as Patton escorted an all-too-familiar-looking woman into the kitchen. Casey could have sworn she'd seen her out at the club, possibly that first night she'd been with Dylan and Josh.

It was hard to remember, though, anything beyond them. She was just about to say something, but the other woman stopped her cold with a quick shake of the head. Casey reversed course and pretended as though she didn't know the other woman after all. It was clear that was what the woman, whom Patton introduced as Angie, wanted. She offered Casey a grateful smile as they shook hands.

She continued to play dumb until Patton moved off to go retrieve a bottle of wine from the study. Almost the second that Patton disappeared from sight, Angie was leaning across the kitchen table to whisper furiously at Casey.

"I didn't know you knew Patton."

"*I* didn't know *you* knew Patton," Casey shot back.

"What were you doing at the club?"

"What were you doing at the club?" Casey asked that exact same question at the exact same moment but managed to answer before the other woman. "Checking the place out for Patton."

"And have you told her anything?"

"Not yet." Casey frowned, sensing a level of desperation in the other woman that didn't match the situation. "Why? What don't you want her to know?"

"That I go there at all."

"But—"

"I'm a travel agent," Angie cut her off to explain as she offered Casey a pleading look. "Do you know how hard a profession that is with the Internet taking over? So to make a living, I specialize."

"And you think Patton wouldn't understand that?"

Angie didn't get a chance to answer before the woman in question reappeared, leaving Casey to mull over the answer on her own. The woman couldn't be worried that Patton would be judgmental about her livelihood. They clearly knew each other better than that. Still, it had to be something.

It was as though there was a missing piece.

Chase didn't want Patton at the club. Angie didn't want Patton to know she worked with the club. Had Chase and Angie had a thing? No. That couldn't be because it soon became quite clear from their conversation that Angie was a virgin, which just seemed too damn weird and had Casey wondering if maybe she hadn't had enough to drink. Even as that thought hit her, it was immediately followed by another.

"Oh my God, it's Lana!"

It had to be. It made perfect sense. Lana was the one woman always there. The one who wielded a position of power that Patton would be jealous of. Casey was even willing to bet that Lana and the Davis brothers used to have a thing.

"Who is Lana?"

That question had Casey blinking and realizing that she'd spoken out loud. Now she had both Angie's and Patton's undivided attention. For her part, Angie looked paler than a sheet of paper, a reminder that Lana was supposed to be a secret.

"Nobody."

That lie probably would have sounded more believable if she hadn't mumbled it, but in her defense, Casey wasn't used to drinking wine...and she'd never been that good at lying anyway.

"Casey."

"She runs things down at the club." Casey cringed, unable to meet Angie's gaze as she spilled those beans in a rush that stood in stark contrast to the way Patton slowly repeated them.

"She runs things down at the club..." Patton went still, her eyes rounding in an almost comical look. "You don't mean Lana Vey? About five-eight with a killer body and an enviable head of black silk that never has a single strand out of place? *That* Lana?"

"Uh..."

Casey wasn't sure what followed that question. All she knew was that she woke up the next morning, passed out in a strange bed, fully dressed, and with a pounding headache. A shower didn't help her memory much. Neither did breakfast, which was conducted by a cheery Patton.

She was strangely happy, given Casey could have sworn she and Angie had spent the afternoon arguing. They must have settled the matter, or not. It made no difference in the end to Casey. As long as Patton was happy, then she could, at least, turn her attention back toward her own problems. She had two of them, and it was time to make her decision.

Flee or fight.

Chapter 23

Feeling worse for wear, Casey gratefully pulled past the sign welcoming her home to the Ansley Creek Luxurious Condominium Complex. It had been a long drive, and her head was still pounding, but she was excited. It wasn't a long drive back from Pittsview, but long enough for her to come up with a few good ideas about how to seduce her men and make a silent but bold statement.

Patton was right. It was seduced or be forgotten.

Nobody forgot her.

Or so she hoped, but as Casey finally pulled to a stop next to the small sports car parked out in front of her building, she felt her stomach start to knot with a sick feeling. Maria had come calling a lot sooner than Casey had anticipated. She couldn't help but worry as she got out of her car that the other woman might have had the same idea she did.

If she did, then she was about to be thrown out on her naked ass.

That thought put the smile back on Casey's lips as she stormed up the path toward the breezeway that separated her condo from her men's. She didn't have any fear of what she'd find as she turned toward Josh and Dylan's door. After all, neither man's vehicle was parked out front, assuring her nobody was around to witness the fit she was about to throw.

Only Casey didn't get a chance. Maria came storming out of the brothers' apartment, fully clothed and depriving Casey of the fun of throwing her out. The woman wouldn't deprive her of the joy of being a bitch, though. Built like a tall, thin boy, Maria might have had the svelte sophistication of a model who had walked the runways in Paris and Milan and possessed the ability to convey a full statement without a speaking a single word, but Casey could smirk...and gloat.

In fact, those were two things she did real well, not that she got a chance to do either. Maria didn't pause as she clicked her high-heeled ass down the path to her tiny, red, over-priced car. She barely even glanced in Casey's way. It was a rudeness Casey would have called her on, but she was glad to see the woman go and didn't plan on slowing her exit down.

If the woman wasn't bright enough to realize what this situation called for, then that was her problem. Casey, on the other hand, knew just what was needed—that thought ended in mid-sentence as everything inside of Casey froze.

Her gaze had shifted back toward Josh and Dylan's condo. Maria had failed to close the door completely, and it had swung back inward, revealing nothing but carpet stains and dusty walls. The place had been stripped, and all that remained were the impressions of the couch feet on the floor and the light squares on the wall where their pictures had once hung.

They were gone.

Gone.

They hadn't said anything. Why would they do that? Why would they flee...unless, of course, they were running away from her. Casey's heart twisted a painful lurch at that conclusion as she wheeled back around to stumble toward her door. She was sniffing back the tears as she fumbled with her keys, knowing she wasn't going to make it to the bed before she broke completely down. She just hoped she made it into her apart— With a sense of déjà vu, Casey watched as her door swung inward to reveal an empty shell.

They'd taken everything, from her toothbrush to the spare can of chili she kept in her pantry. Her clothes, her pictures, the scented dryer sheets she placed in the vents to help her place smell fresh—it was *all* gone.

She'd been robbed, but Casey didn't have to wonder who the burglars were. After all, they'd left a note along with a riddle that brought the smile back to her face.

We have your stuff. Wanna get it back? Solve the riddle. I'm red and blue and you love me, too.

The note was written in Josh's distinctive cursive but must have been dictated because there was no denying Dylan's curt tone in the instructions. It went to prove that they both wanted to play, and that this game was far from over.

* * * *

"This is the dumbest idea you have ever had."

That was saying something, given Dylan had had some pretty spectacularly stupid ideas in his lifetime, but this one...Josh took a deep breath and let it out slowly, telling himself as he did that it would all work out. Casey would be arriving soon, and she'd be welcomed by an entryway covered in zombie targets that were all riddled with bullet holes.

"What?" Dylan blinked in strangely honest confusion. "You let me put them up in the apartment. Just think of how much more important it is for this place. I mean, hell, which would you rather rob? An apartment or a mansion?"

"It's not a mansion," Josh snapped, driven nearly insane by a whole day spent moving and arranging stuff with his brother.

He'd gone out to grab some screws and nails so they could hang Casey's more mature artwork in the front entry, which would have been a thoughtful gesture to welcome her to her new home. Instead, he'd walked in to be greeted by the land of the dead.

In the half-hour Josh had been gone, Dylan had clearly been busy decorating on his own. He'd thumb-tacked up the twenty or so paper targets he used when training with his gun down at the range. It had long been his theory that if a burglar broke into their place, he would turn right around once he saw those targets.

Josh wasn't convinced, mostly because he didn't think the burglar was ever going to show up. Dylan, though, lived in a different universe.

"Look, I just don't think it's appropriate." Josh tried again to be tactful, but Dylan saw through the attempt and responded with his normal bluntness.

"You think it's low class." Dylan leveled that accusation as he crossed his arms over his chest and glared back at Josh, all but daring him to deny it.

"I think Casey will think it is," Josh shot back. He'd agree with her, but obviously Dylan didn't agree with him.

"I think she'll like it. What?" Dylan scowled at the pointed look Josh shot him.

"You can't be that naïve."

"That's just what I was thinking when you suggested it would be romantic to send the woman all around town picking up her own flowers and such."

And such included a gift from the jewelry store that had caused a lot more bickering then Dylan's concept of acceptable decorations. Josh didn't want to go back there, but he did borrow the same line he'd used then.

"Fine, then let's ask her."

This time they didn't have to wait to hear her answer because the doorbell rang as if in response to Josh's challenge. Casey had arrived, and there was no telling what was about to happen. Despite the fact that they had been operating under the assured notion that she did, in fact, care very much about them, they didn't know that for certain.

As Josh moved to answer the front door, he felt the first quivers of uncertainty snake through him, and he took a moment to quell them before reaching for the large brass knob. He took a deep breath, plastered on a smile, and opened the door, but the greeting died on his lips when, instead of looking down into the depths of Casey's amazing eyes, he found himself looking straight into the cool, dark reflection of Maria's gaze.

"Maria."

"Josh." She inclined her head with that cool greeting and stepped past him as if he hadn't uttered her name in unwelcomed shock.

Maybe he didn't have the look down like she did. Maria's features were certainly a mastery of perfected disdain as she paused to take in Dylan's decorations. If Josh hadn't been so taken aback by her sudden appearance, he might actually have been able to appreciate the look of outrage that flashed through her eyes as they settled down on his brother.

"I see you've made yourself at home."

Though it wasn't innately an insult, Maria still managed to fill that comment with enough contempt to leave no doubt of her opinion on the matter. She never had liked Dylan. As bad as that was, Josh realized he'd behaved even worse because he'd allowed her to disrespect his brother. That wasn't right.

"This is his home," Josh spoke up, correcting both Maria and all of his past mistakes as he stepped up to confront his former fiancée. "But it's not yours, so I'm going to ask you to leave."

"Please." Maria sighed, refusing to budge, even when Josh settled a hand on her arm to escort her back toward the open door. "I didn't come over here to fight. I wanted to talk."

"We don't really have anything to talk about," Josh assured her, wondering when the last time was that they did. He couldn't remember.

"I think we do," Maria insisted, digging in her heels and prompting a snicker from Dylan. "What? What do *you* have to say?"

"I'm in love," Dylan declared, loud and proud, before nodding at his brother. "And so is he, just not with you."

Maria's delicate little nostrils flared as her gaze landed on Josh like a ton of bricks. "That cannot possibly mean what he's implying."

"Whatever it means, it's none of your damn business." Josh straightened up and used his superior strength to drag Maria toward the door as he made his position clear. "Nothing in my life is your concern anymore, Maria. I told you that you could keep the ring. My time, though, is no longer yours to waste. Good night!"

He delivered that last line as he shoved her back across the threshold, finally releasing her to slam the door in her face before turning back to confront his brother, who had all but dissolved into laughter in the main hall.

* * * *

Casey's amusement at Josh and Dylan's game waned about three hours in as she was stuck in traffic yet again. The first clue had been amusing. It hadn't taken her long to figure out the "red and blue" reference.

She probably would have gotten it quicker but the "love me, too" kept getting in the way. Those three little words changed everything because they implied that the brothers knew how she felt. More importantly, they weren't running away, which she could assume meant one thing—they loved her too.

That thought had left her giddy, almost giggly, as she finally realized what the "red and blue" meant.

It was the mums.

Casey had once decorated Dylan and Josh's entire apartment in red and blue mums after Dylan had ignorantly declared that if flowers were blue then men might like them, too. He'd been absolutely adamant that there were no blue flowers. Casey had taken great delight in proving him wrong. She'd also earned a reputation for the stunt at the florist just down the street because he'd had to special order all the extra mums.

That's just where she had headed to find her first clue to not only where her furniture was but also in what direction Josh and Dylan were trying to take things. It couldn't have been clearer after she'd visited the florist, the wine store, the sex shop, followed by the jewelers, where she'd picked up two tiny, gift-wrapped ring boxes.

It took all of her formidable self-control not to rip right into them, but it was growing harder the longer she had to sit there doing nothing but waiting for the car in front of hers to roll slowly forward. Casey didn't think she'd make it when finally traffic began to pick up. Not that her trip was over.

She still had to stop by the dessert store and pick up the takeout from her favorite Thai restaurant before finally receiving an address that led her deep into the heart of Buckhead and the multi-million-dollar mansions tucked in amongst the curvy, manicured roads.

Unfortunately, the drive she ended up pulling into wound around statues of half-naked cherubs peeing into fountains. That was still more tasteful than the oversized box with the two-story-tall columns that the drive wrapped around. Casey stared up at the building in horror, wondering what the hell Josh and Dylan had been thinking and praying to God they hadn't actually bought the place. It was as tacky as…Maria.

Sighing as she spied the other woman's little sports car parked in the wide curve of the driveway, Casey knew in that moment just who had picked this place out. Josh probably had bought it for her before Maria had dumped him. That thought soured her mood even more.

Pulling her compact up behind Maria's car, Casey killed her lights just as the front door opened. A wash of light fell around the silhouette of a woman, and Casey could make out Maria's arrogant features as she shoved past Josh, who didn't even spare a glance down the drive to see Casey parked there. Instead, he disappeared into the house, leaving her to collect all the bags on her own.

As if that wasn't just the perfect statement about how her day had gone, he even managed to shove Maria back out the door and slam it in her face just as Casey started up the steps. That left her to confront the seriously pissed-off woman barreling toward her. This time Maria didn't leave her thoughts unspoken.

"Slut."

It was just too much. She'd put up with enough that day and wasn't about to be talked down to by anybody, much less Josh's ex-fiancée. At least she was in love with Josh and Dylan. Casey suspected that was more than Maria could have ever said.

That certainty hit her hard, and Casey felt all her worries and concerns vanish as she set down her bags on the first step, fished out a big purple dildo, and thrust it at Maria.

"Here, consider this a parting gift. You're going to need it more than me."

Maria didn't accept her offering but let it plunk down on the steps below her feet. That didn't mean she didn't look at it. When Maria's gaze tipped back up, Casey knew she'd pushed too far. Her concern was proven a second later as Maria growled and launched herself down the steps at Casey.

Before she knew it, Casey was rolling around on the drive with her hair being pulled and nails digging into neck as the crazy lady actually tried to claw at her. Just when her shock started to wear off and the pain had her fingers curling into fists, Maria disappeared, replaced by Josh's concerned frown.

"Are you all right?"

"Do I look all right?" Casey shot back, instinctively responding with her own outrage, even if it was misplaced.

"I'm sorry—"

"Oh, just shut up." Casey shoved Josh's hand away as she scrambled up to her feet unassisted. "I don't need your apology. I need you to step out of my way."

There was no mistaking the intent behind that command, which was probably why Josh stepped up instead of away. He blocked her view of Dylan dragging Maria back toward her car and refused to let her pass when Casey made to follow.

"Just let her go."

"And what? Let her get away with a cheap shot?" Casey gaped up at Josh, unable to believe he would even suggest such a thing.

"Cheap shot?" Josh snorted, his features relaxing into a smirk as he shook his head at her. "You gave the woman a dildo and basically told her to go screw herself. That's a mature response?"

"She called me a slut," Casey muttered before narrowing her gaze on him. "And if I do let her go, I expect to be compensated."

"Is that right?" Josh stilled, proving he knew exactly what she was thinking. "I'm not doing another striptease just so you and Dylan can have another laugh."

"Oh, no. I got a whole new idea...so, are you going to owe me?"

"You going to tell me what the idea is?"

"No."

"But I will be totally humiliated by it, right?"

"Yes." Casey grinned. He probably would be, but not in a bad way, and he knew it. After the past week, Josh must have figured out how her mind worked. More than that. He loved her for it.

"Fine." He heaved a deep, aggrieved sigh as though she couldn't see the anticipation gathering in his gaze. "But if you go too far..."

Then she'd be the one paying.

"Deal."

They shook hands, sealing their pact just as Maria slammed her car door. Together they turned to watch as the other woman squealed her tires against the asphalt as she shot out her parking space and tore off down the drive. Hopefully that was the last they'd see of her.

Unfortunately, the same couldn't be said of the monstrosity looming behind her. Turning her gaze back to the oversized brick building, she couldn't help but sigh. It was depressing to even look at.

"About this house—"

"Don't sweat it," Dylan cut her off as he sauntered up to throw an arm around her shoulders. "It's going on the market tomorrow, and we'll start looking for a new one the day after it sells."

"We will?" Casey arched a brow at that presumptuous bit of arrogance. She wasn't the only one.

"Will we?" Josh blinked in outraged surprise. "Do you know how much that would cost me? In taxes alone, we're talking tens of thousands of dollars. I don't think so. We have to live here for two years."

"That's it. I've had enough." Dylan held his hands up as he gestured for both of them to shut up. "I've put up with both your and Josh's craziness now for a whole week, but I'm done. So, yeah—it's *we*. You got a problem with that?"

Casey bit back a smile and shook her head slowly. "No."

"Good." Dylan nodded as he heaved out a deep sigh as though a weight had been lifted off him and turned toward Josh. "And you, if Casey and I give you two years, what do we get?"

"What do you want?" Josh's gaze narrowed on them.

"A full-sized basketball court in the backyard," Dylan suggested, forgetting in that moment that it was supposed to be a "we" gift and not a "he" gift. Two could play at that.

"I want puppies." Their apartment complex hadn't allowed dogs, and the urge for something cute and cuddly had been gnawing at her for years.

"Puppies?" Josh frowned. "How many are we talking here? One, two…three—"

"Six!"

"Oh, *hell* no!" Dylan looked at her as if she'd lost her mind. "Do you know how much poop six dogs will generate? Think about my basketball court."

"Build it downwind," Casey advised with a shrug. "I want puppies."

"Yeah?" Dylan straightened up in a blatant attempt to lord over her. "You know what I want?"

"Enough!" Josh stepped between them and shook his head. "Here is what we'll all get. Dylan, a half-court behind the garage, good?"

"Fine."

"Casey?" Josh turned on her, and she quickly cuddled up to his side, wrapping her arms around his waist and blinking up at him sweetly.

"You know, I always think of you as the *bigger* brother."

"Oh, come on!" Dylan objected, but Casey knew she had just won that round when Josh sighed and nodded.

"You can have *two* puppies."

"Three," she couldn't help but press.

"Two," Josh insisted.

"And a kitten."

"No," Dylan objected. "The Kacey kitty doesn't tolerate any competition. He's a jealous pussy."

Casey narrowed her eyes on him at that taunt. "Fine, but we're changing his name."

"You can't do that," Dylan scoffed. "Don't be ridiculous."

"Can we call him the Little D?" Josh perked up. "Or Baby D?"

"I like it." Casey nodded as Dylan's gaze narrowed in on them, but he didn't respond to their teasing.

"I'll second that motion," Josh assured her. "But only if I get to have what I want, which is a romantic celebration in our new home."

"Oh, please," Dylan huffed. "You had the woman pick up her own ring and had the audacity to suggest it's romantic?"

"Yeah? Wait until you see what Dylan did in the entry hall," Josh shot at her before casting a superior look at his brother. "He calls it *decorating.*"

"No, I call it *preventative security,*" Dylan corrected, and Casey could see that the argument was clearly getting to that point.

If she didn't do something now, something fast, something radical…she'd probably end up having to carry all the bags in herself. That wasn't happening. Stepping up between the brothers, she turned to face Dylan first, interrupting him mid-sentence with her own quiet declaration.

"I love you."

Stretching up to catch his startled lips in a quick kiss, she didn't give him a chance to respond before she turned toward Josh, who was frowning as though she'd just said something profane.

"I love you, too."

That wiped the dirty look off his face, not that he had a chance to respond to the quick kiss she brushed over his lips either. Instead, he stood there alongside Dylan as she stepped back and gave them each a pointed look.

"And you..."

"Would do anything for you," Josh swore.

"That's sweet." But that wasn't what she was looking for.

"And I would pluck the stars from the sky and drape them around you if I could," Dylan vowed, not to be outdone by his brother.

"That's very poetic," Casey assured him, knowing he meant his words, despite the laughter coating them.

"I would beg the gods to live forever just to kiss your feet."

"Now that's—"

"I would beg the gods to give me gills so I could scour the ocean for the finest pearls just to please you."

"I don't—"

"I'd get an implant," Josh cut her off, not even bothering to look at Casey as he shot that challenge at his brother, who snorted and rolled his eyes.

"Is that how you plan to make up those three-eighths of an inch?"

"Oh God," Casey groaned, amazed that they were back to that argument and knowing how long it could go on if she didn't interfere.

"At least they can fix length," Josh shot back. "There is not much they can do about meatiness."

"Meatiness? You really want to throw that challenge down?" Dylan dared his brother. "Because I'll get a scale, man."

"No!" Casey bellowed out that denial, drawing both Dylan's and Josh's scowls in her direction. "We're not weighing anything here.

We're confessing. Now I want to hear it and don't give me those innocent looks. You two know exactly what I'm talking about."

"She's bossy, isn't she?"

"Dylan," Casey sighed, wondering if he could ever be serious.

"It's a good thing I love bossy women, huh?" He shot her a smile that had Casey's frustration melting away as she returned the gesture with a small twist of her lips.

"Women?"

"Woman," he corrected himself before going to his knees. "I love you, Casey, and would be honored if you would agree to spend the rest of your days letting me show you just how much."

"That's better." Casey nodded. That's just what she wanted to hear.

Not to be outdone, Josh went to his knees as well and gazed up longingly at her. "I love you, too, Casey, and would be honored if you would agree to let me spend the rest of my days proving to you just how much."

"And that is perfect." Everything was perfect. Sauntering past them and up the steps, she paused at the top to glance back down at them and smile. "Now I'm going to go take a nice, long bath. The two of you can join me after you both put those rings away because I expect a better proposal than one where I had to pick up the takeout."

With that, she turned and sauntered into the house, smiling as she heard both her men rush to follow her. Lana had been right. This was only the beginning of her education.

THE END

WWW.JENNYPENN.COM

ABOUT THE AUTHOR

I live near Charleston, SC with my biggie, my dog. I have had a slightly unconventional life. Moving almost every three years, I've had a range of day jobs that included everything from working for one of the world's largest banks as an auditor to turning wrenches as an outboard repair mechanic. I've always regretted that we only get one life and have tried to cram as much as I can into this one.

Throughout it all, I've always read books, feeding my need to dream and fantasize about what could be. An avid reader since childhood, and as a latchkey kid, I'd spend hours at the library earning those shiny stars the librarian would paste up on the board after my name.

I credit my grandmother's yearly visits as the beginning of my obsession with romances. When she'd come, she'd bring stacks of romance books, the old-fashioned kind that didn't have sex in them. Imagine my shock when I went to the used bookstore and found out what really could be in a romance novel.

I've worked on my own stories for years and have found a particular love of erotic romances. In this genre, women are no longer confined to a stereotype, and plots are no longer constrained to the rational. I love the "anything goes" mentality and letting my imagination run wild.

I hope you enjoyed running with me and will consider picking up another book and coming along for another adventure.

For all titles by Jenny Penn, please visit
www.bookstrand.com/jenny-penn

Siren Publishing, Inc.
www.SirenPublishing.com

Lightning Source UK Ltd.
Milton Keynes UK
UKHW02f1520050318
318915UK00005B/491/P